Etham's Dawn

A Novel

M.W. Powell

John Bryant

ALSO BY M.W. POWELL

Blind Running
Across the Mountain
Buzzard Ridge
A Tangled Binding

ALSO BY JOHN BRYANT

Killing the Darkness

1

Whirling blades chopped through the air as the helicopter rushed away from Etham to save the preacher. The roar of the turbine engine swallowed everything inside the cabin as a pale man clutched the gurney bars with fear and confusion. His entire body vibrated from the chopper's motion as nausea rushed through his body. The preacher's wide eyes focused on the helmeted figure above him tapping a large syringe. Hot sharp pain pulsed from his tightened chest and darkness closed in on him. Coldness rushed through his arm veins as the figure pushed the plunger. His mind faded from the IV lines and irritating vibrations of the medevac chopper. He drifted to blurred fragmented scenes of trees rushing past him; a thundering clack of a pistol and then a familiar young woman running at his side. It replayed in slow motion over and over as the chopper headed to its destination. "Caleb, you're going to be okay, stay with me. You've got to stay awake. You can't leave your congregation. They need you." The EMT yelled as he applied more pressure to the chest wound while scanning the vitals monitor.

The sentences were jumbled and muffled from the noise. The EMT's eyes were young, but strong. Caleb saw that as he studied them. Every detail was etched into his mind as strength drained from his body.

Darkness closed in on Caleb as he tried to spit out words through the oxygen mask secured to his face. Blackness swallowed the preacher and transported him to a void where he was not alive, but not dead.

2

Professor Josh Webb jogged up the Warner Hall steps, pausing to take in crisp spring air. He gripped his leather book bag and made the final ascent to the third floor.

No elevator for me today. Can't let myself get too out-of-shape.

As he topped the stairs, a cold sensation pulsed through his body. His heart thumped hard and his head swirled. A wave of dizziness swept over him and for a moment, lost his balance. He pushed against the wall to keep from falling. Each step towards the classroom became increasingly difficult. Reaching the desk chair became a goal, which he achieved after some effort. Beads of sweat ran down his face as he sat and looked at his watch, 9:45 A.M. His students would be arriving soon. He knew he was getting older, but this seemed different. This was more than exhaustion; no, this was much more intense.

I guess I'm more out-of-shape than I realized. May need to schedule a doctor's visit.

"Mr. Webb, are you okay?" A female student said as she stood in the classroom doorway.

Josh took a breath and pulled himself to his feet. He straightened his shirt and rubbed his out-of-place hair down.

"Jenni, I'm fine. Just feeling a little under the weather today. I'll be better in a moment."

A perplexed look appeared on her. She cocked her head to the side.

"What I mean is that I am not feeling well. Must have eaten something that does not agree with me."

"Oh, okay. Hope you are not too sick. Any chance you will be canceling class today?"

"I'm not that sick. We are going to have class no matter what."

Jenni looked down at the floor and went to her desk. Five other students came in. Two were holding hands laughing. The others were moving like the dead with half-open eyes and the scent of beer on them. Students were so much different these days than when he began teaching fifteen years ago. They were less formal in every way, from the way they dressed to the way they addressed him. It was as if they had lost all respect, not just for authority, but for themselves. Most of the students these days were nice kids, they just lacked the proper teacher-student professionalism and mental bearing. He wondered how hard it would be for them to adjust to the real world after college. Perhaps it would have to adjust to them. They were lost, but he tried not to make it a dilemma in his mind. Josh shook his head, half in disgust and half in resignation.

What a world! It's a crazy one for sure, but I'm sure my parents and grandparents said the same about my generation.

The clock hand finally hit 10:00 A.M. and Josh rose to his feet. He cleared his throat, a subtle motion for the class to shift their attention to him. He was a professor and he loved having a role in shaping the lives of America's future. He didn't feel that well, but he was a professional. He looked over the class, making eye contact with each student as he began his lecture.

"Today, we will continue our discussion on the American Civil War and how its events shaped modern society."

Low groans echoed through the classroom. Eyes rolled back and fingers began to scroll social media sites. Texts were typed and attention to the Battle of Gettysburg waned as Josh continued his lecture with all the enthusiasm he could muster.

"Jenni, can you tell the class your view of the war and its effects on current American culture."

"I'm sorry, what did you say?"

"Are you paying attention? I asked about your view on the American Civil War and its effects on today's culture."

Silence fell over the room. All the students looked at Jenni. Some with smiles and others with solemn eyes. Josh stared at her without emotion with the goal of waiting her out.

"I don't know what to say. I'm not really interested in a war that nobody cares about."

"I see. Well, maybe you can explain why it is that nobody…."

His words blurred, and he felt a dull pain in his chest. Veins in his hands enlarged. He closed his notebook.

"Please read chapters 22 and 23 in your textbooks for the next class. Class is dismissed."

All the students gathered their things with speed and rushed out of the room. Jenni stopped at the door and looked at Josh.

"I didn't mean to offend you, but we don't care about history. It's just the way we think these days. You just have to understand."

Josh sat in his chair and watched his student walk out the door. He wrenched his hands together. A movement outside pulled him over to the window. An object came closer in the blue sky. He had seen the helicopter many times before. Sometimes its arrival and departure formed a pattern, as if the team was training. This time was different due to the speed and direct flight path. Approaching from the southeast and coming in fast made it a real-world emergency. As the helicopter got closer, Josh's heart pumped harder as if it were in sync with the chopper's blades. Anticipation pulsed in his veins as a thin layer of sweat formed over his brow. Every detail of the craft was noted. The rising sun reflected off its cockpit windows as it slowed to a hover and lowered to the university hospital. It dropped out of sight to its landing pad.

What's going on? I've seen that thing come and go many times before. How's this time any different? What is going on with me?

The stabbing pain in his chest turned to a numbing tingle, which spread throughout his body. Ticks of the clock caught his attention and took over his mind. Each second lulled Josh into a trance that almost took him to another place altogether.

Oh, my god, I must be having a heart attack or losing my mind. Something is wrong.

Vibrations and rings from his cellphone pulled him back to reality. Josh reached for his phone but bumped it further across his desk. He leaned farther over to pick it up. The screen was lit up with a campus number.

Damn, it must be the department dean. I forgot to save the number last time he called. I'm sure another disgruntled student is complaining about a grade they got; some think they're so much smarter than they are. Or, probably, I've offended one of them that doesn't comprehend reality.

"Hello."

"Is this Joshua Webb?"

"Yes, it is."

"Your brother, Caleb, is here at State University Hospital. He is in critical condition. Please come to the emergency room as soon as possible. His condition is deteriorating quickly."

Silence took over. Heavy breathing came from Josh's end.

"What? My brother? What happened? Was he the one in the medevac chopper that just came in?"

"Mr. Caleb, your brother is in critical condition and yes, he has just been brought in. According to the documents we have, you are the next of kin and we contacted you immediately. Your presence is required at this time, due to the nature of your brother's injury and condition. That is all I can say over the phone."

"Be there in ten minutes. Tell him I'm coming. Please tell him that. Promise?

"Yes, I'll tell him. Please hurry."

Josh hung up, grabbed his leather book bag and ran down the stairs, each step echoing throughout the old building. The pain and numbness had disappeared and he ran across campus to the hospital.

As Josh got closer, his heart pumped faster. Sudden coldness rushed through him as the emergency room desk was reached. The taste of sterile air dried his mouth as he breathed hard.

"I need to see Caleb Webb right now. I got a call saying pretty much that he's dying. I'm his brother. I need to see him."

"Right this way, Mr. Webb. No need to see your identification."

The head nurse navigated Josh through the maze of hallways, bringing him up to speed on what they knew and his condition. Caleb had been shot and brought in by the Medevac helicopter he had seen. The doctors were doing everything they could to stabilize him. Josh heard the words, though they were muted and echoed as if in a tunnel. What was he going to see at the end of his journey? His legs felt heavy, as if he were rushing forward in slow motion and the ER door opened. The smell and feel of death overtook him. He stopped in his steps and looked at his brother hooked up to life support machinery.

What am I seeing? Is this real? I can't believe my eyes. My brother is on his deathbed in front of me.

A slim man with gray slicked-back hair in a white medical coat walked away from Caleb's bed towards Josh. A stern look was on his face.

"Mr. Webb, your brother is in critical condition. A gunshot to the chest has caused massive damage and there is nothing else we can do. The bullet went straight through. We did surgery to repair it, but the damage is too extensive. The internal bleeding can't be stopped. All we can do now is make him comfortable."

Josh's heart almost stopped and he could not move his feet. The slow beeps from Caleb's heart monitor kept time and in Josh's head. Beeps slowed as Josh's heart beat faster.

"Can't you do something. He can't die, not yet. We need more time. He's a tough man. Please, tell me you can save him."

The doctor shook his head. He looked at Josh and nodded for him to go to his brother for the final time. With feet that weighed hundreds of pounds, Josh stepped closer. Finally, he made it to Caleb's bedside.

"I'm here. What happened? Who did this to you? Tell me. I'm here. Please talk to me if you can."

Caleb opened his eyes wide and motioned his brother towards him with a nod. Josh felt what needed to be done and said, "What do you need to tell me?"

Caleb pointed toward his bedstand and looked towards the ceiling with an expression that Josh was intimidated by. Silence consumed the room. An intimate connection was established between the twin brothers. It had always been there, but now it was stronger than it had ever been.

With care, Josh opened the nightstand drawer. Its contents made him feel somewhat better. Slowly, he lifted his brother's Bible and handed it to Caleb. The embrace of the sacred book produced a cough and smile behind the clouded oxygen mask.

3

Driving through pouring rain to Etham was hard enough with limited visibility and slick roads, but traveling there to bury your brother made the journey even more grueling. The experience was surreal and beyond any pain he had ever known, even worse than his parents dying. Three years had passed since him and Caleb had parted ways and began their estranged relationship. Josh had not come back to his hometown since that altering Sunday morning.

Should have called or visited him. Time is so short, and we took that for granted. I should have made amends with him. We are brothers for God's sake. Damn, we were brothers; we will be forever.

Time dragged with each mile, compounding the aching in Josh's gut. His finger's tapped the steering wheel hard, keeping time with the wiper blades as he took a sharp curve a bit too aggressively. He eased off the gas, more instinctively than from any fear of danger. His memories shifted left to right with the mountainous curves, reminiscing from childhood to Caleb's last breath, and many times in between. Episodes were sometimes bad, but most of his memories were of the good moments. Breathing was hard, but he somehow managed. Josh's brow squinted as he tightened his grip on the steering wheel. Someone was going to pay for this.

Who would kill a preacher? That is beyond evil. It's just pure evil. I've never heard of such a thing.

Josh had his ideas but tried not to focus on one. Caleb was a man of the cloth, but a crazed addict desperate for a fix and needing cash wouldn't hesitate to shoot him down for a few bucks. Still, killing a preacher was going too far, even in this day and time in Etham. Sunlight peeked through the dark clouds and the rain stopped. Josh passed the town sign and slowed down. Red and blue neon lights illuminating the word *Tattoos* welcomed him. That parlor had not been there the last time he had visited. Numerous cars were parked out front and people were milling around inside looking at the artwork on the walls. Across the road, the gas station that had been there since he was a kid was still pumping gas and peddling grab and go items. Things looked and felt different. Even the air seemed to suffocate Josh when he rolled down the window.

Etham, the seat of Woodridge County with a population of around 1,200 citizens, was only a shadow of what it was in the heyday of coal mining. Back then, it boomed with stores and bars where you could get the highest quality goods and services–along with some of the less moral ones if you desired it. A balance between the two was maintained by the law and the people. At the town's height, it was dubbed the "Little Vegas" of Kentucky by the media and locals. Now, the town was just like hundreds of others across Eastern Kentucky that had dried up and struggled to provide any economic prosperity to its inhabitants. These days the coal industry was dead and people lived on government subsistence and criminal activities. A churning sick feeling erupted in his gut when he thought about how much his hometown had changed so much since he was a kid and when earlier generations of his family had prospered from mining. The invasive industry had produced a lower middle-class upbringing for him and his brother that had given them opportunities to move to other livelihoods.

Thoughts shifted back to who had shot Caleb and left him for dead. He eyed the sheriff's department as he drove through town. He clinched the steering wheel and pushed hard on the gas pedal. Josh's mind drifted from the road. Blue and red lights came up behind him with the always corresponding siren. Josh snapped out of his daze as the blaring sound pierced his ears and a cruiser closed in.

Damn it, my mind is mush. Should have been paying attention. Sure, don't need a ticket. Bet it's a state trooper.

Josh pulled into the local dollar store parking lot. He fumbled inside the center console for his insurance card and dug out his driver's license from his wallet. The flashing lights reflected in the rearview mirror and added to his already growing headache. Josh looked into the mirror again as a police officer walked closer with a hand gripped on a holstered pistol.

"Sir, keep your hands where I can see them. Slowly, hand me your license and proof of insurance out the vehicle window with both hands showing."

Josh did as he was instructed. What to say to the officer eluded him. His mind wandered from one crazy thought to another.

The officer walked the final step with caution. He grabbed the license and insurance card. Minutes passed as the man scanned the items. He stared at Josh, who turned his eyes forward and tried not to look at the officer's face.

"You were hitting 55 in a 35-mph zone and that's a little too much."

"Sir, I didn't mean to speed. My mind was in a different place because I've been on the road for a bit. My eyes and mind are tired."

The officer eyed Josh. "That's your best answer? It's a good idea to keep your mind and eyes on driving. You need to keep your speed within reason for your safety as well as everybody else on the road. Do you understand what I'm saying?"

Josh rubbed his eyes and looked up at the officer. After a few seconds, the officer's face came into focus.

"Sheriff Harris Bell, how are you? I'm sorry about speeding. There's so much on my mind these days. I swear I thought I was going the speed limit."

"Josh Webb. I'm tracking your situation, but you can't be running up and down the road at high speed no matter what your situation. Have you been drinking? It would be a shame to get locked up with what you've got going on right now. But don't think I won't do it."

"Sheriff, I've not been drinking. Believe me, I could sure use a drink with my brother being shot down in cold blood. But no, I am definitely sober. I just dazed out for a few seconds and I'll be honest I wasn't paying attention to the road."

Each one eyed the other and both felt sweat form on their foreheads. Tension was thick as mud, despite their similar backgrounds. Bell had always been friendly to him when they were growing up together in Etham. He was seven years older than Josh and was well-liked in town. As a result, he had been reelected as sheriff for years with nobody even running against him. His behavior now was not what Josh expected at all.

"I figured you'd be acting this way, since Caleb got himself shot. Why don't you get out of the car and we can talk for a bit?"

Rage ran through Josh's bones as he thought about the sheriff's words and tone. Patience and restraint were key at the moment due to needing information from Bell. Josh hoped he would do his job and find Caleb's killer. Josh opened the door and straightened his back. The drive and stress had taken its toll on his body. The cracks and strains were evidence. Bell stepped back due to his training with self-protection in mind.

"I was going to stop at your office, but I thought it would be better to head up to the funeral home first. Need to get the arrangements done. I'm the only person left. You know that, don't you."

"Guess Caleb never found a woman to settle down with, now did he? He just messed around with a few here and there. Maybe one too many."

"Sheriff, I take offense to you putting down Caleb. He was a good man, a man of the Lord and a preacher. He never wronged anybody. I don't know what crazy stuff you're talking about."

Bell took a cigarette out and lit it. He sucked in the smoke and blew it out with force. With his hands on his gun holster belt, he walked to the front of Josh's vehicle.

"I guess the definition of being wronged is different from one person to another. Just like the changing of the seasons."

The sheriff's lack of empathy was repulsive and out of character. Had the depravity of Etham made him so calloused? An inclination to punch the guy in the mouth swept over Josh, but he refrained knowing he needed the sheriff. But the urge to hit something was too strong to contain.

"Who shot Caleb? That is what I need to know." Josh said and slammed his fist on the top of his truck.

"Calm down. Your anger won't get you any answers and it will not be tolerated around here. You get me?"

Sweat ran down Josh's forehead. He hoped his direct approach would change the playing field. Bell took his hands off his gun belt and took a deep breath.

"I guess you're not your brother, despite looking just like him. You twins always throw me for a loop. I'll be honest with you, I didn't care much for him. But at this point that doesn't matter. We

16

are conducting a full investigation in conjunction with the State Police. We don't have any solid leads yet, but this county is small. Something will turn up soon. I have a lot of informants around. You just need to relax and let me do what I do best."

Josh paced back and forth. He looked up at the sky and breathed in the cool air. The aroma of Mountain Laurel and Eastern White Pine seeped into his nostrils. In a moment, composure and inquisitiveness overcame him.

"I've got to ask one question. Where was he found?"

Silence filled the air. Bell looked at Josh. Their eyes locked and then Bell looked towards the center of town.

"Why are you asking that? You need to leave all this to me. I'm the sheriff and it's my job. I'll make sure his killer is brought to justice, no matter my opinion of your brother or you."

"Why won't you tell me? You owe me that. You know my family. I know you."

"Alright. Only, if you promise not to go messing around there or anywhere else in the county. This place is different these days. It's a dangerous place around here, very different from the last time you were here."

Josh nodded his head and sat on the top of the truck hood. Bell lit another cigarette.

"You want one."

"Sure, why not?" Josh said as he thought about that day at Carr Reservoir Lake when he almost drowned and his brother saved him.

"He was found a mile up the trail from the resort. Some hikers came across him on Boone's Trail that leads north. Due to the investigation being an open case, I can't give you the exact location, but with all the gossip in town it will not take you long to know where it is."

Josh looked at Bell with a confused look. Each one stared at each other for an uncomfortable moment that seemed to draw blood.

"Resort? Didn't know Etham had a resort. When did that happen?"

"Yes. Opened up two or so years ago. The biggest in the region. It's brought everyone back from the edge. The economy was suffering all day every day, but it is turning around."

Josh was stunned for a moment. He had not heard anything about that, but he had not kept up with news of any kind. This was due to him being on sabbatical for the last year working on a Colonial America project at Williamsburg, Virginia. Etham having a resort was one thing, but solving the economic problems was another. He decided not to pursue the topic with Bell.

"I guess I understand why you're not giving me the exact location. You don't have to worry about me. I want you to do your job and whoever is responsible to pay."

Bell walked away from Josh's truck as he puffed on his cigarette. He took one final toke and put it out with his boot.

"I forgot you've not been here for a few years. The town got a grant to revitalize the community and the city council voted on building a trailhead center. It's a stopover for hikers that use Boone's Trail."

"Really. That doesn't seem like a booming business to me. You'd have to have thousands of hikers to make a profit."

"You're totally right. No benefit to the community at first, but a businessman came in and purchased a lot of land. He developed the trail center and built the resort, complete with high-end cabins spread out over a section of the trail. The accommodations cater to rich clientele. Within six months, business was booming. The center is the hub and is bigger than downtown Etham. Seems like the local economy is getting stronger each season."

Josh jumped up from the truck hood. He put his hands on his sides and thought about what he had just heard.

"So, you're telling me this dying town is now thriving due to a tourist business based on hiking and cabins? I'm not an economic expert, but that is hard to believe."

"I tell you that it's true and it's a miracle. Everyone around here should be grateful for that businessman."

Josh looked across the road at two homeless men flashing cardboard signs begging for handouts. He looked back at Sheriff Bell.

"From what I have see the citizens are not benefiting. What's the name of this resort and who is this bigwig who built it?"

"Things will take time to get totally better. The resort is called Stepping Stone Mountain Resort and Trailhead Center. You know the man, G.W. Fields."

Josh's eyes widened. The name ran fast through his brain.

"G.W. Fields?"

"Yes, the one and only."

"I really don't give a damn about the resort or that Mr. Fields built it. Do you know who killed my brother?"

Bell stopped his pacing and looked at Josh. He put his hands on his gun belt again causing it to creak from pressure.

"Listen to me. We don't have anything solid yet. I'll keep you informed. Like I said, I'll find his killer. Now, you go on and take care of your brother's arrangements."

A nod was all that Josh could muster. His gut and judgment swayed him towards knowing there was no validity in Bell's words.

Bell stretched his neck and took a deep breath. A clenched fist formed and he hesitated to talk for a moment. Finally, with effort he spit out some words in a different tone.

"Me and my wife will attend the funeral out of respect. That's the only reason. The town folk expect it. If it was left to me, I'd rather be fishing."

Josh stared at Bell. Veins popped up on his forehead and anger pulsed. He let his temper fade.

"Out of duty, I checked on your old homeplace. I was just out there today. It's just like your brother left it. I guess the place is yours now."

Both nodded their heads in mutual respect and got into their vehicles. The air was charged with both men's resentment, but a gentlemanly stance was settled upon.

As Josh headed towards the funeral home, images of Caleb looking at him in the hospital plagued his mind. The significance of the town's name resonated in his mind. He had heard the story of the name as a kid from his grandmother, who held the Bible in high regard. A place, "on the edge of the wilderness." It was a location that the Israelites camped on their exodus from Egypt. Now, as he drove the meaning became more meaningful.

4

Nine years had passed since Josh had been to the White and Talbott Funeral Home, a converted Victorian house with a steep gabled roof and ornamental woodwork that sat on the edge of town. In the late 1800s, it was the most expensive home in town. Now, it's the last earthly stop for local residents. Caleb's and Josh's mother, Barbara, had passed away in her sleep due to sadness from losing their father six months earlier. A heart drowned by grief, some said. A familiar weight pressed against his chest as he sat from the parking lot looking at the house. Memories of his mother's funeral flooded his mind, especially of seeing her frail body in the coffin.

Dark clouds pushed to the west and a blue sky appeared. Josh looked himself over in the rearview mirror. A pale face looked back at him with red, puffy eyes. He needed rest, but he doubted he'd be able to sleep. The funeral home door stared coldly at him and he stared back. His heart thumped rapidly; each breath quickened. Seeing Caleb die and feeling his soul leave his body weighed on him like iron chains. His wildest imagination would never have placed him here making funeral arrangements for his brother, his last blood relative. That day in the hospital–the image of Caleb looking at him and then fading away had been etched forever into his soul. It played repeatedly as he sat looking at the front of the building. A chill ran up his arms and brought him back to reality.

Just need to go get this done. Nobody else is here to do it. I'm the last of the bloodline.

The front steps seemed different than the last time he had been there. Were there more? The question went through his mind as he opened the door and walked in. He expected to see old man Talbott at his large oak desk filling out forms and talking on the phone. A younger version was there, instead, with a tablet and texting on his smartphone.

"Good day. Come on in and have a seat. Let me finish up this coffin order and I'll be right with you." The man smiled and typed at a frenzied speed.

Josh took a seat in the same comfortable red wingback chair he had sat in years earlier. Old pictures adorned the front office. One was of the house when it was first built and another was of Mr. Talbott standing proudly in front of it when he opened the funeral home back in the late 1960s.

"Sorry to keep you waiting. My name is Eric Talbott. I don't think we have met before. I'm here to ensure all the arrangements for your brother are done down to the detail."

He reached out his hand. They shook hands and sat back down.

"How do you know who I am? Where is Mr. Talbott at?"

"First of all, can I get you something to drink, a water or cup of coffee?"

Josh shook his head, already dizzied by swirling emotions of anger and grief, and now with an unexpected funeral worker to deal with—and young, at that.

"My grandfather died a year ago. I took over the business, due to Dad not wanting to deal in death. Guess he had enough of it when he was growing up. As far as knowing who you are, I guessed from you being Caleb Webb's twin. I examined your brother when the coroner escorted his body here."

"Right. I guess you do know that I'm here to make my brother's arrangements."

Eric leaned up in his chair. His mustache was too thin and his face too pointed, a look that was expected from an undertaker.

"Mr. Webb, everything has been arranged already. Your brother came in months ago and took care of all the details."

"What do you mean everything?"

"Please forgive me. I would have contacted you, if I had known how to get in touch with you. Caleb picked out his coffin, flowers, music, and paid in full for everything. That is normal for the older generation. COVID and drug overdose cases are totally different, which the last one is the predominance of my business these days. Sorry, I shouldn't talk about business, when your brother was murdered...passed on."

Silence consumed the room. Josh locked eyes with Eric. An uncomfortable minute passed.

"Eric, you're okay. It doesn't surprise me that Caleb prepared everything. That is how he was. I guess he picked a cheap wooden coffin and chose a plot next to Mom and Dad at Chestnut Flat Cemetery?"

"You know your brother quite well. Like I said, everything has been arranged. The visitation will be here tomorrow night at 7:00 and the funeral will be the next morning at 11:00. Will those days and times be okay?"

"Yes. Caleb always prepared for everything. I guess his funeral was no different. Sounds like he made things like he wanted them."

Eric leaned back in his leather chair. His normal customers didn't have enough to pay the bill and they tried to make deals. Most times he didn't get what he was owed, but this time was so easy that he thought of it as a reward.

"Yes, he did."

"Is there anything else that I need to do?" Josh said.

"No, Caleb even wrote his own newspaper obituary. Of course, I put in the date and location of death. Everything else was authored by him. This is the first time I have had someone do that."

Josh leaned forward in the chair. He eyed the younger Talbott.

"I'm at a loss for words. Guess I don't have anything else to say."

Eric texted someone and pulled up a document on his tablet. He hit the print button.

"Here is the receipt just in case you need it. Paid in full. The death certificate should be back from the State Capitol in a few weeks. Where do you want me to send it and do you need more than one copy?"

Josh couldn't believe he was giving instructions on where to send his brother's death certificate. Nothing seemed real.

"One copy will be fine. Send it to Caleb's address. I'm sure you know it."

"Yes, I do. I'm sorry for your loss. Caleb was a good man with a matching reputation. I've heard of his contributions to the community. You have my condolences. I hope whoever ended his life pays for it in kind."

"I hope so, too."

"I'll make sure your brother looks really good for the visitation and funeral. He will look like he did when he was living. As far as his clothes, Caleb brought in a suit that he wanted to be buried in. We'll make sure everything is done as he instructed."

"I'm sure he would appreciate that. I do too."

Josh got up from the familiar chair and shook Eric's hand. Both of them looked at each other.

"Do you mind me giving you some advice?" Eric said with a grim face.

"I don't mind at all, these days. Any that I can get will do me some good."

"See that your brother is put to rest and then leave this place. There's nothing good here. I'm going to leave this town soon. An opportunity has presented itself out west and I'm going for it."

"What about the funeral home when you leave? Who will run it?"

Both looked at each other and knew the answer.

"It will end how it should. I'm moving on. Just like the souls and families that my family have helped. We have done enough to help Etham. There's no helping what can't be helped. Like I said, I recommend that you do your grieving and get out of town as soon as you can. Nothing good is left here anymore."

"I understand, Mr. Talbott. Hope you find what you are looking for. I appreciate everything you have done, I'll see you tomorrow. I understand your angle on the other stuff. I'll be going. Thank you again."

As Josh walked down the front steps, the words "what can't be helped" ran over and over in his mind. The newspaper vending machine at the street corner caught his eye. With the drop of three quarters, he had the paper in hand and was reading Caleb's obituary.

Caleb L. Webb, passed away unexpectedly on September 1, 2022 at State University Hospital. He was 48 years old. His congregation and residents of Etham are deeply saddened by his sudden death.

Caleb is survived by his brother Josh W. Webb. Caleb was preceded in death by his parents, Cyrus and Barbara Webb as well as his grandparents, Abraham and Permelia Webb.

Caleb was born with his twin brother on June 16, 1974 in Lexington, Kentucky. He grew up in Etham and attended State University. Upon graduation, he attended Cumberland Baptist Theological Seminary, which he considered one of the most influential experiences of his life.

He enjoyed the comfort and peace of the outdoors. One of his favorite activities was embracing nature, while hiking Boone's Trail. He considered Etham his favorite place in the world and admired its natural beauty.

Caleb was a devoted soul dedicated to serving his fellow humans. As pastor of The Open Paths Baptist Church he spread his faith and selfless service to his congregation. He was a shepherd of his flock and kept them from harm's way by the word of God and prayer. His soul was illuminated by his work for the community that he loved. He cared deeply for the people around him and was always the Good Samaritan that especially looked after the young. He consistently sacrificed himself to ensure the well-being of the community's younger generations. He was a protector of the young.

As he moves to his next life, he will keep his protected souls in his soul as he did in this life. In the end, he found comfort in knowing he had helped those who could not take care of themselves.

After reading the words, sadness enveloped Josh and time stopped. Images of his brother and fond times from the past made him smile. A passing car brought him back to reality. It was an older couple honking and waving.

They must think I'm Caleb. How could they not know he is dead?

Josh waved, forcing a cordial smile. He watched them head down Main Street towards the supermarket. The old homeplace beckoned him and he got into his truck.

5

Faith and religion had been the lifeblood of his brother. Caleb had always put his congregation and church before anything else– even himself. Anxiety increased with each passing minute as he drove past Caleb's church, The Open Paths Baptist Church. It stood on a steep rocky hill overlooking Etham and had been established in the early 1900s. The church had maintained a devoted congregation, but waned in the current hard economic times and a tendency for the younger generations to move away from religion.

His attention drifted as he drove the last mile to his destination. He wondered how run down the old homestead would be. It had been over three years since he had been there. To be fair, Caleb was busy in the community and likely didn't have time to take care of the property. But something inside him hoped it would be bad, perhaps to prove it had been in the wrong hands or perhaps to simply add justification to the disgust he felt towards his brother for past disagreements. All of that was soaked in sorrow for losing his brother. Josh's ears popped as he shifted into low gear and ascended a hill. Finally, he rounded the curve and pulled into the gravel driveway. Josh grunted and rolled his eyes.

"Of course."

The old place was very well kept and even had a fresh coat of paint. Same off-white color with black shutters and trim that had been imprinted into his brain as a kid. The green shingled roof had recently been replaced with green tin, but no major change in the way it looked. No reason to go change so-called perfection.

He got out and looked down at Etham in between McKinney Mountain and Croley Mountain. It looked no different from decades earlier. The air felt different at this elevation. Clean and unafflicted with the town's troubles down below. It helped his thinking for a moment. A breeze from the north carried the aroma of pines that stood tall next to the house and reminded him of his childhood. Thoughts of why his brother had been shot crossed his mind again as well as why his brother had been alone all these years. He had never married.

Josh climbed the wooden porch steps up to his childhood home. The boards creaked with each step. It was the porch that punctured his armor. Saving for the paint and obvious repairs it had been left unchanged. Even the old wind chimes Caleb hated so much were still there. Feelings aside, Josh couldn't help but appreciate the care put into the place. Hopefully, inside was in just as good condition. But even if it wasn't, the porch was the same; and that was the most important part. Many nights had been spent swinging and looking at the stars. Listening to the sounds of woods at night had always enchanted Josh and took him to another place.

Even the garden was well attended. No big surprise there, Caleb had inherited all the green thumb genes. Josh would have to check it out and see if anything was ready to harvest. That would certainly cut down on whatever groceries he might need to purchase. For all his brother's moral flaws, there was no doubting his work ethic. Josh couldn't deny that.

The door wasn't locked. No surprise there either, knowing Caleb's naive sense of trust. What was disturbing, however, was that it wasn't closed all the way. This was a bit off, even for Caleb, who had enough sense to keep out wandering animals. Josh slowly pushed the door open. With Caleb being murdered, caution was at the forefront of his mind. He peered inside and expected the worst. Nothing seemed out of place, which made him breathe normally again. He remembered that the sheriff and multiple other law enforcement agents had been here, so perhaps they had failed to shut the door all the way.

Sure, thought the place would be trashed or I would have to throw down with an unwanted guest.

Everything was as he remembered. Their home had always been modestly furnished. Only the essentials: nothing more, nothing less. Inside was not filthy, but cluttered, as if Caleb had stopped picking up after himself. That was odd due to everything on the exterior looking pristine. He checked the gun safe, his Mom's jewelry box, his Dad's old money box under the bed. Everything was unbothered. After thinking about what he saw he thought about his brother's traits. Caleb's upkeep of the place didn't include household tidiness, a trait Josh had to admit he shared. His mind shifted.

Brother, you lived a simple life. It must have been faith that kept you happy. It would be hard for me to live here and do what you did. I'm not like you.

The only luxury that Caleb had was his books. Next to the lack of household tidiness, this was one of the few traits that he and Josh shared. In the living room, two walls had built-in shelves that housed numerous books ranging from Plato to modern political theory, with numerous religious works mixed in. Josh was always amazed at this brother's collection in which he strived to surpass himself. He looked into Caleb's bedroom with its simple bed and nightstand. The pull to look in his old bedroom overwhelmed him and made him bypass his parent's bedroom. Their mother had not changed anything and neither had Caleb. A couple of baseball trophies mixed with rock band posters had frozen the room in time. With a smile and self-admiration, he moved to the sparse kitchen that looked the same as when their mother had cooked up the best meals that he had ever tasted.

This is one room that I love the most. Mom was the best. I miss her.

Most of the cabinets were almost bare as was the refrigerator. His stomach growled and hunger gnawed at him. He could not remember when he had eaten last.

I guess some stale toasted bread and strawberry jam will have to do.

Josh pushed the toaster lever down and found a spoon. Several bottles of water were on the counter. He opened one and downed it.

As he sat down on the porch with his feast, the sun slipped over the far ridge and the stars glimmered. The toast and jam were not enough to satisfy him. He remembered the secret place his brother kept a bottle of bourbon for special times and the occasional guest. He went to the kitchen and opened a bottom cabinet. In the back, a wood panel hid a cubby hole and, as remembered, a fifth of aged bourbon was stashed. Josh's eyes widened to see it half empty as he pulled it out.

Caleb never drank a lot. Unless? For him to have had a half full bottle is not a good sign. Something must have had him rattled. The last time he drank a lot was when Mom died. For me, drinking is not too much of a problem and I sure don't need to add anything to mess up my thinking, but a few drinks wouldn't hurt right now.

From memory, Josh knew the cubby hole was also a place Caleb kept other valuables just as his parents had. He reached farther into the space and pulled out an old green metal tackle box they had as kids.

Haven't seen this in a long time. This has seen many fishing trips and some big fish.

With a well-practiced hand, he poured a glass of bourbon from the bottle he had found, grabbed the box, and moved to the living room. His brother's murder weighed on him heavily as he sipped and looked at the scratched-up metal; it was a reminder of their childhood with its good and bad times.

After an hour, curiosity and the numbness of bourbon pushed him to open the box. Folded papers were bound together with a string. With a pull, the bunch revealed his brother's will and an all-access Stepping Stone Mountain Resort pass with maintenance printed at the top.

Sheriff Bell had been right about Caleb bequeathing the house and surrounding ten-acre plot to him. It made sense due to Caleb not having any other family, but Caleb had always been the thorough type. The access pass churned Josh's curiosity.

Why would Caleb put this in the cubby hole? Only important stuff was put there. Why would a poor country church pastor covet this so much to hide it? The man didn't believe in the type of fun the resort offered or any fun, for that matter. The resort pass made Josh even more curious, especially stamped maintenance crew.

Did Caleb work at the resort? If so, why? So many questions to get answers to or try to get answers.

Wind kicked up and swayed the oak trees above the house. Chimes from the porch sounded. Rain began pelting the tin roof, slowly at first and then harder. Lights flickered and thunder crashed in the distance. Josh looked at the pass and the now quarter full bottle of bourbon. Nothing made sense at the moment, but he knew deep inside that he would find out who killed his brother. He poured another drink from his brother's bottle and toasted their unbreakable connection. The wind and rain continued. After an hour, he passed out on the couch.

6

Josh heard the voices as a child hears adults conversing around the dinner table as they lay to sleep in their adjoining bedroom. Muffled, like being in a closed wood box. The whole town had flowed around the side aisles of The Open Path's sanctuary, offering their condolences, each with their own stories of how Caleb had touched their lives.

Brother Caleb led me to the Lord. Brother Caleb helped me with my bills. Brother Caleb always brought such inspiring messages.

Each thankful for such a godly man and deeply hurt by his violent murder. Their eyes told even more of their gratitude.

Who could murder a man such as this? How will the community survive such a loss? But they will.

Josh endured the deluge of sympathy like a conductor punching a ticket for people boarding a train: extend hand, force a smile, nod head, and say, "Thank you. Move along; next please."

If only they knew the real man, Caleb, that they were putting upon a pedestal. They needed to know the whole man. But they only saw the external, the preacher man. The Gospel of Christ was his craft. Winning souls, helping those in need, and encouraging them were his trade.

Cold dark reality would betray the preacher to be every bit as sinful as the rest. They just didn't see it.

Josh continued at his post, occasionally peeking down the tracks in search of the caboose, hoping it would soon come. He wondered whether these ceremonies were ever really for the family members; the ones who hurt the most. Perhaps, Caleb was different, maybe because people were telling him things about his brother that contradicted the man he knew. It didn't matter now. The total shock of the death was in his brain. Knowing that the time for reconciling things with his brother was in the past consumed him.

He doubted his state of mind would be much different, if everything had been good between them. Death was death, after all. At the end of the day, Caleb was his twin and they had been inseparable for most of their lives. And now he was gone, leaving Josh with dark hole in his heart, lots of questions, and a long line of clammy hands to shake. This thing was a charade, a ceremony for everyone else. He was merely a supporting cast member, a stage prop.

To make it worse, he hated the place–this tabernacle of hypocrisy. He desperately needed an escape and to process this in his own way. He needed a different sanctuary, the porch of the old homestead with a bottle. Many of his early life decisions had been made there rocking on that old bench swing. Sometimes with one or all his family; often on his own. The greatest decision ever made on that swing was to get the hell out of Etham, while he could and he did. But he sure did miss the place every so often.

Leaving Etham was not solely his idea. Their father, Cyrus, suffering from black lung at the time of Josh's exodus, had cultivated that seed in his mind from as early as he could remember. He had insisted his sons pursue higher education and leave their destined raggedy coal mining existence behind. But it wasn't just an insistence on the education and good career themselves, it was something more. He instilled in them both a love for learning.

Although he labored his life away at the mines, Cyrus had been an avid student of life. He read books of all kinds and experimented with different gardening methods. He spent time at church and visiting folks in the community. For a coal mining slave, he was quite the Renaissance man. If he had it his way, he would spend all his time learning about the great world in which he lived. But bills must be paid, so he made a point to always clock in on time and head down the dark mineshaft.

Such was the story of the porch. Josh's affection for the bottle came much later. Not that he was a drunkard, Josh had come to use alcohol as a way of winding down after a long week of teaching or to blow off steam after intense research. He thought of the bottle as a therapist and his occasional binges as therapeutic retreats. It was a proven science and it was effective, though some might say the retreats were more frequent than really required. Nonetheless, he figured another night on the old porch with a friendly bottle of Kentucky bourbon would be just what the doctor ordered. If the weather eased up just a bit, he might spend the whole weekend in therapy.

At long last the final hand reached out. It was attached to a man with a vaguely familiar face, "Joshua Webb, son I haven't seen you in, what, ten...fifteen years? Good Lord, look at how fast time slips by!"

"Mr. Fields, yes sir, it's been a while."

"I'm so sorry about Caleb, he was a good man. I can't imagine a soul in Etham he hadn't touched. Just look at all these people, he impacted every one of them!"

"Yes sir, there's a lot of them. I didn't know there were so many people in Woodridge County."

"You'd be surprised, Josh. In fact, Etham has nearly doubled in population in the last few years. And believe it or not, your brother played a big part in it." Mr. Fields lowered his voice, pointing his head to the parking lot, "But listen, you're absolutely beat. Get out of this dismal place and get some rest. These folks will be fine. But let's get together in a few days before you leave town. I'll tell you all about how your brother helped our humble town grow!"

He's right about getting some rest. I'm not going to the funeral or cemetery for the burial tomorrow. Yes, people will not understand me not being there, but I don't owe anybody a justification or anything else. I can't stand seeing Caleb being put in the ground or seeing Dad and Mom's graves.

Josh shook hands with Mr. Fields as he left and thought about him building the resort that Sheriff Bell had talked about. He didn't plan on visiting his father's old friend, though he should. Mr. Fields had always been good to his father. After Cyrus got too sick to work in the mine Fields would find ways to keep his father on the payroll. Jobs that weren't difficult, but neither were they degrading. He understood dignity was at the heart of a man like Cyrus. The pay had never decreased either, though in reality it should have. Mining was a business after all, but Mr. Fields as a supervisor took care of his own and that paid off in huge dividends of loyalty from the miners. From the looks of the sanctuary and Cyrus shaking hands, it looked as if he was still taking care of everyone.

Josh slipped into the parking lot and drove away unnoticed by the sympathizers, who were socializing in the church's fellowship center. Mr. Fields was right, his presence was no longer necessary. He would spend a day, maybe two, at the homestead and perhaps bid his last farewell at the cemetery as he left town. A thought crossed his mind; he could sell the place and be done with Etham forever. A flash of nausea washed over him followed by a wave of chills. Was this an ancestral rebuke from some deep place within him? He would think more about this during the upcoming evening therapy session with Dr. Bourbon.

Getting back to the homestead was a blur. Stepping on the porch, he looked back at the driveway and his truck wondering how he had gotten from the church to here, as if he had been teleported.

My mind ain't right. Forgetting everything these days.

Josh returned to his truck to grab his backpack where he had tucked away a fresh bottle of well-aged Kentucky bourbon, his reading glasses, cell phone charger, and some clothes. His pack would make him better prepared than last night and passing out on the couch. Removing the bottle, he threw the bag on the living room floor and retrieved a glass from the kitchen cabinet. Heading to the porch, he noticed Caleb's pocket Bible had fallen from the bag. He scooped it up on his way out. He set the bourbon, glass, and his brother's Bible on the wicker table as he sat on the swing. It was about an hour or so until sunset and Josh took a final moment of sobriety to relish being home and to set a slow pace for the evening's therapy session.

Cool mountain air soon mingled with a soft, oaky vanilla fragrance as Josh broke the bottle's seal. His normal stock was mid-range, but he kept a nicer selection for the extra hard times. It couldn't get any harder than this. The first glass was warm and smooth, and he savored it as if enjoying it with an old friend. Despite their rift in recent years, Caleb was the oldest friend he had. He imagined sharing this drink with him for old times' sake.

"Here's to ya, you sorry piece of work."

A soft breeze brushed through the wind chimes as to return the toast. Josh chuckled at the chimes. They were Caleb's idea, a Mother's Day gift. But their incessant clanging was an annoyance that nearly drove him insane. However, Mom loved them and thought they added a certain charm and thus found a place of permanence. She had passed away nine years ago and the wind chimes remained. Sentimentalism had immortalized their presence.

He couldn't help but scoff at his brother's contradicting nature. Caleb had that way about him: part savior and part devil. Just like with the wind chimes, he would love giving while despising the gift. Most people only saw the savior side of him, but Josh had seen both sides. And though he could come to terms with a man wrestling with his sins, he just couldn't stomach a man making excuses for it.

The second glass helped advocate for Caleb's flaws. To be fair, Caleb was just a man like everyone else. Hell, Josh had his own inconsistencies. But then again, he wasn't going around telling everyone else how to live. He didn't pretend to be something he wasn't.

Josh resolved to cut Caleb some slack, if only for tonight. They were brothers, after all. No, they had been more than that, friends. While Caleb may have had his devilish side, he had certainly been a savior for Josh on several occasions.

Resting forward with elbows on his knees, Josh thought of that time on the lake when Caleb was just that, a savior. He shook his head with a grin, hating to admit it ever happened. Another breeze blew him gently into another time. The chimes sang again joined by a fluttering chorus of blood-stained pages. Unwittingly, Josh picked up his brother's Bible in one hand while holding the warm glass with the other. He looked out across the western wooded landscape; savior in one hand and devil in the other. Josh gazed dreamily towards the dark red horizon, fully immersed in another time.

7

Sunlight beamed off the water of Carr Reservoir Lake, causing the two brothers to squint their way to the secret honey-hole. They had fished this man-made lake many times with their father and now they were out by themselves. Wind from the west pushed them along in the flat-bottom Jon boat their father had bought for them when they graduated 8th grade. At that time, the boat was everything. It represented a new freedom. They were in control, captains of the ship. Flirting with girls or scamping in the woods took less priority when the fish were biting. Now, as they turned 17 and had started to follow separate paths, fishing was the mutual passion that held them together. Despite their current lives with all the ups and downs, fishing enforced the already physical and mental bonds of being twin brothers. Fishing kept the balance between themselves and the world that consumed them slowly every day.

Ripples and waves hit the side of the boat, pushing it to the deepest part of the lake. Houseboats leisured by and high-speed boats plowed towards party spots scattered across the lake. Their small craft tossed from side to side. Waves from scantily clad females caught their eyes and toasts from beer-handed occupants flashed by.

"Love the scenery, but we need to get up into Shallow Creek. The fish will be hitting hard today. I feel it." Josh steered the outboard engine in that direction.

"I feel you, brother. Stop looking at those babes and hit it. Too much good-looking traffic down here. Maybe our looks would get them talking, but your personality would sure drive them off." Caleb laughed as Josh scratched his cheek with his straightened middle finger. He pointed the boat towards the secluded inlet to the north.

The grinding engine pushed the boat onward, inching the brothers to the sweetest fishing hole they had ever come across. Their Dad had shown them this fishing Mecca and brought them every year since–a sacred event ringing in the annual spawn.

"You remember the first year Dad brought us here? Remember the snake incident?"

Josh rolled his eyes. "How can I not? You bring it up every time."

Caleb's laughter filled the cove. "We were over there swimming, while Dad fished the other side of the boat and nonchalantly asked us what kind of snake that was swimming past." Caleb gave Josh a devilish grin and continued the worn-out story. "You started paddling like a wild man, scared to death, and splashing water all over me. Josh...you were in the boat before Dad could tell you that he was only joking"

"Yeah, yeah, smart guy. I remember you were right up my spine trying to get back in the boat, just like me." Josh reached his hand up to backhand his brother, but then gave him a wink. "Anyways, Dad was always one for a good prank."

"Here we are." Caleb said and pulled a pack of menthol cigarettes out of his shirt pocket.

"Where'd you score those?"

"At the gettin' place. That's all you need to know."

Josh smiled and looked at his brother. Both eyed each other down.

"I sure know where you got them. Old Man Ingram. He's the only one around that smokes those cheap cigs. You went and stole them, didn't you?"

"You think you know everything, but you don't know a damn thing about nothing."

"Guess us being twins, we know everything about each other and what each one does. Wouldn't you say that is the truth?"

They smiled in mischief as Caleb shook a cigarette loose from the pack. Josh took one and fired it up as Caleb lit his.

Both coughed and hacked, but kept smoking like old men. They tried to outdo each other with the smokes, as with everything else.

"Not bad for an off brand." Josh coughed, and both laughed at acting like they were getting away with a major crime.

"Why don't we wager five dollars and a six-pack on who catches the most fish today?" Caleb said as he tossed his line out and took a drink of beer.

"Now, now. You'd be losing that bet for sure, but since you are so sure of yourself it's a bet. I guess you will have to go to the bootlegger for that six pack and borrow the five dollars off Mom." Josh said and threw his line into the water.

"Then, it's a deal. Now, don't be backing out on paying up, if you get drunk and don't catch a damn thing. We will see who'll be borrowing money and buying from the bootlegger." Caleb snapped.

Both shook hands, took a drink of beer, and looked at each other. Then, the competition overtook them. All of this was a ritual they had done every year, until they had the falling out.

Caleb spotted a nice spot to cast his lure between two half-submerged logs. He yanked and reeled a pattern that he thought made sense to him and the fish. Thoughts of bringing in a big whopper and rubbing it in his brother's face consumed him. Josh had always been the favorite one of their father's, despite being twins. To Caleb, Josh was the chosen one. Sometimes it made him jealous, but he loved his brother and was as enamored by him as his father was. The same black hair and eyes with olive skin were inherited from their mother's Native American roots and made them look alike, but their minds were different. Josh was always the life of the party, while Caleb was more introverted. Both sought knowledge, which with their father's push led them to seek a way of life other than toiling in the Eastern Kentucky coal mines.

"Pull the boat over there. Bet there's a heap of largemouth bass in that deep hole."

Caleb pointed towards a dark shadowed area with a large dead tree pointing out of the water. It looked like a prime location.

"Hold your horses. Give me a minute." Josh eased the throttle of the engine and trolled toward the spot.

"Right here." Caleb mumbled and cast his line out.

Ripples radiated across the water from where the lure hit. Crank buzzing and line stretching echoed around the inlet. Sensation pulsed through Caleb's hand as his line tightened after a sudden slapping of the water and his pole bent nearly in half. Intuition and experience ignited a jerk of the rod, followed by a large-mouth bass jumping into the air.

"Fish on!" Caleb shouted, "I told you! It's a big one, too!" Caleb settled down, focusing on bringing it in.

"That's a big one for sure. Easy bringing him in. You'll lose him if you ain't careful." Josh yelled.

Caleb stood as he reeled and pulled with rhythm. Each movement tilted the boat, which prompted Josh to put his arms across and grip each side of the boat. Each second that passed made Caleb's intensity increase. His widened eyes locked on to the fish and its movements. Nothing could break his struggle to bring that fish in.

"Brother, you're going to lose the bet for sure! We will see who the fishing king is around here."

"I don't know about all that. You have to get it into the boat first." Josh teased, hoping he had not lost the bet before even getting in a cast.

Hard jerks from the fish bobbled the boat side to side, but the young angler met each with finesse, giving it line and then bringing it back in. He was letting the bass wear itself out. But the fish wouldn't give in easily and continued to zip back and forth, looking for logs to twist the line around. It hadn't lived this long and get this big without experience.

"Take it easy, Caleb. You're going to flip the boat. Let's not get wet today."

Pride and greed overpowered the angler as he continued his struggle to get the prize in the boat. His balance was tested and was almost lost a few times.

"Here, let me get a net and help." Josh yelled.

"Don't help too much. Don't want you to take any credit for my catch and weasel your way out of our bet."

Josh got up and leaned over the side of the boat with the net. He watched the line rip through the water as he stretched his arm out. Another six feet and the net would finish off the struggle. Caleb took a deep breath and pulled the rod towards him with all his strength.

With a crack the fishing line snapped and the fish's tail fin darted towards a sunken tree and sent Caleb falling back into the pedestal seat.

"Damn it, I lost him!" Caleb yelled as he landed, and then he heard the splash.

The force had whipped across the boat and sent Josh over the side, splashing water like a portal into another realm.

"Josh? Holy crap!" Caleb's bellowing laugh faded when Josh didn't resurface. "Josh!"

Caleb crouched as close to the water as he could and reached down. Nothing to reach for and nothing reaching back. Sweat burst off his forehead as he grabbed faster and deeper. He yelled for his brother at the top of his lungs and thoughts of what to do next. Finally, clarity came. He began pulling his shoes off to jump in. Just as he pulled off his last shoe, Josh's hand pushed through the top of the water.

"Josh! Give me your hand. Don't drown on me."

Outreached fingers signaled life. Caleb reached and grabbed them. Cold fingers wrapped around his hand. No amount of tugging could bring Josh up. His boot was hung between two sunken trees. His head was still underwater. Without thought Caleb jumped in despite not being a good swimmer. Murky water made seeing anything impossible. Down he went, using his brother's body as a guide. He swam down and got to his brother's foot. With all his energy, he pulled and tried to work the boot free. Fast thinking and diminishing air in his lungs, made him untie the boot. Josh slipped out and swam up towards the top of the water with Caleb right behind him. Each gasped for air and coughed as they surfaced.

"What the hell happened down there?" Caleb gurgled as water came from his mouth.

Josh could not form any words. Water and pieces of leaves seeped from his mouth as he looked up at the sun. His eyes glazed over as he floated on his back.

"You okay? Don't you be dead on me."

Caleb swam up to his brother and pulled him up on the bank. He looked down at Josh.

"Say something. Anything. You okay?"

Time stopped and the world became silent. The two brothers locked eyes, trying to comprehend what had just happened. This was a true brotherhood, where one would give his life to save the other. No other bond in the world was as strong.

Josh leaned over and spit out a twig and they both roared into laughter as they looked back at the boat bumping along the bank.

"Catch your breath, I'll get it." Caleb said as he swam back out to get the boat.

Josh lay on his back and watched the clouds float across the sky, encouraged by a gentle breeze. The feeling of the breeze was imprinted on his skin forever. From that point on, every time he felt the wind brush against his skin he was brought back to that day. Caleb had saved him and had never held it over him. He owed his brother and he was determined to pay the debt back, despite any bad feelings he had toward him.

8

As Josh drove up the highway toward his destination, sadness and anger enveloped him. He thought about his brother and who could have put the bullet in him. Memories of Caleb consumed him as he dazed from reality to memories and back. Many times, he and his brother had rode up this road with his mother as they went to pick up their father at the mine. Back in those days, they only had a 1974 sedan that burned as much oil as it did gas. Black Stone Coal Company owned all of Casteel Hollow and many other sites in the county. This one had closed after Caleb and Josh had graduated high school and their father was laid off permanently with black lung as a parting gift. Mr. Fields was not able to help Caleb after the lay off. Now, the hollow looked different; not good or bad, just different.

Josh pulled his black truck from the isolated county highway into the newly paved parking lot of the Stepping Stone Mountain Resort and Trailhead Center. It stood four stories tall, with a wood canopy stretching over a drop-off point to the entryway and two stacked stone pillars on each side. The first floor was also stacked with stone, at least where he could see. The final three floors were faced in cedar, topped off with green metal roofing. There weren't enough people in all the surrounding counties to fill up the place, but judging from the full parking lot it looked as if business was going well.

Stepping through the automated sliding doors, Josh took in the grandeur of the foyer. A large fountain treated arriving guests with a refreshing welcome, as water poured over cascading levels into a serene pool. A large glass skylight let the sun in to nourish all types of local flowers and greenery.

"Sir, I'll be with you in just a moment."

"Huh? Okay, thank you." Josh gave a quick acknowledgement to the receptionist, who had already continued assisting another customer.

The fountain was a grand centerpiece, but it didn't take away from the rest of the foyer. More stone trimmed the brightly painted interior walls, which were decorated with portraits of Kentucky's most famous settlers, trailblazers, and prominent characters including Daniel Boone, Kit Carson, Jim Bowie known for his namesake knife, and Judge Roy Bean who was known as the only law west of the Pecos after settling in Texas. Stopping in front of his favorite, Daniel Boone, he studied the man's rugged features, with lips pressed tightly as if holding in something important. His gray eyes pierced viewers as if they were the ones being observed. What had Boone been thinking of while sitting for the portrait? What other tales had not been told about his blazing of the Wilderness Trail? Josh had played out the historic icon's journey countless times as a kid roaming the nearby hills. He had followed the spirit of the great pathfinder–blazing his own trails, setting traps, and fishing the streams. He and Caleb spent many summer days building forts and preparing for imminent attacks from the natives.

"Sir? May I help you?"

The voice seemed distant, a hollow summoning from another realm. How long had he been staring at Boone or had Boone been staring at him? Josh struggled to form a response, as if waking from a deep sleep.

"Sir, would you like to check in or may I assist you with something else?"

"Oh, sorry. No, ma'am, I'm here to see Mr. Fields. He isn't expecting me, but he said to drop in when I could. I'm Josh Webb."

"I believe he is in, let me check and see if he's available."

"Thank you." Josh turned back to the portrait of Boone, searching the man's eyes again. He saw pain. The frontiersman's legend had come at a high cost, while attempting to settle the nearby area in 1773. The Delaware, Shawnee, and Cherokee tribes had banded together against the settlers and had captured, tortured, and killed his son to send a message: leave, or suffer the same fate. Boone's party had received the message and abandoned their mission. Josh couldn't imagine Boone wanting to leave without wreaking vengeance, but a cooler head must have prevailed in the interests of not losing anymore settlers. It was a wise choice and they would live to settle another day.

Perhaps this was the course Josh should take. If Boone's band had gone out looking for justice, they probably would have all been killed. Such a tragedy would have greatly delayed the American expansion west. Worse, for the legendary frontiersman, he would have been lost in history, as with most men. Worse still, many men and women would have been lost with him. Was Boone telling Josh to follow suit and leave? Let the law handle things? The old generation had sent a clear message. Josh stroked his jaw as a thought occurred to him. Was Caleb's death also a message? If so, by whom? Was it wise to leave Etham and never come back?

But something else in the man's eyes grabbed him, regret. Had Boone lived a life of disappointment, not having chased down his son's killers? Was this the message he had for Josh? Yes, you can run with your tail tucked in like a dog or you can pursue justice for Caleb, even if it comes at a high cost. Josh's furrowing eyes penetrated back at the portrait as he pressed his lips as Boone had pressed his in the portrait.

No, sir, I'm not going to live in regret. Caleb's killer will pay, if it's the last thing I do.

"Mr. Fields will see you, dear." Josh turned half startled from his thoughts to see a different woman, older and better dressed. She had the air of someone in higher management.

"Thank you."

"My pleasure, Mr. Webb. Right this way." Motioning him to follow, the woman led Josh around the reception desk and through a door marked "Staff Only." She introduced herself as Rita Long, Executive Secretary to Mr. Fields. Josh lit up when she motioned him to follow her and that she was an attractive woman. She led him down a long, plain hallway consisting of a maintenance closet, a break room, and another room where two ladies were separating linen. They stopped at an elevator, which opened as soon as Rita pushed the button. Inside the elevator was one, unlabeled button. She pushed it and gave Josh a smile. "Here we go."

The elevator doors opened at the top floor to a spacious lobby, with a more rustic mountain décor with an elegant but simple oak desk and a couple of plush sitting chairs for guests to wait in. He opted to stand and check out the wooded scenery pictures and trail maps that decorated the wall. As Rita picked up the phone to announce Josh's arrival, Mr. Fields opened his office door and held his arms up with surprise, as if greeting a long lost relative.

"Josh, come on in, son. Good to see you again under better circumstances. How are you doing?"

"I'm okay, thanks."

Josh took Mr. Fields' hand and added a grin. "And it looks like you are doing pretty good, too. This place is amazing. You've come a long way."

A sparkle lit in Mr. Fields' eye as he soaked in approval. "Yes, I have, Josh. It's hard to believe I was once just another coal miner digging in these old hills. I never would have dreamed it. And not just for me, but for everything that has happened in Etham. The town and people are doing great."

The office boasted of its local connection with a sitting area that faced a stone fireplace, no doubt sourced from the very hills in which the lodge now sat. On the opposite wall there was a small bar, which was stocked with only premium stuff. A large window covered the entirety of the outside wall providing a picturesque view that stretched for miles. All the furniture matched the same elegant desk Ms. Long was using just outside Mr. Field's office. All of red oak, no doubt from trees harvested, while building the resort.

"Dad would have loved this. He always told us there was more to these mountains than coal. He'd talk about the beauty of it; that something here was more important. He understood the value of coal and how it sustained the economy, but it also came at a severe cost to both the land and the workers. The people were the real casualties of coal mining." Josh said.

"Cyrus was right. Josh, how I miss your father! He was the hardest working man I ever worked with and supervised; by far the brightest. Your Dad was always pointing out random plants and talking about how useful they were as food or medicine. He always had a book in his lunch box. I poked at him some about being a bookworm, but it never bothered him one bit. He considered it a compliment."

"Yes, sir, that was my Dad. He read a lot and spent a lot of time outdoors walking around looking at stuff. Studying everything. Even after he got sick–" Josh paused, "he was always learning."

"He was a good man, Josh. The best I ever knew, I reckon."

"Thank you, Mr. Fields. That means a lot."

"Caleb was a hardworking man, too, just like your father. He was the best handyman I've ever seen and had a lot to do with keeping this resort and the cabins in top-notch shape. I owe him for that."

"Handyman? Here?"

"Yes, he came to me right before I had the grand opening saying he needed a job. Of course, I couldn't say no."

"I sure didn't know he worked here as a handyman. He was always good with his hands. He could fix anything. Guess religion didn't pay well for him."

Mr. Fields looked at Josh with a stoic look. He clasped his hands. "Preaching ain't never been an easy life, at least for an honest preacher. Somehow, Caleb had gotten the attendance up quite a bit, which says a lot for a small-town church." The old stoic thought of a point and chuckled. "But it doesn't really matter how big the crowd is when none of them have any money for the collection plate."

Thoughts of finding out Caleb was a handyman at the resort, the access badge, and the fact he was found dead on the trail up from the resort crossed Josh's mind. His eyes glazed over for a moment.

"Sheriff Bell said that some hikers found him on the trail not far from here."

"That's right, they rushed back here and told the front desk. My staff immediately called 911. I headed up there as soon as I heard about it and found him in a puddle of blood, barely breathing. Just an awful thing to come up on."

Josh closed his eyes. Images ran through his brain and prompted him to shake his head. Fields looked out the window.

"Yep, just an awful thing to see Caleb shot like that. I held his hand, until the ambulance arrived. The EMT's jumped right in, doing what they could. Then, they took him to the resort's chopper pad where he was flown to the hospital."

Josh shook his head again, hoping to erase bad thoughts. He ran his hand over the solid oak desk, noting how perfectly it matched the floors and bar in the far corner of the office. He had worked for a cabinet maker while working his way through college. He might have stayed with it, if the money was right. Only the boss makes money in those kinds of jobs, so he kept pursuing education. He still had a great appreciation for the craft. Whoever did the work in this office was a master.

Mr. Fields picked up that Josh was looking for a distraction. "Just about everything in here comes from these hills. A small grove of red oaks provided for the desk and cabinetry. The fireplace was made from stones collected nearby. I love it. It's much better than the cluttered mess I wrestle around in my Etham town hall office."

"It's beautiful, that's for sure and what a view." Josh walked to the window and looked out over the valley which presented the colors of the season. He could just see the edge of Etham in one direction and the scab of earth known as Banetown in the other. "Yes, sir, very nice!"

"Let's have a seat, Josh. Can I get you a drink? Bourbon?"

"Sure, thanks."

"I know Caleb's death must be wearing on you. How are you doing?"

Josh took the glass as he sat in the leather chair. He stared into the bourbon and swirled the glass hoping he could have this discussion without breaking down in front of Mr. Fields. The past several days had been spent on his porch talking to himself about his brother. Only difference, he was alone then and free to say what was on his mind to the trees. To yell, cuss, and cry. He hadn't expected to talk so much about it here, but now he knew differently and it was upon him. Josh swallowed hard and pressed his lips together. He looked at the window, which showed only blue sky from where he was sitting and gave no help as to what to say.

"I'm okay, I guess. Just been sitting out at the old homeplace, thinking a lot. I have been contemplating about growing up with Caleb and how we had kind of split ways. About how stupid and foolish we were. At least on my part."

"Don't be too hard on yourself. Most families fight among themselves over foolish things. That is how things are and that includes your family, too. The truth is, you and Caleb were bound to make up because you were twins. You know that, right?"

"Maybe, but we waited too long."

"Yes, maybe. But the point I want you to understand is that you boys didn't hate each other. Caleb knew that and so do you. The only difference is that y'all didn't have the chance to make it right and you can't help that now. You just need to come to terms with it all and move on. I know you can move on and help Etham, too. Your intelligence and my backing can make things happen around here."

Josh turned his focus to the empty fireplace, watching invisible flames dance across logs that weren't there. Blood flooded his cheeks as he worked to slow his breathing. He was determined to be strong for pride's sake, but he was having issues with the water forming in his eyes.

Relax, dammit.

"Josh? You okay?"

Josh stood and walked over to the window. Resort guests meandered around the grounds. Some with high-end gear and attire, while others were much more casual and fit more within the range of his means. Josh shook his head and took a drink of bourbon, which helped.

"I don't know if I'll ever be able to forgive myself about me and Caleb. I knew some stuff about him that didn't square with him being a preacher, but I shouldn't have let it come between us. Now-"

"You must let it all go, Josh. Maybe not now, but give it some time. Focus on what you can do. Honor him by doing that?"

"And what is that?" Josh said as he looked into Field's eyes.

"I'm not sure. Be the kind of man he knew you to be. Maybe, you should keep teaching and keep believing in the goodness of people? Maybe, go back to the university and help the younger generations learn? Maybe, you could help people here with me? Just a thought."

"The goodness of people? The people around here?" He startled himself as much as Mr. Fields, but continued, "Like the good people who shot Caleb in cold blood? Or the good people that paid my Dad to breath in coal dust all those years and then cut him off from his medical care when he got sick?"

"You have a right to be angry. It's okay for a while, but Josh, believe me when I say there are good people around. Deep down, you know that's true. It will take some time."

"Maybe so." Josh softened his tone and looked back over the mountainside through the window. "But what now? Leave Etham and just go back to the university, like nothing happened? Just pick up where I left off? Resume teaching, as if Caleb had never been murdered?"

"You should take some time off. Why not stay around here for a while? Relax; maybe do some fishing or check out the trails. Why don't you stay here at the resort? I will arrange the best suite with no charge. We have the best spa in the state, too. You will be able to relax and get yourself together. It will do you some good. Plus, I've had an idea jumping around in my head that I want to bounce off of you. When the time's right, of course."

"Mr. Fields, I appreciate your offer, but I must decline. I need some private time at the homeplace and then I'll probably head back to the university. All that is up in the air. I hope you understand."

"I understand, but if you ever change your mind the offer is good anytime." Mr. Fields smiled.

Josh thought again about the tragedy of Daniel Boone's son and how the score had been left unsettled. His brother's murder was also a tragedy, but this was different. At least the native tribes were defending their territory. Caleb had been murdered for no reason and shot by some thug. Boone's group may have been right to flee and maybe Boone regretted it. Josh couldn't see himself living in regret. Justice had to be served and Josh intended to see it served.

"I think I will stay for a while, but not for fishing. I need to find out what happened to Caleb and make sure whoever did it gets what they deserve."

"Josh, I get it. You want justice for Caleb, but let the law take care of it, son. There's no reason to get yourself mixed up in whatever happened. It could be dangerous. Whoever shot your brother is a person that is driven by different things than you. Like I said, take some time, grieve, and do what Caleb would want; live your life."

"Mr. Fields, thanks for your time and the drink. You've always been good to our family. My Dad always thought the world of you."

"Thanks, Josh. I've always felt the same for him, back then and now. I do for you, too."

Josh rose to leave and was embraced by Mr. Fields. Josh had did the right thing by stopping by and seeing him, he owed that much to his father. But it was good for him, too. Josh didn't know if he could ever forgive himself for not being there to protect his brother that day or if he could ever think of others as being good. Mr. Fields meant well and maybe he was right; maybe he just needed some time. Yes, he would grieve, and he would move on. And he would live for Caleb.

But first, someone was going to pay for Caleb's death. Blood rushed hot through his neck and his face tightened as he stepped back into the elevator. Sheriff Bell wasn't making Caleb's death a priority, at least he didn't seem to be. He also seemed to have some kind of personal hostility towards Caleb. But why? What was Sheriff Bell holding back? Josh had given Bell a chance, but now it was time to press the issue. Perhaps Daniel Boone had lived his life in regret, not pushing back or seeking vengeance. Maybe, the frontiersman's advice was to dig in and bring whoever did this to justice.

It was time for answers. He would pay the sheriff a visit.

9

Cool fall air rushed through Josh's truck windows, bringing in a strong pine aroma and helped cool the heat in his cheeks. He had traveled this winding road countless times, both in his Dad's old pickup and on foot. Times were harder back then, at least financially, but Josh didn't know it. To him it had always been paradise, playing in the creeks, catching crawdads, fishing the honey holes, and exploring the woods with Caleb pretending to be Daniel Boone. A smile formed on his face. As he got closer to Etham, abandoned houses stood out to him. Memories of friends and distant family once living in them flooded his mind. Trash lined the yards and ditches. Previously thriving businesses had become boarded-up buildings deteriorating with each passing year. Etham was now a fragile shell due to coal drying up and no other industries wanting to invest in the region. Most well-to-do families had left for better places, but poor people on the lower rungs of society's ladder were stuck. They did the best they could. From Josh's perspective everything had changed. Hope for the town ran through his mind.

The Stepping Stone Mountain Resort could bring Etham back from decline. Convincing him would be seeing the reality of change.

Sadness seeped back into his heart. Mr. Fields' words, "The goodness of people," repeated in his mind as he rolled through town.

Maybe, I should see the goodness in people? Maybe, I should just let the police do their jobs and not get involved? Maybe, I should just live life and let things go, the falling out with Caleb, and accept his death? Too many maybes and not enough answers.

Horns honked and caught Josh's attention as he pulled onto Main Street. A rusted-out 4x4 truck was stalled at one of the two stoplight intersections in town and was holding up a few vehicles from passing through. A magnetic sign advertising "Stepping Stone Resort" was attached to the door and steam radiated from the engine. A Good Samaritan inclination echoed in his head, which compelled him to park across the street and get out to help. As he walked closer, the driver got out and slammed the door. Josh's eyes could not help from tracing the details of a woman. Unkempt, long sandy hair, curled at the edges crowned the petite frame of a woman opening the truck's hood and leaning in to look at the engine. Tight jeans with rips, black t-shirt, and a tattoo-sleeved arm were not things he expected. A rough but delicate look stuck in his head.

"Can I help you?"

The woman pulled herself from the engine compartment and turned around, wiping her oil-stained hands with a dirty rag. Her bright blue eyes connected with Josh and her face became pale.

Coldness and fear consumed her. Tension and disbelief shot out of her eyes and her body froze into a motionless shell. Tight lips were finally wrested open.

"You? How? You were just...."

Instantly, Josh detected a hidden northern accent with a sprinkling of southern flavor. Questions about who she was and where she was from came to mind.

"Looks like you've got some engine problems. I'm not an expert, but maybe I can give you a hand."

The woman took a step back and lost her balance. She leaned against the truck. Her eyes outlined every feature of Josh.

"You okay?" Josh said and took a step forward.

"You—you look just like that preacher from the church...up that way. But that can't be." She said as she pointed north towards a cross crowned steeple that rose on a distant hill a few miles out of town.

"Caleb was his name. He was my twin brother. You're not the only one that has been giving me weird looks since I've been in town. Hard to believe I was just here a few years back and now nobody knows that I was his twin brother."

"Yes, Caleb. That was him....the preacher."

Disbelief emanated from her. She shook her head and then her demeanor changed. Calmness engulfed her. The woman straightened up and lit a cigarette. Smoke swirled around her as she took a deep draw. Smoke and aroma seeped into Josh's nostrils. The combination had irritated him ever since that day at the lake and he had not picked up a cigarette since until the other day with the sheriff. Right now, he craved another as the memory of Caleb saving him from a watery grave flashed through his mind.

"You, okay?"

Josh nodded as he focused back on the woman. Her movements and eyes captivated him. The mix of beauty blended with a bad, good girl vibe intrigued him. Something about her made him think and see things differently in a flash. Deep down his gut told him that she was a person who was destined to be part of his life in some way. At this point, he had no words, an issue he had never had before.

"My name is Kristol Engel. I'm sorry for acting all weird. You look almost exactly like him. Forgive me and I'm sorry for your loss. What's your name?"

She reached out her hand. Her lips tightened and eventually formed a smile.

Josh produced a clownish grin that he regretted and jutted out his hand, which was grabbed with firmness. The feel of her hand sent pulses up his arm.

"Josh, Josh Webb. I guess you knew the last name already."

"Nice to make your acquaintance Josh, Josh Webb. You asked if I needed help. Well, honey, I sure do. You said you ain't an expert, but whatcha know about motors? I don't know a damn thing, except where to put the gas in."

He had never met a woman like this before, even at the university with all its different types. He had been hit on by young, attractive students who wanted to improve their grades, even older teachers who were divorced and lonely. Some, he resisted and others he embraced. History would be the judge of his choices. At this moment, him being thrown off guard and out of his element was an understatement.

"I know a little more than that. Let me take a look. I'm glad we introduced ourselves before I got under your hood."

Kristol looked at him and laughed. He looked back and tried to hold back a mischief grin.

"I didn't mean that like it sounded. Please forgive me."

"Honey, you're forgiven. No bad feelings from me. Just glad a man with humor and grit is looking and feeling under my hood. Haven't had that for a while. Not many men around here would come and help me. Most men around here are worthless slugs."

Smiles between them made Josh feel more comfortable. He walked over and looked under the hood. Pain from his hand pushed him back and then he went back in.

"Damn, hot. The cap burned my hand."

Radiator fluid fumes curled both their faces. Fluid spewed onto the engine and the pavement. Gawking looks from people going around the stalled truck didn't faze them.

"I'm sorry. What can I do to help?" Kristol said as she leaned against the fender.

"I'm fine. Not my first time being burned."

She smiled. With well-practiced motion, she pushed a sandy brown curl out of her eyes.

"Right here. Your radiator is low on fluid and you'll probably need your thermostat replaced. Filling up the radiator with coolant will put a band-aid on it for a bit. The gas station right down the road will have fluid, I'm sure of that. I'll drive down there and get you some."

Kristol was silent. She looked at Josh and examined every detail of his face. His swept back black hair and green eyes kept her attention, but his glowing nature captivated her more. Then, she analyzed every inch of his body and concluded he was not too bad for an older man. Also, he was the spitting image of Caleb, the preacher. She didn't care.

"You look just like your brother. It's hard to comprehend and I'm amazed. I just don't know what to say."

Josh looked at her. Words failed to form in his head. She continued.

"Well, not exactly like Caleb. Some things are very different."

"Sounds like you knew him. Did you?" Josh said.

Silence pushed and pulled them with the force of a river. Multiple honks from the vehicles stopped behind Kristol's truck repeated.

She waved her hand at the irritated drivers. They honked more and agitated her. Again, she motioned them to go around.

"Listen, you don't have to go fetch me coolant. I knew that already. I've been putting it in for a few weeks. You're right about the thermostat and there's a leak in my radiator. I've patched it

71

before, but it just won't hold. I've got coolant in the back of the truck. Appreciate you stopping and helping me. Sure, nice of you. Most people will not even stop and spit on you, even if you're burning unless they get a dollar out of the deal. Sure, do appreciate you."

Josh blushed and looked at her. Words swirled in his head. He realized that she knew more about engines that she had let on.

"I don't mind at all. If you ever need help again, let me know."

Kristol looked at the ground and back at him. The hissing radiator did not stop, nor did their eyes stop scanning each other. Steam and fumes pushed both from the truck.

Honking cut through the conversation and hissing. Both looked at a faded blue Blazer stopped on the street.

"Hey, Kristol! Looks like you need some help."

"Billy Dalton, from the way your heap is smoking and missing, you don't know a damn thing about vehicles. I don't need any help."

Billy nodded with a scowl. With effort, he tried to spin his tires and show out, but with disappointment. The result made him turn his head and slink out of town.

The exchange triggered a change within Kristol. Her eyes became darker to the point of being unnatural and she put her hands on her sides.

"I can handle this. Just like I handled things at Cincinnati University and handle things now at the resort. I don't need anybody taking care of me or telling me what to do."

People of Billy's kind and the way that they pushed her were nothing new, but she had an edge. Hard times and pain were close friends to Kristol and she had learned to deal with them. Her parents were killed in a car wreck when she was nine. From then on, she fended for herself and became hardened. She had struggled to get accepted to the university and worked multiple jobs while attending. There were always temptations before she came to Etham, some she shrugged off and others she embraced. All of it made her rough around the edges and she was not one to let anybody too close to her.

She looked at Josh and sensed he was a good man. Nothing kept her from thinking he was bad with her experience, but something stood out about him. Kristol walked around Josh. Both continued to eye each other and debated what their next words would be.

Josh spoke first, "Totally understand. Just wanted to help a person in distress. That's all. Sounds like you work at the resort. You must know Mr. G.W. Fields?"

Kristol froze and her eyes widened. She was at a loss for words. Something within her changed for a moment, the calming of a storm.

"Yes, I know him. He's my boss. He takes care of me, always has. G.W. is a good man."

"He has always been good to my family. From what I'm seeing he is trying to help the people of Etham by building the resort. It may all work out, who knows."

"Yep. The town is going in a direction for sure." Kristol said with tight lips.

Josh smiled and walked back towards his truck across the street. Thoughts of Kristol consumed him to the point of having issues of putting one foot in front of the other. Steps continued to be hard to take, and breathing was almost impossible. Trying to shake her from his mind, he set his attention to the ridge lines above Etham. They were the same wooded hills he remembered as a kid coming to town for whatever reason, a soda, or his first job at Rudder's Grocery Store.

"Hey, Josh! I appreciate your offer of help. I mean that."

Josh turned and smiled. Wind blew and muffled his words. He had to repeat them and walked back up to Kristol.

"No problem at all. Glad to be here at the right time."

She smiled. Then, cocked her head to one side.

"Where are you laying your head, while you're in town?"

"Up at my brother's, the old homeplace. Nowhere else to stay."

"I know the place. Everybody knew the preacher and his good works."

Josh looked at Kristol and a feeling of coldness wrapped around him. A shroud that he could not control. Caleb's face came to mind. She cocked her head to the side again and smiled.

"Come up to the Stepping Stone Resort, sometime. I'm the grounds manager there. You need to embrace nature and Boone's Trail. It's big business and the only one we have these days. When you come up just ask for me. I'll give you the big tour. Then, you can make your own decision about the future of Etham and if you want to stay longer."

"I've been inside the resort, but not explored it. I have to ask a question."

Kristol eyed him. His response made her adjust her head.

"Alright. Just one. Don't want you becoming clingy to me." She laughed.

"How did you get here? I'm just asking. You have a hidden northern accent and I can tell from your background, educated. If you don't want to tell me now, maybe you can when I visit the resort again."

A long minute passed. The question hung in the air and lingered.

"I guess you'll have to come to the resort to find out. Now, won't you?"

With a spin of her feet, Kristol reached in the back of her truck bed and pulled out a gallon of coolant. She went about filling the radiator.

"By the way, this piece of junk is my work truck. I do own and travel around in a better truck. Didn't want you to think I was a local scrub with no class." She laughed.

"I would never think that about you. I assure you of that."

Josh reflected on her answer. Elation formed a smile as he started walking back across the street. He turned and watched Kristol roll out of town. An impression had been made.

10

Goosebumps peppered Josh's arm as he opened the truck door. Thoughts of Kristol generated strange sensations. Something about her sent vibrations through his body, especially in his heart. Anticipation of seeing her again consumed his mind, until thoughts of Caleb crashed in again. Despite Mr. Field's and Sheriff Bell's words about letting things be handled, his gut pulled his eyes toward the police station on the corner. Crisp air hit his skin and chills went up his back. With white-knuckled fists, he walked down the sidewalk with angered propulsion. An old man sitting on a bench stared at him with scared eyes.

Hey, preacher. Sorry I've not been to church in months. Just been caught up with living. Well, I wouldn't say living as much as being here and almost dead."

Time had weathered the man and a look of confusion was imprinted on his face. His hands shook as he gripped a curved handle cane and pushed the top of a whiskey bottle deeper into his jacket pocket. Josh stopped. He recognized the man underneath the long, white beard and octagon-shaped bifocals.

"I'm Josh. You're thinking about my twin brother, Caleb. Aren't you Mr. Edwards? You live up on Blanton's Ridge. My Dad used to bring me and my brother to your house all the time. I remember that time when your wife cooked up some chicken and dumplings soaked in butter. The best that I have ever had. Do you remember that day?"

"I do, just like yesterday. Those days are long gone. Never to come back. Lost my homeplace on Blanton's Ridge. Lost my Betty, too. She's long passed on to the other side. Bad times. Was made to sell it. Damn the government and banks. They've ruined everything. Damn them all."

Josh looked at the man, who was only a shell of the man he remembered from his youth. A weird feeling came upon him. The old man and his prophetic words hit hard. Thoughts about his family's old homeplace crossed his mind. It could be gone in the wink of an eye. Deep down, he had always known that.

"Mr. Edwards, please take care of yourself. Maybe, one of these days you'll get back to church with the new pastor."

"New pastor? What happened to the old one? Kinda liked him."

"He's moved on to a better place, like Betty." Josh said and put a twenty-dollar bill in the man's hand.

"I won't take a handout. Never have and never will."

"Consider it a payment for those chicken and dumplings I had back in the day."

Mr. Edwards nodded and smiled. Josh turned and walked up the sidewalk to the County Sheriff's Office. The brick annex connected to the stone block courthouse, and it looked out of place just like a lot of pieced-together things in Etham. It had been there as long as he had remembered. The full glass door was the same one he had pushed open as a kid when his father had come to pay his property taxes.

A change of approach was decided as Josh walked in. Different this time due to Sheriff Bell's previous attitude and tone. Yes, he was the law around here and needed to provide answers, not words with no meaning. Josh walked into the office with a smirking deputy behind the front desk.

"Mr. Joshua Webb, as I live and breathe, you came to visit the homeland from your university throne."

"Well, well. Seems like the washed-out basketball star who lost the regional tournament and popped hot for drugs is a deputy now. Now, isn't this a crazy world we live in. What is your unbiased opinion, now be honest? I understand honesty may not be one of your strong traits."

With gritted teeth, Deputy Earle Tullos stood up. He grabbed a police baton from his desk drawer and walked toward Josh.

"That's enough. Back down, Tullos. I've got this. I welcome Mr. Webb to our office. He must have a reason for coming to visit. Right, Josh. I figured you would have been on the road after your brother's visitation, because I didn't see you at the funeral or when they lowered him into the ground."

Josh looked at Bell and reevaluated his different approach idea. Both men eyed each other as Deputy Tullos displayed a goofy smile that made him look even more stupid.

"Yes, you're exactly right about having a reason to come here. I'm here to discuss Caleb's murder. As far as my presence at my brother's funeral, that is my business."

Bell continued to look at Josh and studied him up and down. Silence smothered the room like a wet blanket, except for the noisy window mounted air conditioner and flickering fluorescent light tube above them.

"Tullos, put in a work order for the AC and get that light fixed ASAP. They annoy the hell out of me. Josh, let's go to my office and talk things over."

The deputy nodded his head and walked out the front door, while fishing a cigarette out of a pack. Josh watched him exit and had an uneasy feeling about the man he had just made fun of. Something told him that he would have issues with him sooner than later.

"C'mon in and make yourself comfortable. I would offer you some coffee, but I drank the last cup just a while ago. Can't do without my coffee."

"That's okay. I didn't come to drink coffee."

Josh sat down and looked at Bell, who leaned back in his worn-out leather chair. Cheap cologne, which was applied in hefty amounts could not cover up Bell's cigarette and body odor, which overpowered the room and made Josh feel even more disgusted by the man. Both felt unnerved being in each other's presence again and kept up their manly stances. One finally welled up some courage.

"Sheriff, who killed my brother?"

Bell leaned forward and took a deep breath. He ran his hand through his graying hair.

"I told you the other day. I'm working the case and don't have any leads right now. What did you not understand when we last talked? I find it hard to believe that I have to educate an educated man, again."

"As far as being educated, I only know what I'm told and what I've verified. To me it's hard to believe a church pastor was gunned down in this small town and nobody knows anything about it. I grew up here and know the people. I'm Caleb's twin brother and I feel things, deep things. We had a connection that can't be described in words."

Bell stood up and walked to the window and looked out at the boarded-up restaurant across the street. Then, he put his hands on his sides and turned around. "You remember Johnson's Grocery Store and how Ebb Johnson used to slice the best tasting ham anyway you wanted? You could get it on a sandwich or just on a paper plate, if you liked it that way. And it was real cheap."

"Yes. What the hell does all that have to do with my question?"

"You can't get that anymore. Things like that are long gone. Things have changed around here. More than you'll ever know. Your brother had changed and was not the same man that he was years ago. I think you know that, now don't you?"

Josh leaned up and stared at Bell. Thoughts of what to say next crossed his mind. He knew deep inside his brother had changed but letting that bit of information slip out was not something that needed to be done at the moment.

"I don't think so. Caleb was a good man. He kept his church and parishioners as his utmost priorities."

A cell phone vibrated on Bell's desk. He picked it up and looked at the text.

"Well, I think you're naïve to think people don't change over time in this messed-up world. Your brother did care for his flock, but I think he cared a little too much for a few and led many astray. Now, in my opinion that's not a good shepherd."

"I take offense to that. Caleb was a good preacher. Maybe, with some flaws, but he was a virtuous man. You going to do your job and bring his killer to justice?"

The front door opened. Bell's face tightened and he sat back down. An attractive middle-aged woman with bright blue eyes and auburn hair walked in. From the purple scrubs she was wearing, Josh figured she was a nurse. He had seen her before but struggled to remember. Then, it dawned on him that he had seen her at church that day when he and Caleb had parted ways. She was his brother's mistress.

"Julie, come on in. Perfect timing. You remember Josh don't you, Caleb's brother?"

All eyes were on her. She stopped abruptly and looked at Josh. Her glowing eyes and smile told many things, each one different to her husband and Josh. Within seconds, she looked at Bell and regained her composure.

"I didn't mean to interrupt."

"No, not at all. Me and Josh were just finishing up. Right Josh? Sorry, this is my wife."

Both men looked at each other with clenched teeth. Josh was thrown off balance by seeing Julie. Thoughts raced back to that Sunday.

"We're done here. Sheriff, as you promised, please investigate Caleb's killing. I'll be staying at the old homeplace."

"I'll come up that way, if anything comes up." Bell said and then tightened his lips.

Julie stared at Josh and her eyes followed him as he walked out of Bell's office. Words formed in her mouth, but she stuttered at first.

"Josh, it's nice to see you again. You have my condolences for your loss. Caleb was a good man."

She looked down at the tiled floor. More words swirled in her head that she wanted to say, but it was not the time. Sounds of Josh shoes hitting the tiled floor echoed as he walked out of the building.

Sheriff Bell looked at his wife with intense eyes. He sat down and clasped his hands. His dark eyes looked at his wife.

"Looks just like Caleb don't he. How does that make you feel? I seen you looking at him. You should be ashamed of yourself. You should not have mentioned Caleb's name."

"Listen, I've had enough of you bashing me for what I've done. Either kill me or leave me. I can't change the past, but I won't be a prisoner of it, either. I was not looking at Caleb's brother any differently than anybody else would."

"But, he is his identical twin. I know you looked at him in that way. Didn't you?"

"Josh is not Caleb. That is all I'm going to say about it. I just came by to tell you that my mother fell again and father is out of his mind as usual. I'm going up to take care of them for a few days. They don't have anybody else."

"Yes, I know. Your sister is in rehab for another six months and your brother is in jail. Same old story, just a different day and year. Okay. Go on and take care of them. After all, they did thank me when I made a better life for you."

Julie looked at him with repulsion. Thoughts of why she had been fooled into marrying him came to the forefront of her mind. At this point, she decided to let it slide, because other things were more important. One of these days they would have to either make up or just call it quits and move on from each other. Today was not the day to fight that one out. Julie didn't have the energy.

"My loving husband, if you don't mind, I'll leave now and head up to Frankfort to take care of Mom and Dad for a bit."

Bell was at a loss for words at the moment. Anger swelled within his heart. It gnawed at him, just like it had for years. As time passed, his heart became darker to the point of not really caring about Julie or the people he was elected to protect. His allusion was that everybody knew about the affair between Julie and Caleb. He knew that they laughed at him behind closed doors and from a distance. In reality, all the people knew was that he straddled the law now depending on the day and circumstance. No one really trusted him and his rage helped contribute to the decay of Etham. He knew that he had not been there for Julie and he had always wanted that to be different. Regret filled his brain, but anger overpowered it.

"Go on. If I need you, I'll give you a call or text."

"Whatever. You better start being a better husband to me, like you were when I married you. If not, I may decide to leave you."

Julie walked out the door. Bell sat in his chair and pulled a half-empty bourbon bottle from the desk drawer. With a gulp and a draw from a cigarette, he put his feet up on his desk. Memories of their newlywed years flooded in; late nights of coming into a candlelit dinner and cuddling afterwards. Going on impromptu romantic trips on the weekends made the relationship so sweet back then. Those times were gone and so was the closeness. The question of what had happened between them plagued him as much as the sting of infidelity. He knew he had been guilty too, but it was always different due to perspective. A deeper question was whether there was any love left.

Deputy Tullos ran in. His eyes were wide and he seemed to salivate like a dog.

"What's Josh Webb doing in here?"

"What do you think, Tullos? He's here about his brother."

Tullos pushed past the Bell's desk and watched Josh stop at his truck. He looked back at the office window, but the deputy was sure he couldn't see him through the glass. Tullos couldn't help but feel the man was looking directly at him. Tullos snapped the blinds shut.

11

Smashing Sheriff Bell's face in with a right hook wouldn't help get answers, but Josh felt it might make him feel better. A few nights in the slammer might be worth the trouble, but it would only make whatever help Bell was planning on giving disappear. Still, it felt good thinking about it as he made the trip back to the homeplace. The sheriff's wife crossed his mind, too. Josh had met her once before. And it had caused a lot of grief back then. No doubt she was part of the problem now, due to her being Bell's wife. She made things worse. The last time Josh had visited Etham turned out to be regrettable, as it would be the last time he and his brother spoke before having to watch him die at the hospital.

Josh faded back to that last time. Caleb had bragged that church attendance had been up lately and that morning the congregation was looking upright and ready to receive the sermon. Not quite elbow-to-elbow, but enough pews were filled to satisfy any self-respecting pastor. Some of the entitled felt a need to come early enough to retain their rightful seats. Thanks to generous donations, the small country sanctuary had been updated a few years earlier. Lighter colors painted over the dark paneling and new light fixtures brightened the once drab, uninviting room. And to the great pleasure of most everyone, a new heating and cooling system had been installed.

Holy words poured out from the pulpit as men, women, and children leaned forward, engaged with spiritual utterances. An elderly lady was wrapped in a knitted blanket kept on a pew just for her. Other women snuggled against husbands for warmth; single ladies wrapped themselves in their own arms. Veterans of the pews were easily distinguishable from those visiting by the layers of clothing they wore. All of them thought, would it hurt to lay off the A/C just a bit? They contented themselves in knowing their suffering was for the Lord.

"Brothers and sisters, I will close with a final thought. Whatever temptation you may find yourself in, God can get you out its binding, but you must be humble and rely on His power. Remember, take heed lest you fall!"

The "Amens" and "Praise the Lord's" echoed across the sanctuary as the Holy Spirit gave communication through the preaching of God's Word. Pastor Caleb Webb's calls to humility and dependence upon God were akin to the prophets of old. Each week he would fan the congregation's embers aflame, stoking renewed passion for the souls of man. Each week God's Army would march his banner into a world of lost sinners to seek and to save that which was lost. Each week they would retreat back to their sanctuary, broken as ever, looking for assurance from the preacher that they weren't as bad of sinners as the rest of the world.

From all accounts the congregation loved Brother Webb. Josh hadn't been around in a while. Caleb had become quite the orator. Experience and effort pays off, even for clergy.

Not that Josh was devoted to church. Like Caleb, he'd been dragged to church every week whether he liked it or not. He didn't hate it, but there were just too many inconsistencies for his taste. He observed contradiction growing up, seeing the holy men and women of Etham doing the same sinful things as everyone else: smoking, drinking, cursing, and committing adultery. What rubbed him raw was seeing the church run off a younger pastor some years back for getting the youth involved in an outreach program to bring in less-appealing kids. Seems like they wanted everyone to be saved, but some didn't need to be saved in their church.

Regardless, Josh was proud of Caleb. Perhaps in time his brother would bring him back into the fold. Not today, mind you. Besides, this Holy Ghost-filled army was probably enough to save the world, at least for now.

Josh waited for the congregation to file through and compliment Preacher Caleb on another great sermon. He was on a roll. They would then file out and head to the Burger Shack or Fudd's Restaurant down the road. Man doesn't live on the Bread of God alone.

While Josh waited for his brother, a few familiar faces stopped by to say hello. One was an old family friend, Mr. George Wesley Fields, called G.W. Josh drifted back to what he knew now.

Mr. Field's had been their father's supervisor at the Black Stone Coal Company, until Cyrus Webb got black lung and was finally laid off. When the company relocated their headquarters to Cincinnati, Ohio and moved operations out west, Mr. Fields moved away for a while and then came back to Etham. He said to all that asked he just couldn't stay away from the community he loved and came back to be part of the solution to the community's struggle. He had gotten involved in local politics and was instrumental in transitioning the town's economy away from coal to tourism. This created jobs for a growing number of laid off miners and brought in revenue for the town. He was unanimously elected as a councilman. From what Josh remembered from Sheriff Bell's conversation, Mr. Fields built the Stepping Stone Mountain Resort. He had been good to the Webb family and to the community and expected rewards in kind.

Josh drifted back to that day at the church. He turned back to watch his brother finish sending off his flock. The last in line was a very attractive lady who was around the same age as he and Caleb. The two were certainly acquainted and spoke for several minutes about something.

A new addition to the church caught Josh's attention. A stained-glass mural of Christ ascending to heaven was centered above the altar. The cathedral on campus had a similar one, albeit much larger. Caleb had mentioned that a local artisan handcrafted it at no cost, a work unto the Lord. The craftsman hadn't attended the church in over a year and now mostly kept to himself. Caleb thought it was a shame, saying that the man was a quiet doer of goodwill and never wanted compensation or praise.

The mural elegantly illustrated Christ's ascension: the glorified Savior rising from the earth, encompassed by clouds with hands outstretched bearing the marks of sacrifice and with stupefied men gazing up in wonder at it all. The brightly smeared colors capturing the last moment before the disciples would be chastised by angels for staring at the sky. The portrayal captured the essence of the gospel, that men were filled with power from being on high to not just stand there, but to do something! Go, and make disciples.

Looking again to his brother, Josh watched Caleb close his conversation with the woman with the typical shaking of hands. Except that most handshakes don't transfigure into a lover's-holding-of-hands kind of shake. The consensual hold was released in a blink, as if both hands agreed that this wasn't the place. Josh thought it was imagination on his part, but the woman's blushed face betrayed her before she turned away. These two had feelings for each other, but the feelings were not open to the public. He was sure of it; Caleb and his lady friend were a thing.

Of course, there was nothing wrong with that. Protestant pastors married all the time, it was not forbidden. Relationships often begin with the simple holding of hands. Perhaps Caleb had found the "one". It would be good for him to have a partner, both in life and in the ministry. It seemed to be hush-hush here, so he'd wait until later to get the scoop. Of course, he couldn't wait to rib Caleb a little for old times' sake.

The lady was a bit of a looker, too with long auburn hair. Her slender body was a trait that Josh found attractive. Caleb's taste impressed him. There would definitely be some questions later.

As the brothers rounded the curves in the church van, curiosity swelled in Josh. A few times, he almost asked his brother about the auburn-haired woman, but he turned to relaxed topics like fishing and what each other had been reading lately. Small talk is all they seemed to do during the last few visits. Caleb pulled into the driveway and started walking towards the garden.

"You go on and get cleaned up. I'll dig up some fresh potatoes and get the grill going. I've got some nice sirloins chilling in the fridge and ready to be flamed to perfection."

"Now, you don't have to be cooking and serving me. I can help."

"No. I got this. You're my guest for the week. Go on now."

Josh shook his head and walked up the porch stairs. Deep down he didn't mind being cooked for. It had been a while since he had enjoyed a home cooked meal.

The grill coals were just right when the steaks went on and sizzled. Caleb hadn't begrudged Josh on having a beer. He was just happy the two could hang out in happiness. They hadn't seen each other since their mother passed away. So tonight, it would be Caleb the brother and not Brother Caleb. He could not resist one question about church.

"How did you like the services? Be honest, how was my preaching?"

"Everything was great including your preaching. Everyone treated me like royalty. You haven't told your congregation I'm a heathen, have you?"

The brothers laughed. "I figure they can find some things out on their own!" Caleb smiled.

"Tell me about that lovely looking lady you were talking to at the end."

Caleb choked on his bottled water and feigned ignorance. But hesitation kissed his cheek like Judas Iscariot.

The goading began, "I knew it! You and that pretty church lady are a thing. Don't be shy, it's not like you're Catholic."

"No, it's not like that. Not at all. She has been going through stuff at home with her husband and I have been providing therapy."

Josh nearly spit out his beer. There was no way on God's green earth that the moment Caleb shared with that lady–that married lady–was anything short of intimate. Surely, others in the church had noticed.

"So, you are telling me that interaction was only pastoral and not anything else?" Josh cocked his head with a smirk, "Caleb...brother, this is me you're talking to. I know you inside and out, my twin; I know the romantic dolt you used to be back when you were younger."

"You've got to believe me, there's nothing there, brother. Forget about it."

"Look, man, it's alright if you have a lady friend and that she is a wife to someone else. You're a grown man and grown men have needs." Josh said as he lifted his beer for another sip.

"Easy, Josh! Give me a break! You think you know every little thing, you always have. Let it go!"

Caleb turned the steaks over, looked across the yard, and then flipped them again. Josh watched his brother fidgeting with the tongs, face flushed red and in thought. He had struck a nerve.

"Listen, I don't want to cut too much into your business. It's just that I looked over and saw what I saw. Looked like you two were in a moment. Kind of obvious is all. I don't see what the big deal is. It's not like you aren't allowed to have a girlfriend. I mean, maybe if you went too far, you know, and–"

"Stay out of my business, Josh. You can't just barge into town and start making accusations like this."

"Easy there, big guy. Okay, maybe I read too much into what I saw. Maybe, I didn't. Whatever. It's none of my business what you do with your life, but you oughta not be parading around telling folks not to "fall into temptation" while you're messing with members of your flock, who are married." Josh said as he finished his beer and opened another with an intoxicated buzz in his head.

"Hey man, watch your words."

"No, Caleb, you watch yours. The problem is you think everyone around here is too stupid to see what's going on. Maybe folks around here are, but don't think I am. If those dumb hillbillies at your "Christian" church can't see what a hypocritical scumbag they have for a pastor then they deserve you."

"Hillbillies? Scumbag? Have you forgotten you're a hillbilly, too? Get the hell out of here and don't come back! You drunk fool."

"Sure thing, preacher man; have a great life!"

Three years later and no reconciliation materialized. During this period, Josh had figured they'd make amends after some cooling-down, as they had in the past. Time passed and Josh's optimism waned. Mom and Dad were gone and the absence of Caleb in his life had been crushing. He had lived in the hope that somehow, they would find a way to put this petty thing in the past. Eventually, hope totally disappeared and that void exposed the permanence of his aloneness. Now, Caleb was six feet below ground. Reconciliation would never come and he would now be alone. Josh didn't have a family, no one to pass on his legacy. Birds began to chirp and gently called Josh back to the present.

12

Damp, brisk morning air was perfect for hot coffee. Josh pulled on his hoodie and wrapped both hands around the cup to knock off the chill. He rocked easy in the swing and watched the world awaken. The sun had brightened the sky enough to see across the yard but had not yet made it over the mountain trees. Rich, bold flavor from his cup provided a soothing enjoyment as the last bit of darkness retreated into the woods.

A family of deer meandered out past the garden along the tree line, occasionally pecking at the grass as if they were on their umpteenth holiday meal.

They've probably already wiped out half the peas and lettuce in the garden.

There were no fences keeping them out of the garden. The Webb family philosophy was to plant enough for the animals, too. That way they would have a little more meat on the bones come hunting season. The small herd faded with the shadows into the forest.

All was calm as if the wind was sleeping in, a typical mountain morning. The porch was a place for the elderly who had toiled, labored, and had finally passed the torch on to younger souls with stronger backs. They would find something of purpose later in the day. In the meantime, they would rest. These leisurely mornings were the rewards of the older generation that had invested in a lifetime of hard work. Perhaps Josh would enjoy this daily, if he ever made it to retirement. That was a long way off.

With the first cup put away, Josh refilled and returned to the swing. The wind woke with a startle and slapped at the wind chimes and pushed his cardboard coaster to the porch floor. Fluttering pages beckoned Josh to his brother's pocket Bible. It sat on the wood patio table, a patient courier waiting to be called forth to present its tidings. Josh studied the old book with its familiar words and verses, fanning the pages back and forth.

Blood stained the book, Caleb's blood. It hadn't crossed his mind before, but he was holding a part of his twin. It was more than just blood, but the Bible. Josh wrestled with that. Caleb had carried his pocket Bible everywhere he went and often joked that if the whole Bible was the Sword of the Spirit, then his New Testament was a dagger. Smaller, but every bit as piercing.

But why cling to a teaching that you clearly didn't uphold? Josh was sure of the affair and with Sheriff Bell's wife of all people. Worse, Caleb had lied to his face about it. How could someone on the one hand love God–treasure His words–and on the other not obey the teachings? How many people refused to go to church, or believe in God because of hypocrisies like this in the churches?

A crease caused the Bible to keep opening to the same page, no doubt caused by Caleb's tight grip after being shot. A final beseeching to God, in vain, but for what? And why would God help him after he had desecrated his pastoral calling? He examined the page, noticing a heavy blotch of dried blood covering the page. He had somehow smeared the form of a cross, perhaps making some last confession to God. The smudged cross covered a passage in the Book of Acts. Josh softly traced the stain with his finger.

A cross, or an X?

Josh heard the words of the chapter being read before he recognized his own voice. It had been some years since he had read the Bible, and had to admit the King James' Version's poetic language was soothing:

"But ye shall receive power, after that the Holy Ghost is come upon you: and ye shall be witnesses unto me both in Jerusalem, and in all Judaea, and in Samaria, and unto the uttermost part of the earth."

A thick, crimson blotch made the following passage hard to read. Studying it closer he could make it out. It was the part about Christ being taken up into the clouds. Josh was taken back by deja vu or was it something else? Something familiar, like thinking about a friend you haven't seen in ages and then running into them by chance at the store. A chill crept up his back straightening the hairs on his arms.

Josh sipped at his cup while searching the yard for an answer. Something about it was important but eluded him like a name on the tip of his tongue. Maybe, Caleb was pointing to a person or reason he was killed. And then it hit him–at the church! Josh remembered the stained-glass mural, depicting this very passage. The wind swept through the porch knocking the chimes and thrashing at the pages. Josh sprang to his feet, erect, like every hair on his body.

"Caleb?"

13

The large wooden door creaked open to reveal the small sanctuary. Windows along the side walls brought in enough light to find the switch. Josh hesitated, taking stock of the church as it was, as if opening an ancient treasure chest. He took in the smell of aged hymnals mixed with lavender-scented candles as his eyes adjusted to the unlit room. He had never been alone in a church before. He felt like a ghost standing there and wondered what other spirits might be there watching him. He scanned across the wood pews as if looking under his bed to show himself there were no monsters. And then, on cue, an abrupt darkness washed over the sanctuary proving his suspicions were correct and that there were indeed monsters under the bed.

Josh found himself back outside, having made a hasty retreat. He held the walkway rails with sweaty hands and tried to calm the thump-thump-thump of his heart. A cluster of clouds moved on from blocking the sun and the sudden warmth on his back was ushered up to his cheeks.

Get a grip, numb-nuts. It was just a cloud. Not the monsters coming for me.

Josh stepped back into the freshly brightened sanctuary. He quickly found the lights again, confident he was alone, but not taking any chances he flicked the switch.

Okay, stop playing games and get down to business.

Josh walked up the center aisle between two rows of creamy blonde maple pews. He paused at the center section on the left where his family had sat for years. At least until he and Caleb were old enough to sit with the youth up in the front. Josh could see his Dad wrapping his arm around Mom. She would smile or blush at something he whispered. They were reverent, for sure; but they were playful.

Josh released a long-held breath and turned back to the objective, the stained-glass mural on the wall past the pulpit and baptistry. Caleb had said that sunrise was the best time to see the mural, because it faced towards the east. It was then you would experience a manifestation of God's grace as the sun's light danced through the mural's colors. It was one of Caleb's special moments, he had said. A time of communion with God.

Looking up at the mural he could see why. Josh didn't altogether dismiss the idea that God communes with people but had never experienced it himself. He knew something of meditation and could see how the light pouring through the art could amplify such an experience.

I'll have to come by sometime at sunrise.

Caleb had pointed out the stained glass wasn't merely a work of art, but an illustrated sermon. It proclaimed Christ had indeed risen from the grave and had ascended into Heaven, to sit in his rightful throne at the right hand of his Father. A glorious comfort for believers and a dire warning for others. In the mural, he is presented in an upward motion, with clouds beginning to envelop him. The disciples are standing there flabbergasted when angels appear and question their actions.

"We are watching Christ ascend to Heaven. It's amazing; can't you see it?"

"Yes, but you must stop looking into the sky and get busy spreading his message of redemption!"

The mural was certainly the work of an artist, but the idea must have belonged to Caleb. This scene was a favorite of their mother, who loved to tell her day-dreaming twins to get their heads out of the clouds and do something. The memory of his mother warmed him and Josh whispered, "Thank you," to the mural, or perhaps to Caleb.

The mural certainly had an effect. Josh underscored the thought of returning for the sunrise version. He walked past the pulpit to the backside of the choir loft. There was a large cutout in the wall that opened so the congregation could see into the baptistry. The place where he, his brother, and countless others had been baptized in the name of the Father, the Son, and the Holy Ghost after professing their faith in God. An allegiance many held dearly for the rest of their lives and some, like Josh, had abandoned. The mural was framed into the back wall of the baptistry.

Quality of craftsmanship was more apparent the closer he came. He wouldn't have been surprised by some minor imperfections; after all, it was the work of a local artist. But as Josh looked at a piece of work, it was strangely out of place. The mural was something you would find in the great cathedrals: brilliant and patinaed due to centuries age. Instead, it was here and new, in a backwoods mountain church. Caleb had told him the artist was local and had done the work at little to no charge. Local and free is usually associated with inferior craftsmanship and rightfully so. In this case, the only thing that proved to be inferior was his own premature judgment of the piece.

Something Caleb had said about the artist popped into his mind. The man had been a regular for years and had presented the mural as an offering of love for the church. Then, he stopped coming rather abruptly if Josh remembered correctly.

Why would a man so dedicated to his church and produce this masterpiece stop coming? Maybe, he decided to go to another church? Maybe, he knew something about Caleb?

Josh sorted out the puzzle pieces scattered in his mind. So many things pointed at this mural, as if Caleb were calling out from his grave and leading him to it. But why? It's true that both would have wanted to reconcile, but it was too late now. It didn't make any sense, but here he was looking at the mural and convinced there was something to this.

Might as well see where this leads.

Josh thought back to the artist. If Caleb were leading him to the mural, then maybe he was leading him to the mural's creator. The man had stopped coming to his beloved church for a reason. Why? What did he experience or see? What did he know? Judging by the man's willingness to walk away and by his meticulous craftsmanship, he must be a man of integrity. He could be trusted. Perhaps, that was a stretch having not met the man, but the seed was planted in his mind.

The mural invited him to come and touch; to not just see its beauty, but to feel its passion. Josh swallowed, trying to release the tension building up in his throat. With a grunt, he hopped into the empty baptistry and reached out to the work of art as if to a friend. The smooth, wavy glass was warm from the sun. He felt oddly intimate and at peace. He was drawn to the mural emotionally. He wasn't here for nice feelings but looking for something more specific; something to identify the artist. A signature of some kind, but none was found. Even if there was one it might be unreadable. Maybe, there was a record in his office? Feeling around the side of the mural, his hand came upon a thin piece of metal on the frame. Shining his cell phone light, he found a brass plate that read: *Randall Boyd, 2012.*

14

Randall Boyd lived about four miles northwest of Etham. He wasn't too hard to find thanks to the internet. BoydArtworks.com was a bit outdated and looked as if it hadn't had any views in years, but it placed him in Woolridge County. The young clerk at the gas station knew Randall and was happy to sketch out a strip map. From it, Josh knew where the house was. Randall had made small pieces for the station to sell along with cheap magnets and what-nots. The clerk wasn't sure if he was still creating them because he hadn't brought any in for over six months. His small works were hot items with the influx of resort tourists.

Boyd lived on a small county road off the main highway that went to Hazard. He and a neighbor were the sole residents on the road and they couldn't see each other. If Boyd was concerned about his lawn, he had some catching up to do. The grass was getting beat out by chickweed and dandelions. A long cluster of purple deadnettles bloomed half-heartedly along the railroad ties that lined the gravel drive. Seemed odd for an artist, but maybe he spent most of his time working the stained glass and trinkets.

A sixty-or-so year-old woman came out of the house as Josh exited his truck. Mrs. Olivia Boyd stood on the porch with one hand on her hip and the other held over squinting eyes as if she was looking into the sun.

"Well, you must be Brother Caleb's brother...John, is it?"

"No, ma'am; Josh. I am Caleb's brother. I was admiring the mural up at The Open Paths Church and saw that Mr. Boyd was the artist. I was wondering if he might be around."

Mrs. Boyd studied Josh as if doing some kind of psychic reading on him or judging whether he was worthy to proceed to the famous gallery. The reading was brief, but uncomfortable. She then turned towards the wood line as if suspecting someone was spying on them from the trees.

"Well, if you're wondering about the art then Randall is in his shop out back. He ain't done much lately, but maybe he'd like some company other than the snakes he's currently with."

Snakes? I ain't much on dealing with snakes.

"Yes, ma'am, I'll keep my eyes open for them. Thank you."

Please tell me this guy isn't keeping a bunch of snakes back here. What kind of whacko mess am I getting into?

Josh heard a group of men talking as he came to the opened roll-up door of the shop. It looked to be a converted garage. He couldn't make out what they were saying, but one was laughing at something.

"Hello?"

The men stopped their conversation and turned to look at Josh. They obviously knew his brother by the way they looked at him, but not in a very neighborly way. The two younger men didn't seem very friendly, at all, so Josh figured to not be too forthcoming on anything.

"How can I help you, young man?"

Boyd looked at him with the same look as his wife. He eyed him and knew who Josh was.

"Yes sir. Are you Mr. Boyd?"

"That's me. I forgot your first name, Mr. Webb. What can I do for you?"

"Josh. I figured you would know I was Caleb's brother. I came by to talk about your art. I understand you work with stained glass. Is that correct?"

"Art? Is that why you're here? You want Randall to give a tour of his gallery?" The snarky laugh came from the shorter of the two young guys.

"Easy, Billy. Why don't you and Dave load up and make that delivery. I'll be okay, nothing to worry about." Randall said.

"Dave can go, I'm going to stick around and help you move these pallets." Billy pointed to a couple that looked as if they had been there for a while and weren't planning on moving anytime soon. He continued, "Go ahead, Dave. And tell the Boss I'll be by later."

"Yep, too easy." Dave turned to leave and gave Josh a mocking wink.

Billy made a half-hearted attempt at looking productive by shuffling tools around on a workbench. "Don't mind me, fellas, I'll just work on a little project over here. Randall, don't be forgetting our arrangement."

Josh noted a pair of faded-green snake tattoos wrapping around Billy's forearm. His mind opened.

Ah, the ones Mrs. Boyd warned about.

Good sense was tugging at Josh's shirt sleeves and suggesting he leave. Something deep down made him hold his ground.

"Mr. Boyd, I feel like I have come at a bad time. Maybe I can visit you later, if that's okay?"

"You're okay, Josh Webb. I knew your brother, Caleb. We can talk, now."

"Yes, sir. Were you close to my brother?"

"No, we weren't close. Look, if you are here about my art then you're out of luck. I don't do that kind of stuff anymore. It only got in the way of real work."

"Oh, okay. Well, I have seen the piece you did at the church It sure is a nice one. Doesn't seem like a passing hobby. I was hoping.... you...."

"Forget it. Look, I don't do that stuff anymore. To be honest, whatever it is you're looking for," Mr. Boyd's eyes pierced into Josh's, "you need to let it go. I'm sorry about your brother, but I can't help you. Go back to wherever you've been all these years and let the sheriff sort it out. You'll be better off."

"Listen, Mr. Boyd, I don't want to be a bother. It's just that me and Caleb had…."

"No, sir, you listen. I can't help you. All I know is I made that stained glass mural for the church and that's that. I think it's best you go."

Josh looked over at Billy who was coiled up along the workbench listening to the conversation. Josh hadn't expected the visit to go anything like this. Looking back at Mr. Boyd, the two men locked eyes. Josh didn't see anger or resentment as if Josh had come to rub salt into whatever art meltdown the man had experienced. Instead, he saw fear. He saw eyes pleading for help.

But for what? What's going on here?

Light footsteps crunched against gravel and brought a welcomed distraction as Mrs. Boyd walked into the shop. She had three cans held together in both hands.

"I thought you guys might be thirsty, so I brought some sodas."

Mrs. Boyd's presence calmed the tension between the men. Josh grabbed the back of his neck as he looked away trying to figure out what had happened and what to do. Maybe, the old guy was just out of his mind. One thing was for sure, this was a waste of time.

She offered the first can to Billy, who took it so she would leave him alone. This freed her hands to separate the cans and offer the other two a drink in unison. Like many southern ladies, Mrs.

Boyd was a natural hostess seeing that the men had what they needed to get their work done.

"I was just leaving, ma'am, but thanks."

"Oh, that's okay, dear. Take it with you."

Like the snake man, Josh didn't argue. He just wanted to get away from this hellhole. Josh grabbed the can of soda which was wrapped in a couple of napkins. Perhaps the drink was too cold for Mrs. Boyd's hands. He thanked her for the drink and bid them farewell.

Randall Boyd walked up to his wife and held her hand. As Josh rounded the house, he looked back at them. They watched him like a shipwrecked couple watching a ship cruise by, unnoticed and condemned to remain. Then Randall Boyd turned away, beckoned by the snarky man with the snake tattoo.

15

A patrol car sat hidden in a thicket at the intersection of the Old County Line Road and Route 15. Deputy Tullos watched unsuspecting travelers pass by, while waiting for the end of his shift. He slumped behind the steering wheel for extra headroom, adding to the hide-and-seek thrill of his job. Most folks called it a speed trap, but he liked to think of it as a honey hole. The spot sat at the intersection of a service road and the main highway as it curved past a speed limit sign meant to slow traffic just before town. It accounted for two-thirds of his monthly quota. Folks had complained about it for years, saying it wasn't necessary to drop the speed that much so far out of town. Besides, it was kind of unethical. Etham disagreed, citing safety concerns. Of course, the revenue it provided didn't hurt.

When the monthly ticket quota was met, Tullos would relax his standards. On rare occasions, he'd let cars blast by up to fifteen miles per hour over the limit. It also depended on how much longer he had before his shift ended and what kind of mood he was in. In this case, the car that throttled past him at 3:32 pm caught him on an okay day but didn't quite make the deputy's relaxed standard. He flipped on the blue lights and had the guy pulled over in less than a quarter of a mile.

Theatrics played a prominent part for Tullos and it showed in how he exited his patrol car. Standing up behind the door, he stretched upward to his fullness, revealing a lean, but toned body. He took time to observe the vehicle and get a sense of the occupant's temperament as he adjusted his uniform and straightened his hat. He slowly approached the vehicle, pressing the trunk with his hands. It was an old trick he'd learned at the Academy to leave his fingerprints on the vehicle in case things got ugly and the prints might be useful in indicting the guilty.

The heavy-footed driver was a college kid passing through on his way home to Elkhorn, located in the next county over, for a family emergency. He recognized the young man as having played against the Etham basketball team in the playoffs the year before. They had eliminated the deputy's beloved high school in overtime. In turn, they were eliminated in the next tournament round.

"I oughta give you a ticket for stealing hoops and dreams."

Tullos had a soft spot for fellow athletes and let the kid off with a stern warning. The young man thanked the officer and vowed to never speed again. With that, Deputy Tullos returned to his car and back to the honey hole. One more hour to go until quitting time. Tullos decided to stop watching the cars and enjoy a cigarette or two outside his cruiser.

His phone buzzed as he lit his first smoke. It was Billy Dalton. Tullos let the phone ring a few more times allowing himself a couple nice draws from his cigarette. Writing tickets was his day job; answering calls like this was his night job.

"What's up, Billy?"

"Check it out, Tullos. That preacher's brother came out to the Boyd's place earlier. He's asking about that old man's artwork. You know, that glass mural at the church?"

"Did Randall talk to him? What did he say?"

"No, he kind of cut him off pretty fast. Maybe, too fast. Then his wife comes out, giving everyone one a soda."

"So?"

"So, she don't normally offer me a damn thing. Seemed kinda shady."

"Yeah, I suppose so. Look, keep the Boyds under check. I'll let the Boss know, but–and I hate to say it–lay off Josh Webb for the moment. I'll check in with the Boss and see if things need to be escalated. I think there's some kind of history there."

"You got it brother. I'll stay on the Boyds for now, but let me know if anything changes with the Boss."

"Thanks, Billy. You'll be the first to know."

Tullos took a final puff of his cigarette, mashed it out under his foot, and fired up a second with a hard drag. Blowing smoke in the air, he considered what needed to be done about Josh Webb. He figured Webb could be encouraged to make tracks out of town easy enough. The real problem was Sheriff Bell. He didn't like the guy as a supervisor, nor did he think the man could be trusted.

True, Bell had been convinced to turn a blind eye to some of the Boss' shady dealings, due to something the Boss knew about Sheriff Bell that would hurt his re-election efforts. In return, Bell was given information about a lot of the small-time competition. It was a sweet deal; he got to make just enough arrests and the Boss didn't have to worry about the law interfering in his business. It didn't end with petty drug deals. No, even that was a cover for something more insidious. Bell's blind eye would only turn so far, so he could not know what was really going on in Etham and the Boss made sure of that. Bell was already starting to pick up the trail of the preacher's murderer. That made the sheriff more of a liability than Josh Webb. It was a fine line, one that Tullos wished the Boss would stop walking. The best thing to do was to get rid of Bell, maybe through a drug bust gone wrong. That would be simple enough. Hell, the guy would even be made into a hero. It was time to make the case. Tullos awakened his phone and scrolled to the Boss' profile, a picture of a scraggly stray cat. He chuckled at the cat and pressed the phone icon. The line picked up on the fourth ring.

"What is it?"

"Hey, Boss, I just got a call from Billy Dalton. Josh Webb went out to the Boyd place. Billy said the old man didn't say much but was acting weird. The old lady was too."

"What was weird about it, did he say? Other than Josh being there in the first place?"

"Just that Randall Boyd cut him off pretty quick. Then Mrs. Boyd came out with drinks, even gave one to Billy. She hates Billy. He thinks they were sending signals or something."

"Son of a... Okay. Tullos, listen. Get one of the boys to tail Mr. Webb. Make it twenty-four hour surveillance on the downlow. Make damn sure they ain't seen. We need to get him out of town before he stirs up trouble."

"You know, I can just go over to his house and make the case, straight up. I could take a few of the boys along to drive the point home."

"Don't even think about it, Tullos. We need to get him out easy with no fuss. We've got too much riding on this. Stay the course, for now."

Tullos closed his eyes and let out a slow breath. Surely, the Boss must know doing nothing isn't going to work. They had to get Webb out of town, but whatever relationship the Boss had with the guy was deep. He shook his head.

"What about Sheriff Bell?"

"What about him?" The Boss was getting annoyed, but Tullos was a key player in keeping the law off his back, so he listened.

"Listen, Boss, I know you're trying to keep things quiet with no bloodshed, but Bell is getting too close. I can set up a drug bust and make sure he gets eliminated."

The Boss' silence indicated consideration. Maybe Tullos' opinion of being too soft was right.

"Not now, but you are right. We'll deal with him soon. First things first, let's get Josh Webb out of town. But we need to do it carefully. Remember his brother, the preacher was just shot and killed. If something happens to Josh now, then it will draw way too much attention. We don't need that, understand? Wait him out and make sure nothing comes to light for Josh. He'll eventually leave."

"How do you know that? He seems pretty set on finding out things to me."

"No, Josh Webb hates this place. If nothing opens soon, he'll leave."

16

Josh followed the old, curved County Road back up to the highway and then home. Nothing about his visit to the Boyd place seemed normal. Why was the old man so defensive? Did he sense that he was there to ask about his brother? Even if he was, so what? It was such odd behavior for country folks around here. Sure, the world isn't as friendly as it used to be, but that was an odd way to treat a guest, even if he was a stranger.

Then, there was the look in the old man's face when they locked eyes. Maybe his words had been unnaturally harsh, but his eyes said something else. No, it was a lot more. Randall screamed for help in his own way. Something in it was meant for Josh and not for the man, one of the snakes, pretending to work behind him. Was he listening in? For what reason?

The truck came to a stop at the homeplace and Josh turned off the engine. He sat still in the seat replaying the events in his head searching for something he may have missed. Remembering the soda Mrs. Boyd gave him, he popped the top and took a drink. Something felt stiff between the can and the napkin. Inside it was a small sheet of paper with a set of numbers on it, followed by one word.

755.12LIN, Help

The note confirmed what Randall Boyd's eyes were conveying. Both he and his wife, Olivia, were in some kind of trouble and needed help. Questions rushed through his mind in chaos like impatient children vying for a teacher's attention.

What kind of trouble could these people be in? Drugs are certainly an issue in these parts, but people aren't normally forced into it, are they? Are the two men–the snakes–somehow holding them hostage, perhaps using their property to traffic the drugs? What do these numbers mean? Is it a date of some kind? And what of the letters?

Josh unconsciously took another drink of the soda, restarted the truck, and headed to town. There were no answers yet. Perhaps the drive would help. Maybe, going to the sheriff was the way to go. Judging by their last interaction, on top of the revelation of his wife, Sheriff Bell didn't seem to have any real interest in helping. To put it simply, Josh didn't trust Bell or maybe it was the other way around. Either way, the feeling was mutual. But what were the options? When someone slips you a note asking for help you take it to the law. Why had the Boyds not reached out to the law themselves or had they?

Nothing about the note made sense. It may as well have been an Egyptian hieroglyph, with a meaning meant to be sealed for several millennia into the future. Driving to town seemed to be a waste of time, but sitting at the old homestead wasn't likely going to offer any solutions either. Josh pulled into a parking spot along the street across from the sheriff's office and reconsidered reporting. A female deputy came out the door and trotted down the steps while waving at an elderly couple as they walked past. They responded in kind, the old man waving with a book in his hand.

Josh smiled. Simple acts of hospitality like that were what made small towns great. Even if you don't know everyone by name, you still treated them as friends and they treated you the same way. The old man said something to his wife, and she covered her face with one hand and swatted his arm with the other. The man bellowed a laugh that Josh could hear from his truck and held up his book as a shield.

That's it, a book! The note is a Dewey Decimal book number.

Shifting the truck out of park, Josh drove around to the far side of the town square and came to a halt in front of the Woolridge County Library. It hadn't changed much since he was a kid when his family would come just about every week. For a moment, he thought he might look back and see his father and mother coming up the steps behind him. The library was old back then and even older now. He thought the flag was the same one, faded and slightly tattered.

Old books permeated the air further stirring memories of his family's weekly venture to the library. Most Saturdays would find them gathered around one of the wooden tables scattered across the lobby. He and Caleb were allowed to check out two books of their own choosing. They would all spend about an hour reading at the library, a ritual Cyrus Webb held sacred. He believed being well read added an extra layer of discipline to a man and made them all better humans.

Just inside the entry was the same annual gallery display of elementary school art; drawings of animals, family members, and flowers. The only change being the name of the kids on the drawings. Josh remembered several of his masterpieces being displayed at another time in the past.

He looked down at the strip of paper to refresh his mind of the number and made his way down the aisle labeled 700-800. From his research background, he was familiar with the section number. About a quarter of the way down, he began seeing 755 numbers and then 755.12LIN, a book about religious paintings. The number he was searching for was not there. He searched the adjacent shelves hoping the book had been misplaced. Still nothing. Maybe, he had been wrong?

Josh sat at one of the tables where he sat as a kid. He had been certain the number was a book classification identifier. What else could it be? He had considered it being a date of some sort. But how would that be helpful?

"Josh Webb? Son, is that you?"

Josh looked up to see a grandmotherly woman smiling at him in surprise. Beatrice Price held both hands to her cheeks with black frame bifocals and a gray hair bun, although much thinner now. He couldn't believe she was still the librarian after all these years. He stood with a smile and opened his arms, the anxiety of his purpose forgotten.

"Ms. Bea, how are you doing!"

The two embraced and Beatrice stepped back just enough to look in his eyes, taking him in as if being reunited with a favorite student from long ago. A big smile appeared on her rosy cheeks.

"Bless my heart, Josh, it's been so long. Seeing you sit at this old table brings back happy memories, it sure does. Makes my work here seem more important than it is."

"Oh, Ms. Bea, your work is important, at least it is to me. This old library is a special place and helped shape me more than anything outside of my family."

"From what I hear, now you're shaping young minds. How are things going at the university?"

"Things are well. Young folks seem so different these days, especially the ones who come to college. You'd think they would be more serious about their education. They have a way of making you feel like you're just a road bump to something more important to them. Maybe, they're right."

"I know what you mean, but do you know what? They'll come around. The next generation always seems to be worse than the last. But they are not, they're the same." Beatrice's smile was calming and had a way of making sense to Josh. Her wisdom was highlighted by humor, as always and followed with a wink,

She continued, "The only difference now is you and I are older and wiser. And they are young and immature like we were back in the day. They always come through, just like you did before them, and I did before you."

Her wise words made an impact and Josh softened. The two sat down and Beatrice poured out how hurt she was about Caleb. How she thought the world of their parents and how he and his brother were like sons to the old librarian. Josh remembered how she babysat them a few times and how they quickly learned to stay out of her kitchen. The two talked, laughed, and even shared a few tears for about an hour.

"Josh, I'm so glad you came by, it's made my whole day, but you didn't come by here to visit an old lady. You looked so distraught earlier, what are you looking for?"

"Well, it's kind of silly, but I think I was looking for something that was never here. But you know what, I did find something better," Josh reached out and touched Beatrice's hand, "You've made my day, too!"

"Awe. I appreciate you. What exactly did you expect to find?"

"Like I said, it's kind of silly. Someone is in some kind of trouble and I think they were reaching out to me for help. They gave me this note."

Beatrice read the number and her warm smile disappeared. Leaning her elbows on the table she tightly squeezed her mouth with a wrinkled hand. She closed her eyes with a nod and let out a breath.

"The Boyds?"

Josh straightened abruptly; eyes widened by her knowledge of them. They looked at each other.

"How...how do you know?" Josh said.

Beatrice led the bewildered man past the counter into a cluttered office. Reaching in her desk she pulled out a book and handed it to Josh. *Famous Art of the Great Cathedrals.* The number on Mrs. Boyd's note matched the white strip of paper taped to the book's spine: 755.12LIN. He had been right; it was a book. Thumbing through the pages he found a folded sheet of paper kept hidden a little over halfway through the book.

Please help us! Our daughter Elizabeth Dawn Boyd is addicted to drugs and is being forced to sell her body to keep up her habit. She works at the Honeycomb as a dancer and is forced to have sex by some kind of pimp. My husband and I have been threatened and believe our daughter will be killed if we go back to the law. We told the law, but they haven't done anything to help.

Looking back at the book he saw a picture of a stained-glass mural of the Lord's ascension. He studied the picture, noting the similarities between it and Randall Boyd's rendering at the church. The attitudes of the two thugs at Boyd place, the snakes, began to make more sense. Was the law involved in this? Was Sheriff Bell heading all this up?

"Josh, things have gotten bad around here. Drugs, theft, and in the past few years, prostitution. And more recently full-blown sex trafficking."

"What do you mean, sex trafficking? Here? In Etham?"

"I know this is hard to believe and to be honest it's not very evident to most people. They think it's just the crackheads selling their bodies for more drugs. They don't suspect that some are being forced to do it and right under their noses." Beatrice said with sad eyes.

"But how do you know about it? I mean, you have this note, but why not reach out to the State Police or even the FBI?"

Tears welled up in Beatrice's glazed eyes as she looked away. Covering her mouth with trembling hands she blew out a sigh. "We're afraid, Josh. I know it's wrong. It's shameful, but there is something going on around here that is deeper than anything we can imagine. Josh, I'm so sorry."

Josh held Beatrice, feeling her sobs. She had been holding the secret inside for too long. It angered him that such a sweet person and others had to live in constant fear, especially in a town like Etham. They couldn't even trust Sheriff Bell; a man Beatrice had also watched grow up and no doubt sat at these same tables.

Was Caleb's death related to all of this? The mural had led him to Randall Boyd. Had Caleb been involved with drugs and prostitution? He knew his brother had been involved in a sexual scandal–with the Sheriff Bell's wife, for goodness sake–but he was certain Caleb wouldn't have sank lower. Would he?

Olivia Boyd had entrusted her friend Beatrice with the secret message, hoping she would find a way to get it into the right hands. When Josh came along, she decided to take the risk and reach out to him. Maybe, it was because he was an outsider, having been gone so long? Maybe, it is because his own family had been thrust into the chaos and he would also want answers?

No, he wanted more than answers. He wanted justice.

17

Banetown wasn't really a town. It was a loosely scattered strip of bars and one rather nasty gas station that made as much money selling beer, lottery tickets, and porn magazines as anything else. The place in the road existed as a blotch on the map nicknamed for its propensity for destroying lives. Josh parked in the side parking lot of an exotic dance club called the Honeycomb, hoping no one would recognize him.

He had waited until dark, hoping most of the eager clientele would get in ahead of him to decrease any embarrassing encounters. He didn't want to be seen in such a place and he didn't want anyone mistaking him for his brother. Most people by now should know that Caleb was dead. Josh had been to strip clubs a few times when he was younger. He'd awkwardly went along with the boys when they'd get the calling. Why it was called a gentlemen's club was beyond him. A real gentleman wouldn't come close to such a despicable place.

Now, here he was about to go into one, but not for a show or a tease of the flesh. He was looking for Elizabeth Dawn Boyd. Maybe, if he could get her alone, she might tell him something? Josh wasn't sure what that something could be or if she would even talk to him. He knew enough about pimps to know they were very protective and were always nearby watching over their property. He'd have to be careful. He also knew she was addicted to drugs and may not want help, except for another hit of whatever she craved. He had to try, if not for the girl or her parents then for the chance of finding answers about his brother. Someone in this shady place probably knew something about Caleb's death.

A couple men were finishing their cigarettes, bantering around outside while waiting on a third friend to join them. One of the men said something to the arriving member who responded with an expletive suggesting what he should do with himself. This initiated a hearty bro-hug and the three men hee-hawed through the front door to join the debauchery.

Josh chewed his lips between taking drags from his own cigarette. Sliding back into smoking was easy. He would have to stop while ahead, but he wasn't planning on it tonight. He paced the length of his truck back and forth and finally mustered up the fortitude for the task.

You can do it. No one here is going to judge you for going in there. They're here, too. They won't even notice or care that you are here. Just go in and do what you've got to do. Come on, let's go.

The internal speech didn't inspire him much, but he crushed the cigarette under his boot as he started forward. The walls vibrated, echoing the music inside, which was not the type he liked to listen to. His clothes transitioned into glowing neon versions of themselves as he stepped through the door. After paying the entrance fee to the rather large man at the door, he stopped and acclimated himself to the black light of the bar. Cheap perfume and body sweat called more to his sense of disgust than arousal.

Men gathered around small tables watching young women dance their way out of skimpy costumes and lingerie like Sirens luring them to the stage to part ways with their hard-earned or ill-gotten money. There weren't any tables available, so Josh found an empty stool at the bar.

"Hi there, handsome! What can I get for you?"

"What's that? Oh, yes, I'll just have a glass of water, thanks."

"One glass of water coming up, but–" she pointed to a sign that stated customers had to purchase a drink with alcohol. "Sorry, it's the rule. You don't have to drink it; you can give it to one of the girls."

A drink with little alcohol, but a hefty price. Always the rules of the house you visit, especially houses like these.

"I'm sorry, it's been a while since I've been out like this. I'll have whatever is on draft."

"You've got it, honey. Is there anything else I can hook you up with, perhaps some company?"

"Actually, I'm kind of looking for someone and was hoping she still works here. Her name is Elizabeth Dawn Boyd. Do you know her?"

The mischievous bartender studied Josh with a teasing smile. She pointed to the stage and then waved her open hand across the room, "Yes, I do! They are all Elizabeth Dawn Boyd. They can be whoever you want them to be." She continued with a devilish wink and smile, "If you're really nice and generous, they can do whatever you want."

Josh hung his head down toward his glass, slowly shaking his head with a you-got-me grin. The bartender's playful banter showed that he was wasting his time. He figured there would be no harm in finishing his beer before heading out. The challenge would be to not get captured by the action on the stage.

A woman sat down on the stool beside him and introduced herself. She was older than most of the other girls, around forty. She was likely a manager of some sort, but no more dressed than the others. Josh noted that she was no less attractive, either.

"Hi, I'm Tiffany."

A warm flash spread through his face and his stomach fluttered. "Hi, Tiffany, I'm Josh."

"Josh or Joshua? I like that name. It means something like a rescuer, or something. Doesn't it?"

He laughed at the irony of that and looked at Tiffany. "Yes, something like that. It's just Josh."

The seductive hostess was pleased at having summoned a little life from the man. "You know, all the action is in the other direction. What brings a dignified fellow like yourself into a place like this and you don't even want to watch the girls? You aren't a real gentleman, are you? Oh, or maybe you…," Tiffany raised her brows and tilted her head as if to suggest he might prefer something other than women.

"No. No!" Josh nearly lost his last sip of beer through his nose, "Good Lord, no, it's not that."

Laughing at himself and about how he was coming across, Josh leaned back on the stool and stretched his arms and legs. With some restraint, he turned to the dancer on stage, now topless, and then back to Tiffany. He searched her eyes, wondering whether she could be trusted with the question about Elizabeth Dawn.

Tiffany's eyes revealed an amused curiosity for Josh, but he sensed that she was more here for the sake of business than she was for conversation. She wasn't to be trusted and if he asked her, then he would probably be shown to the door the hard way. No, he would tell her it was nice to meet her and then get the hell out of there. but she continued.

"Well, Josh, we can't have you sitting around here, surrounded by all these beautiful honeybees and looking so depressed. Now, you pick out a girl and we'll get you a nice little space to enjoy a distraction from whatever troubles you."

"Thank you, but I guess I'll get going. I guess I made a mistake thinking this would cheer me up."

Tiffany leaned in close to whisper seductively, "There are some men at the door that think you are trouble by what you asked the bartender. I'm starting to think that, too. You're going to order another drink and I'm going to fetch you a hot, little honey and you're going to enjoy her show. Then, you need to tip her well. Otherwise, you will probably get roughed up by my friends and that would cause a setback in business. I don't like setbacks, Josh. Do you understand?"

Josh thought about the options. Then, he thought some more and understood what needed to happen. He offered a friendly smile and ordered another beer.

18

Marilyn was aptly named for her striking resemblance to Marilyn Monroe. Short, tousled, bleached-blonde hair with playful eyes, seductive red lips, and with all the right curves. She was a near spitting-image of the sex icon, but with less clothing. She led Josh to a secluded spot in the rear, close to the office area. The wall had a mirror so clients could watch from both sides of their selected honeybee. It was obviously a two-way mirror so that security could watch to ensure the client kept their hands off the merchandise.

Marilyn was left alone with Josh to do as much as he would pay for within the confines of the law. At least as much as the law was paying attention to. Management would ensure the dancers wouldn't go too far. The girls knew their limits and typically knew when they weren't being watched. The dancer circled around Josh, who was seated facing the mirror. She teased him with a feathery scarf and gyrated her hips as she passed around him. She leaned over to him as if to whisper but blew softly into his ear. Her perfume swirled about, toying with his senses and seducing his mind.

Hell of a distraction.

Josh snapped himself out of arousal, remembering why he was there. He made an effort to feign enjoyment while hoping to somehow find a clue. He decided he would get further if he played along, so he leaned back with a boyish grin, as if finding his old man's porn stash. When she drew in again, he leaned his head against the side of hers, careful not to touch.

"I'm looking for Elizabeth Dawn."

She playfully pushed his head away with her finger and then waved it in front of him in a "No, no, no," gesture. She smiled and unlatched her bra while straddling his lap.

Josh swallowed and struggled to hold on to any decency he might still have. Marilyn bent forward and let gravity send her bra to the floor. Josh closed his eyes and said a prayer for mercy, assuming God was within hearing distance of the place.

Her scent increased and he felt her breath against his ear. Sweat began to form on his head and he felt her lips against his face.

"I'm looking for Elizabeth Dawn Boyd? Please. Do you know where I can find her?"

His whispered voice cracked causing Marilyn to giggle. She looked with drowsy eyes, noses almost touching, and bit her bottom lip as if nearing climax.

Will this damn song ever end?

Hopping off Josh, she slowly walked behind him and grabbed the back of his neck as if to massage. Her hands slipped over his shoulders, feeling his chest, and she drew in as if to kiss his neck.

"Elizabeth Dawn was up at the Resort, last I knew. Works one of the cabins. I didn't tell you that. When I come back around, grab my ass and prepare to be slapped."

The words were light with feigned seduction. Josh couldn't believe what he had just heard. Not the actual words, but that she actually said them. He held back the temptation to ask her to repeat.

The Resort? Working one of the cabins? That didn't make any sense.

Marilyn straightened and with another giggle messed with his hair. When it was properly messed up, she kept one hand on his shoulder and teased her way to his front. In case he might forget her last words, she tugged his ear as if it was a blow horn. He winced and she gave a playful laugh, followed by a stern eye and with pressed lips mouthed, *"My ass."*

It came more simply than he would later admit. He reached up and grabbed a handful of the dancer's backside which prompted a surprised shriek followed by sound slap. Josh thought he had misinterpreted her instructions, but before he could give her an explanation, he was being hauled off by two very brawny individuals dressed in black suits. One was bald with a tattoo that ran up his neck and the other had greased-back jet-black hair with a large gold chain around his neck. They didn't say a word, only smiled. Josh looked back one last time before being thrown out the front doors. His dancer winked at him and blew a kiss, Marilyn Monroe style.

19

Sunlight peeked through the trees as it rose over Spruce Mountain and warmed Josh's cheeks. Last night's dance with its revealing words coupled with no sleep added to his anger and anxiety about Caleb's murder and the whereabouts of Elizabeth Dawn Boyd. Each passing minute made his blood pump harder as he sat on the old homeplace porch. Thoughts about who, why, and where traversed his spinning brain. Something caught his attention for a moment. Fluttering movement in the flowerbed that his mother had always kept prompted focus. The blurred wings of a lone hummingbird grabbed his squinted eyes. It moved from flower to flower gathering nectar. The extreme speed of the bird had amazed Josh from the first time his father had pointed them out when he was a kid. Something clicked in his head and Kristol's tattooed arm flashed.

She had a tattoo of a hummingbird blended into a background of flowers. Damn, she invited me to come see her at the resort. It must be the resort that Marilyn mentioned.

With haste, he downed the rest of his coffee, grabbed his truck keys, and sped down the driveway. Fog and mist shrouded the lone highway as he took each sharp curve as fast as he could. Thoughts of Kristol consumed him. Thinking about that day in town, every detail and her scent excited him, but he was smothered with the memory of holding Caleb's hand as he passed on to the next life. Each mile blended into his hazy attention.

As he hit the straight stretch on Highway 15, the Green Valley Mobile Home Park on the right caught his attention. Seems like it had always been there, and most of the trailers were the same ones that had been there when he was younger. Back in high school, the kids that lived there barely scraped by and most were troublemakers. Junky old cars and piles of trash were normal sights then just as they were now. Slowing down to look the landscape over, a lot of folks sat on their porches, emaciated with the look of drug-induced zombies with no hope of regaining life. On the corner of one of the streets, two scantily dressed women with short skirts and skimpy halter tops leaned against a junked car. Green Valley had always offered commerce enterprises that were known by all and catered to ones that strived for that kind of lifestyle. The difference here was that the quality was at the lowest level and to the point of them barely making any cash for friendship.

The highway turned to fine gravel as it twisted up towards the Stepping Stone Mountain Resort and Trail Center. His phone vibrated as he pulled into the parking lot.

606....That's the local area code.

"Hello?"

Silence.

"Hello, who is this?"

More silence. A silence that consumed multiple seconds.

"Anybody there? Hello?"

Josh hung up and shook his head. One bar of reception didn't surprise him.

Bustling activity amazed him more now than when he visited the resort before, or perhaps he had not been as keen on the details the first time. People in expensive polo shirts and pastel slacks mingled with young couples in hiking boots and shorts came in and out of the main entrance. Expensive sports cars and SUVs were scattered about the parking lot which made Josh think about his passion for high performance vehicles. Rounded wood columns accented the steep-angled A-Frame log building; he seemed to notice more detail this time. As he walked towards the entrance, he looked at his watch and noticed he had some glitter from the dancer that had enlightened him in many ways the night before. Embarrassed, he rubbed the top of his hand against his jeans. With effort, the mark of his visit was erased.

As he got to the two front doors, a well-dressed older man came out and nodded his head. Too much cologne lingered as the man went past. It reminded Josh of his ex-fiancé's boyfriend that he had caught coming out of her apartment. The smell had been imprinted on his fist as well as his brain. He shook his head and wiped away the memory as he walked in. As before, the large wood beams spanned across the ceiling, the waterfall splashed, and a stone fireplace at the end of the great room seemed out of place in Woodridge County. Places like these were up in the Smoky Mountains or some place that people paid top dollar for. With wide eyes, Josh walked up to the front desk.

"Welcome, sir. How can I assist you?" A young woman with pouty lips and bright blue eyes said with a smile.

What a beautiful woman, even more beautiful than the desk clerk that greeted me last time. Maybe, if I was ten years younger and a bit more handsome, she would look at me without getting paid to work at the desk.

"This place is nice, and busy."

Now, that's not the best opening sentence.

"Sure is. The cabins stay booked year-round and the trails are always filled with hikers from all over the world."

Josh looked around the resort with amazement like before, but this time was different with his increase in knowledge. Like Mr. Field's had said. Things are looking up for the county and its people. Mining is dead, but tourism might be the future.

"Sir, please don't mind me asking, but you look very familiar. There was a maintenance man we had that took care of everything. You look like him. Sorry, I'm mistaken. I heard he died recently. Have you stayed here before?"

If Josh had a dollar every time he had heard about him being familiar lately, he would have a bulging wallet. Thoughts of his brother and his murder crossed his mind again. He looked at the

138

metal name tag pinned to her maroon polo shirt. A thought of Caleb's resort badge flashed across his eyes.

"Ms. Rawlins, you don't have to call me sir. Makes me feel old and broken down. No, I've not stayed here before or hiked the trails. You are correct about my twin brother dying recently."

"Sorry, I didn't mean to offend you. Please forgive me and you have my condolences. I didn't know him personally, but he was a polite man. Always said hello to me and asked how I was. Please call me Susan."

"You didn't at all. I appreciate your words. My name is Josh. I'm here to see Kristol Engel. She said she worked here. Do you know her?"

The smiling bright-eyed look disappeared. Her pouty lips tightened, and she tried to hide her anxiety. She looked down at the polished wood floor and thought about the time Kristol had cussed her for not checking in a guest correctly. Going from having a cordial persona with a fake smile to a demon with pointed teeth was the truth that Susan had learned about Kristol that day. She looked back at Josh.

"She does work here. She's a manager. Let me get her for you."

Susan unclicked the small walkie talkie from her belt and pressed the talk button. She turned and looked out the large window to the side of the front desk.

"Kristol, this is the front desk."

Susan put her free hand on her side and shook her head. Disgust was displayed on her face, but she tried to hide it. She pushed the button again.

"Kristol, this is the front desk again. There is a man here to see you. He says he knows you."

"Front desk. Escort the man down to the maintenance garage. I'm taking care of some business up at the Mountain View cabin. I'll be there in a few minutes."

"I'll do that. Be right down, ma'am."

Susan looked at Josh and slightly shook her head. Words formed in his mouth, but he decided not to vocalize them.

"Josh, please follow me. I'm sorry you're inconvenienced with a wait."

"I don't mind at all. Please lead the way."

He could not help but notice the curves that Susan's black skirt provided. Thoughts of himself being a dirty old man ran rampant in his brain. Being single for too long wore on him and last night's dance didn't help. He shook his head and tried not to have any thoughts at all. His goal was to talk to Kristol. The connection with the hummingbird grounded his focus. Maybe, it would lead to something. He wanted to find out exactly where Caleb was killed and maybe a few other questions would be answered.

The elevator to Mr. Field's office refreshed memories of his previous visit. Questions and deductions crossed his mind but were quickly dismissed as they went down from the main floor to the level below.

As they walked along the stone path to the maintenance building, Josh noticed a few women getting into trucks with the resort name and logo on the doors. They were dressed as if they were going to a high-class event. Seeing that convinced Josh he was onto something and reinforced his determination to talk to Kristol. Maybe, she knew something. She had been very flirty and talkative that day in Etham.

"Right down here."

"I appreciate you escorting me. I think I could have found it without causing you any trouble."

Kristol told me to escort you and that is what I'm going to do. That's the way it is around here. Do what you're told and don't ask any questions."

Her tone of voice and the last sentence made Josh look more intensely at the woman in front of him guiding him down the steps that led to a massive six door aluminum garage. ATVs, golf carts, a couple of zero turn lawn mowers, all kinds of tools, and a shiny new tractor were inside. What she said made him wonder what kind of manager and employee relationship they had. It seemed strained at the very least to him.

"Miss Engel. Here is the man that wants to see you. His name is Josh Webb."

Butterflies flew around Josh's stomach and a lump formed in his throat. A bent-over woman in tight faded jeans and black t-shirt was looking over a stack of papers.

"Sweetie, I'm so glad you took me up on my offer to come visit. Just got back from cabin number 2 on the ridge way up there." She said and pointed.

The lump in Josh's throat got bigger from the word sweetie on. He smiled and thought of what to say. Words were lost to the abyss that was created in his brain when he saw her. The feeling was more intense this time he laid eyes on her.

"Susan, appreciate you escorting Josh down. Please get back to the front desk. I'm sure our valued customers need your assistance."

Both women stared at each other with contempt. Communication turned from words to intense eye contact. The memory of the check-in altercation still resonated in their minds like salt in a fresh bloody wound.

"Yes, I'm sure I'm needed back at the front desk. Josh, it was a pleasure to meet you. If you ever need any assistance, please come to the front desk. I'll be sure to provide you with VIP treatment." She said and walked back up the step towards the elevator with Kristol watching every step with angered eyes.

"Thank you so much, Susan."

"It's hard to get good labor these days. Sorry. It's good to see you again. What do you think about the resort and trail center? It's really nice, don't you think?" Kristol said and batted her eyes.

"Yes, hard to believe it is here. Right over there was an old mine that dried up years ago and now this is here. I'm sure all this is helping the local economy." Josh said as he scanned the hills that flanked the holler. The summits looked the same as he had remembered them.

Kristol filed some documents in a cabinet and leaned up against one of the mud-covered ATVs. Her tattoos caught Josh's attention. The hummingbird on her arm brought him back from being stricken with her to why he had come to see her in the first place. Josh knew he had to tread lightly to get what he was looking for.

"There's a lot of questions I need to ask you. I just don't know where to start."

"Josh. Ask me anything. I'm an open book. I owe you because you offered to help me out when no one else would."

That statement piqued his attention. He tried to figure out how to reply, but her nature did not wait for him to find an answer.

"I guess you came up here to find out about your brother, Caleb. Yes, I knew him. He was a maintenance man here. Top-notch in my book and kept this place going. He was a good man, a man of God as some people say. I don't believe in all that, but he was a good man, nonetheless. He helped the community and the locals liked him a lot. It's a damn shame that someone shot him. There's a lot of bad people around here these days. If I could have done something to prevent him from dying, I would have."

"Bad people. What do you mean? Could you have saved him?"

Kristol walked towards a new green tractor that was in the last bay of the garage. She rubbed the top of the engine compartment.

"Things change over time. Bad and good people come and go. That is the nature of things. I'm sure you understand with you being an educated university professor."

"I agree. How do you know I'm a professor?"

"I have my ways and word gets around. You know how small this place is, since you grew up here."

"What do you mean about bad people? Did you see him get shot and could have saved Caleb?"

"I mean the world is full of bad people. People like him don't deserve to die, I would never want anybody to die like he did. I didn't see him die."

Josh studied every inked design on her arm. The colorful hummingbird reminded him of the real one he had watched in the garden earlier that morning. Her eyes captured him as she looked at him. She walked closer.

"You look so much like Caleb. It's hard to distinguish, but you are different from him. A different kind of difference. I know that sounds crazy. Do you understand?"

"I do. I'm very different from him. A lot more adventurous."

How could he be so lame with that last statement? The struggle to be separate from his brother had plagued him from the beginning. He loved his brother, but both had wrestled with being twins. Caleb's death made it worse. Did he live in his brother's

144

shadow in his mind or was it real? Was it the other way around and Caleb had lived in his?

Josh looked at Kristol. Something about her pulled his strings. He wanted to know everything about her. At this very moment, he wanted that more than he wanted to know about what happened to Caleb. That disturbed him for a moment.

"I know you're not from around here. How did you end up here? Remember, you told me that you would tell me?" Josh said and tried to clear his mind of Caleb.

Kristol squinted her lashes. She was not one to open up to anybody, but something about Josh clicked with her. It was his tone and demeanor, but even more was his tenacity and true appreciation of everything.

Their eyes exchanged signals and Kristol decided to talk about her past. Had he penetrated her hard exterior or had she opened up as part of something larger that maybe she didn't really understand at the moment?

"Well, since you are so curious. You're right about me not being from here. I'm from Cincinnati. Been here for a few years. The trail center brought me here. I worked as an intern for a government funded project that helped start the trail. Powerful people thought that tourism could be a way of pulling this land and its people out of the mining slump. So, I got a job due to Mr. Field's. He was awarded grants and built the trails. His connections and outside investments led to the resort and twenty cabins being built along the trail. In my opinion, all of this is pulling the region out of dire straits. Etham is starting to reap the rewards. It's a road to recovery. So, here I am. I like it around here and Mr. Field's takes care of me."

Josh thought about every word she had just said. His mind grinded on all of it.

"Sounds like you know Mr. Field's well?"

"Yes. I guess you could say he treats me like a daughter. I feel that you came up here for more than a visit and a boring story about how I got here. Maybe, even more than finding out information about Caleb, because you have a look on your face. Am I right?"

"Well. Something like that."

"Go on. Ask your questions and I'll do my best with what I can answer."

The word "can" threw Josh's mind into a frenzy. Words and feelings formulated, but he decided in an instant to stick to his mission.

"Do you know Elizabeth Dawn Boyd? I've been told she worked here and possibly knew my brother."

Kristol's smile disappeared. She walked out of the garage towards a large oak tree circled with black mulch. Josh followed her and Kristol turned around.

"I knew her. She came up here and worked for a bit. Then, she moved on just like they all do. I heard she went out west. A pretty girl, but her mind was not right to work here."

Kristol seemed sincere in her words, but her body told a different story. Everything from the words to her pulling the leaves off a nearby limb made Josh feel uncomfortable. All of it prompted more curiosity.

"I was told she was a local girl. Going west doesn't seem like something she would do. What do you think?"

"Sounds like you know her. I don't know enough about her to speculate on anything. Just heard she went out west or at least talked about it with some of her co-workers."

"Nope. Just know of her from some locals."

Silence fell between them. Kristol walked back towards the mower and the way she floated towards it enamored Josh. Despite wanting more information from her, he was lost in himself and her. He had not felt this attraction in a long time and questioned whether he had felt this ever before. Every move she made entranced him more.

"Can I ask you one more question?" Josh said.

"Shoot."

"Where was Caleb killed?"

Kristol turned around. Her eyes connected with his.

"I liked your brother a lot. You look so much like him. Even got his good looks, but not his personality." She laughed.

Her words and smile threw him off balance. He did not know how to respond.

"Don't be uncomfortable. We are adults here. Your brother provided for the community and individuals in need. Really, I don't know anything about where Elizabeth Dawn Boyd ended up, but I'll tell you where your brother was killed. I owe you that."

Cold wind blew across the resort. Goosebumps jumped up on both of them. Josh looked up at the hills and watched the limbs sway. Then, he faced her.

"Go up the north trail." She said and pointed her finger towards a well-worn path out from the garage. She continued.

"You'll pass two cabins. The next one is the place. It's named Elkhorn Cabin. The sign will be hung from a post. Walk to the water well in front of the cabin. That is where Caleb was shot down."

"Who shot him?"

Kristol paced back and forth. A tear rolled down her cheek.

"Nobody really knows around here. This place is the death of many. Not a place to come to and stay. There are many ways to die, some slow and some fast....even some die that are already dead, but just don't know it. You're from here, but you need to leave and go back to your teaching. Forget about this place and what happened to your brother. Things happen and they happen for a reason. Sheriff Bell will take care of things. Just let it go and be happy. You deserve it. Your brother would want it that way."

Josh looked at her and then pivoted towards the trail that Kristol had pointed out. Struggle raged within him. Kristol's words didn't sit well with him.

"Your outlook has changed from light to a dim view. Understand. I guess I'll have to find out what happened and why by myself. It has always been like that for me. Caleb needs justice and I intend to see he gets it."

"I didn't mean to offend you." Kristol said and tightened her lips.

"You didn't. I promise you that."

Gravel crunched under Josh's feet as he walked toward Boone's Trail. As much as he wanted to look back at Kristol, he could not. Her eyes watched every detail as he disappeared into the dark woods. Higher up the hill, the trail zig-zagged back and forth in a series of switchbacks to make the terrain easier. After a half mile, his calves and hips hurt. No doubt, he was out of shape and he knew it. Every step made him regret not working out more like he had told himself he would many times. Getting to the spot where his brother was shot pushed him on. Adrenaline pulsed. The trail leveled out and began to parallel the road. The thought of being able to drive to the cabin made him shake his head. Of course, the resort guests could drive up to the luxury cabins and unload expensive luggage filled with stuff they didn't need. He laughed.

Sweat ran down his forehead as the tree canopy opened and he was able to see the blue sky. Josh walked past the first cabin, which judging from the kids playing out back and a high-end van out front, a suburban family paid a lot of money to get away from the grind of the city. As Josh made his way up some steep terrain, he looked at the valley below and awed at the beauty he had forgotten. After a quarter of a mile and a lot of sweat, he saw the second cabin up ahead. Wood shingles topped the manufactured logs of the structure. A large balcony off the back provided a scenic view of Middle Fork Creek which ran into Carr Reservoir Lake. A large black SUV was parked out front. Light from inside gave Josh a view. An older man and younger sultry woman were naked sitting at the bar sipping from wine glasses. Embarrassed for looking, Josh looked away as he passed the cabin. Another quarter of a mile up the trail, the third cabin, The Elkhorn, came into view. As Kristol stated, a well was in front next to a stone path that led to the cabin entrance.

I feel Caleb. I feel him here. This is the place.

Josh walked up to the well and touched the stones. Each mortar filled crevice scratched against his palm. His reflection from the water deep inside made him think of Caleb and who had shot him. Heartache ignited in his chest and a few tears ran down his cheeks. As much as he tried to hold back his feelings, it was difficult. He leaned up against the well and looked around. A red foreign-made car parked to the side of the cabin caught his eye; a model with high performance tires and hood intake vents. He wondered if the current occupant knew anything about his brother being shot. It was a longshot, but he knocked on the door.

"It's about time, I called an hour ago. When I pay for service, I expect it to be rendered in full with no delays."

Slicked-back black dyed hair with tight angled eyes that were the result of too much Botox made the man look even more menacing than his tone. Josh looked at him with a loss of words.

"I see that you are not here to assist me with the service. What do you want?"

"I'm not sure what you are talking about. Can I ask you something? Were you here a couple weeks back when a man was shot right over there, next to the well?"

The man was silent as he pulled back his head with awe. With a step forward, he scanned the yard and driveway.

"Shooting? Don't know about any of that business. I just checked into this cabin yesterday. Nobody told me about any shooting. I'm not involved in any crazy business like that. Guess I can't help you."

"I guess not, sorry to bother you."

The crackling of tires against the road with a grinding engine distracted their attention to a 4x4 truck pulling up. The Stepping Stone sign was on the side. The driver with a billed cap pulled back and exposing his forehead was easily identified as one of the men from Randall Boyd's place. He smiled with his yellowed buck teeth jutting out and said something to his female passenger which prompted her to get out of the truck. Josh's eyes met the woman's as she passed with a shy wave. Instantly, he was drawn to her for some unknown reason. Every detail about her jumped out at him. Her short skirt and stiletto heels were out of place in this wooded environment. She looked at him with heavy mascara and bright lipstick. The way she looked back at him as she walked to the cabin door projected mixed signals.

"Hey, we meet again. Probably not a good thing that we keep running into each other like this." Billy Dalton yelled out.

Josh squinted his eyes. Contempt and anger raged within him. His toleration for an individual like Billy went only so far. He nodded and turned back towards the cabin door. The young woman looked back at him with her full dark eyes as she was led into the house by the man that had answered the door. Josh took a step forward and stopped himself. Minding his own business when it came to the girl hit his mind. As he walked towards the well, Billy crossed his arms.

"You need to get to stepping and leave these resort patrons alone. They don't need any more hassle. I brought the man's girlfriend up here. I guess he didn't book her travel arrangements correctly and she arrived late." He laughed.

Josh knew it was not a good situation and he had finally found where Caleb had been shot. He nodded his head.

"Glad you have good sense, Josh Webb."

Billy pulled out of the driveway and went back down the dirt road. Dust settled as Josh regretted not beating the hell out of its occupant.

None of this feels right. Caleb must have known something about all this.

A cold breeze turned the leaves up and put a chill on his skin. He felt the stones and mortar of the well one more time and shook his head.

Guess I'll walk the road back to the resort. That trail is too rough for me right now.

Someone watched Josh walk down the dirt road. Then, the eyes looked down the trail and towards the valley.

20

A pair of cheap, green-faded snakes slithered around Billy Dalton's arm as he slammed his vehicle into high gear. Zipping around a patrol car, he honked his horn and gave the unexpecting deputy a proud middle finger as he passed. Blue lights jumped from a deep sleep and quickly caught up with him.

Billy's own vehicle was a classic 1985 Chevy Blazer, dark blue paint and silver trim with only a few dents and scratches to show from his off-road adventures. It had originally belonged to his uncle from his mother's side, who had kept it in pristine condition, until he met an untimely death in 2001. Billy was sure it had something to do with drugs, though you wouldn't dare mention that to his churchgoing mother. But folks don't normally get shot in these parts for being good neighbors.

Billy's father had passed away from pneumoconiosis, which was a big word for the black lung disease. Like most other men in these mountains, his father had worked in the mines and like many had become another victim of the horrendous disease. Billy was eleven at the time. His father had been promptly replaced by several of his mother's deadbeat boyfriends, more out of financial survival than a need of a relationship. Young children don't have the luxury of understanding any of that and he had held a grudge against his mother ever since. She tried hard to hold on to him, but he didn't care about her or anything else. Her death a couple years back didn't bother him at all.

What Billy did care about was his Blazer and the one true goal in his life was to keep it in mint condition. Well, maybe not mint condition, but as close as possible. He kept that goal and to him the Blazer looked pretty darn good, if he did say so himself and he did often.

Locking eyes with the deputy in the rearview mirror, he puckered his lips, blew a kiss, and smacked the steering wheel with his tattooed hand and gave a hearty laugh. He then turned on his blinker like a good driver and pulled to the side of the highway. He lit a cigarette, while he awaited the deputy.

"I ought to jerk you out of that piece of junk and pistol whip your ass!"

"Wow, Tullos. Baby, calm down. You know you love me. Plus, I do good work for you."

"Yeah, whatever. Get out and give me a smoke. Then you can tell me what that circus show was all about. Don't mess with me because I'm not in the mood today and don't feel like messing with you."

The two men stood leaning against the patrol car, facing the wood line as cars passed by unaware of Billy's earlier driving antics. He told Deputy Tullos how he had seen Josh Webb up at the cabin where the preacher had been shot. He had been talking to the guy staying there, but Billy didn't know about what. The girl he was delivering got out of the truck before Billy realized it was Josh, otherwise he'd have kept her inside until Josh left. Billy was not sure Josh knew who the girl was.

The last part stopped Tullos from hearing anything else. A group of dried mullein stalks were growing on the far side of the drainage ditch, their limp leaves fluttered in the wind, reminiscing of recent months when their flowers had been proudly displayed. Soon they would be gone, but they had left their seed, as was the way of all nature. Tullos blew smoke through clenched teeth, and studied the dying plants as if they might have the answer to how Billy could be so stupid. Billy stopped talking at some point realizing that Tullos was somewhere else in thought.

"So, Tullos, what are we going to do? I mean, if the Boyds have somehow talked and now he's snooping around and recognized...."

"Yeah, that's a problem, isn't it? We should have gotten this guy out of the picture on day one, but, no, the Boss is soft on this guy–some kind of history or something. Now, you go dropping off one of the girls in broad daylight like the freaking milk man in a resort truck. What the hell, Billy? You know better."

Both men flicked their cigarette butts into the ditch in unison and Billy lit up another with twitching hands. He'd thought the blunder with the girl was kind of bad, but it had happened so fast. What the heck was he supposed to have done? Yelling for her to get back into the truck would have caused more of a scene, so he had let it ride and made up the lie about the girl's travel arrangements. He figured talking a little smack to the preacher's brother might have caused a distraction. Hearing Tullos' reprimands after the fact made him feel like a fool.

"We've got to step up the pressure and make things happen." Tullos rubbed his chin, conversing more with himself than with Billy. "I'll go to the Boss and explain how this works on the ground level. The Boss has got to see how bad this is getting. We've got to wrap it up with this Josh Webb."

"Whatever you want, man. Just say the word."

"You go find Dave and standby in town. I'll call you when I get the go ahead."

Billy started toward his Blazer and stopped, "What if we don't get the go ahead?"

Tullos considered that possibility. This would take more than a call, he needed a face-to-face meeting with the Boss. Urgency was better communicated in person when they could look each other in the eye. The Boss would have to put aside whatever feelings he had for Josh Webb and let them take care of business.

"We'll get the go ahead. Just be ready. That is all you need to worry about."

21

After the encounter on the trail, there were many things for Josh to think about and make decisions on. The first decision was a no brainer, he needed food and beer. He had neither at the old homeplace. So, Josh found himself parked outside of Fudd's Restaurant. A faded sign boasted serving *World Famous Hamburgers and Fries*. The original proprietor, Charlie Fudd, had concocted a secret ingredient ketchup that made his otherwise cheap fries into something of a legend. It was more of a blend of barbeque sauce and chili peppers than traditional ketchup. Some patrons teased that Charlie sprinkled in a little cocaine or weed, as well. Having a variety of locally brewed beers on tap sealed the experience of eating at Fudd's.

The other things to think about included his reaction to Billy Dalton threatening him and the big one was that he finally knew where his brother had been shot. His mind struggled to process it all. A distraction came at an opportune moment.

His waitress was dressed in black leggings and an orange t-shirt with the Fudd's logo on the back, an updated version of the boastful sign by the front entrance. She had a pair of orange and white checkered skateboarding shoes that matched the shirt and a name tag that identified her as Tammy L. Under a Fudd's ball cap was red hair pulled up in a bun and a very familiar face that Josh couldn't quite place, likely the daughter of someone he had went to school with.

"Hi, my name is Tammy. I'll be waiting on you today. What can I start you off with?"

"Hey Tammy, I think I'll have…the Smoke Mountain IPA."

"Sorry, we're out of the IPA. We have some good lagers, though. I recommend the Black Water Lager. It's locally brewed in the next county over. They just opened up last year."

"If you say it is good. I'll take it."

"Good choice, it's our best seller. You'll love it. I promise. You ready to order?"

"I'll take the Classic Fudd Burger with fries. Don't forget the special ketchup."

"Coming right up."

Tammy had the large beer on his table in a minute. Josh sipped his beer as he waited for his food and contemplated the events of the day. His first thoughts, which he could not help, went to Kristol. She's a hybrid in every way from her looks to her profession and even her emotions. A mixed bag, but charming just as he remembered her from their encounters. Her long, sandy brown hair, sky blue eyes crowned with a brow piercing, an arm covered with tattoos unhidden by a sleeveless tank top, and tight jeans revealed fearlessness to be different. Maybe, even a hint of naughtiness covering niceness.

Then, her emotions showed something else. When he asked certain questions, she would turn away, almost as if hurt or ashamed–as if she had something to do with the whole world being a mess. Especially, when he asked about Elizabeth Dawn Boyd. Her teasing smile had vanished as she turned away, as if stunned by a jab to the chin and hoping to recover before another question could send her to the mat. She was hiding something, but what?

Then, his mind drifted with reluctance to Billy Dalton and where Caleb had been shot down. Why there of all places? Caleb working at the resort would have put him there, but something was not exactly right. Feeling his twin, Josh knew that Caleb was there to do something important or find something. Both him and Caleb were naturally curious and always went with the side of the helpless, downtrodden, and defenseless. They always wanted to help people like that. Hence, they picked their paths, Josh a teacher and Caleb a preacher.

"Here ya go, enjoy!

Tammy interrupted his thoughts with a plate loaded with a world famous Fudd burger, hot French fries with the concocted ketchup, and another beer.

"Wow, that was fast. Thanks!"

"You're welcome. Let me know if you need anything else." She said with a smile that caught his eye and made him feel younger.

Thinking back to Kristol, Josh considered her position at the resort. She was a maintenance person, but she was also in upper management. She had come across the job on some kind of internship and loved working outdoors. She was hands on; not afraid of getting grease on her hands, but she seemed a bit aggressive with the girl from the desk. Was that a typical female drama, or something more? Then, there was the fact that she had a close relationship with Mr. Fields. That connection made Josh question everything. Fields had been a close family friend, but he wasn't exactly an equal. He was his father's supervisor and gave things to the family, so that put him at a different level. He couldn't help, but feel like the man had a hidden agenda, at least going off their last conversation. Had his benevolence always hidden something more? Kristol being like a daughter to him was something to think about. What was he expecting from her or what was she expecting from him?

Perhaps Kristol was not much of a people person, but she appeared to be okay with him. Sure, she seemed a bit emotionally confused with questions about his brother, but she did point him to the place where Caleb was shot. Maybe she shared in the trauma of the incident. After all, it did happen on her grounds. That made a lot of sense. He would make a point to ask her how she and the resort were coping the next time they talked.

The burger was dry and unseasoned, and the bun wasn't the same as it was back in Charlie Fudd's day. It wasn't stale, but it wasn't fresh either. In the small plastic cup next to the fries was some kind of generic ketchup, not the famous secret sauce of old. Charlie must have taken it to his grave and would be rolling in it now.

Sheriff Bell was right about one thing, everything seems to have changed and for the worse.

Josh scarfed down the food, more out of hunger than enjoyment and washed it down with the last drop of his beer. At least, beer was drinkable. When Tammy asked if he needed another he declined and asked for the check. He figured he'd grab a six pack on the way home and maybe some bourbon. No use in spending all his money in a terrible establishment like this.

He thought again of the Sheriff's subtle dig at the local establishments, like Johnson's Grocery being high priced and a dump. Add Fudd's to the list of terrible changes.

He had said, "Things have changed around here. More than you can ever know." At the time, Josh figured the lawman was just making excuses. Then he thought of Mrs. Boyd's note about Sheriff Bell and how he might somehow be involved. If not directly, then for some reason turning a blind eye.

Things have certainly made a change for the worse. Sheriff Bell has changed too and must be involved. What does that mean? Is all this his doing? Or someone else? One thing seemed certain,

*someone with a lot of clout or money was pulling the strings. How
high does this go?*

Leaving a good tip, Josh paid his bill and started towards his
truck. He turned the corner from the restaurant to go into the parking
lot and nearly ran over a couple of ladies. The first was his old
librarian friend, Beatrice Price and the other, Olivia Boyd. The
women stared wide-eyed at Josh as he looked around searching for
anyone who might be following them. Josh reckoned that if whoever
was responsible for Elizabeth Dawn's disappearance kept tabs on the
Boyds at their house, they were likely to follow them around as well.

"Mrs. Price, Mrs. Boyd. How are ya'll today?"

Mrs. Boyd looked around, having the same suspicions as
Josh. Her face was drained of color as she looked back at him. Her
eyes strained red and filled with water as her voice cracked, "Fine,
Josh, how are you?"

"Mrs. Boyd, I don't think we can talk here in the open. But
quickly, do you have a picture of your daughter? If not, could you
get me one."

"Yes. Yes, here in my purse."

Mrs. Boyd fished through her purse and quickly retrieved a
photo of Elizabeth Dawn.

"It's a couple years old…but she can't look too differently,
can she?"

'Don't give it to me now. I'll tell you when to hand it over."

He continued looking around as if he were buying drugs and
feared the police were watching. As he scanned the area, he talked.

"Why did she leave home? How did she ever get involved in all this? I don't mean to pry."

"It's a long story. She started hanging out with some bad friends at school. We found pills in her room and she started to stay gone weekends. Then, she just left home without warning."

"I understand, Mrs. Boyd. Listen to me, I think whoever killed my brother is linked with whatever is going on with your daughter. I'm trying to figure it out, but I need to stay away from you and Randall for the time being, due to eyes watching everywhere. If you see me again, you'll need to avoid me. Shake my hand and give me the picture."

"Okay." She did as she was told.

Josh took the photo and put it in his pocket without looking at it. He began to walk away, not wanting to put the women in danger. When Mrs. Boyd called his name, he ignored her and began walking faster. Josh felt the agony seeping out from her voice, but with the way these people were keeping tabs on the Boyds he was sure they were being watched. He had to get away from them as quickly as possible.

It was too late.

22

There were no vacancies at the Stepping Stone Mountain Resort. A perfect storm had played out in favor of outdoor getaways. For one, an early spring heat wave had pushed itself into what seemed like summer, enticing many to flee from their congested urban existences, especially coming off two years of mandated COVID lockdowns. People were tired of being cramped up and were eager to get out in the fresh air. Travelers from as far away as Chicago and Washington, D.C. had made their way to the resort since its grand opening. Though not planned as such, the timing had been perfect. What had looked at one point to be a financial disaster for many businesses had turned out to be a boom for the resort and Etham. The right time and right place, with a little bit of luck to boot makes for good business. Mr. Fields smiled warmly as he gazed from his office window at the full parking lot below. People were swarming in and out like a hive of honeybees. He lit his briarwood pipe and enjoyed the fresh cherry cavendish tobacco as it swirled around his distinguished gray head. His phone vibrated in his suit jacket pocket. He smiled at its message. Everything was going better than planned.

Hope you are taking your medicine and not smoking. Things are good with the cabin on Hope's Ridge. The roof is repaired.

A knock on the door pulled him away from his phone. He looked at the wood barrier with dread due to not wanting to deal with anyone right now, but he knew there was no way of getting away from business.

"C'mon in."

The door opened with hesitation. Fields took a deep draw from his pipe. He didn't like Sheriff Bell, but he was necessary for the good of his operation. He feigned a welcoming smile and turned to greet him, as if he was the most important man in the world at the moment.

"Bell, how is everything going in town? I bet you are taking care of business."

"Business is booming. Your guests are getting down to the shops on Main Street and spending lots of money. Some find their way to Banetown, which is okay by them and me, but I'm keeping the peace, too."

Fields' grin became more genuine with the good news. Visions of the future crammed in his mind and then cleared.

"Good to hear. Just make sure to keep our visitors safe. Hard to believe this whole county was dried up. The government nearly destroyed us by taking the mining industry away. I thought it had destroyed me, too, having to move away like I did. But if I hadn't got out when I did, none of this would be here. I learned a lot from scraping by and building a business in Cincinnati."

"You sure have built a big enterprise here and getting bigger every day. That's raising some eyes in the region and the state." Bell said with a raised eye and tightened lips.

"Don't be holding back on me, Sheriff. What are you hearing that I'm not?"

Bell put his hands on his gun belt and took a deep breath. He looked Fields in the face and thought about what to say. Silence prompted Fields to take a seat in his desk chair.

"Sit down. Relax, Bell. Tell me what all these people are saying about me and the resort."

Bell did as he was told, just as he had always done. His gun belt creaked along with the leather chair as he sat down.

"A few of my friends up at the State Capitol told me some officials are curious about how things are booming so much and how the county used the grant money. They seem to think they need to be getting a bit more tax revenue, as well as some kickbacks from what they helped fund up here."

"Those damn leeches want to suck us dry. They didn't help with anything here. Sure, we got a grant, but that was Federal money; those state yahoos didn't invest a damn cent. Everything else I funded. As far as the taxes, I go by the rules that's on the books. Nothing more and nothing less. I'll be damned if I will line their deep pockets with kickbacks, unless they come to the table with something. I built this place and run everything that goes on around here for the interest of the citizens and myself."

"I agree with you. From what I'm hearing they aren't tracking anything illegal; they just can't figure out the town's boom. They're just trying to rattle our chains for cash. I'll let it be known through my channels that there is not much money to be made up here, until we can expand some. How does that sound?" Bell said and leaned back with the air of a proud rooster.

Fields stood up and looked out the window again. Veins twitched in his temples, but he managed to cool himself with slow breathes. Self-control was a virtue of the powerful and he prided himself on having it. A few rumors coming from the Capitol was a small issue at least at this point. A knock at the door prompted him to turn around.

"Sir, you've got another visitor. I told him you were busy, but he insisted." A trim brunette, who looked a bit too young to be working said with a smile.

"Who is it?"

"It's me, sir." Deputy Tullos said as he walked around the assistant into the room.

Bell stood up and turned around with an annoyed look. Both men locked eyes trying to figure out why the other was there.

"What brings you up here? I thought I told you to patrol Banetown." Bell said and straightened himself.

"Nothing going on down that way. So, I figured I needed to come up this way."

"Like I asked, what are you doing here? I didn't call you." Bell said with a scowl.

"Need to talk to Mr. Fields about some professional development and investments," Tullos said as he looked at Fields.

Fields took a seat at his desk. He eyed both of them and decided to settle things.

"Both of you calm the hell down. Maybe, I want to hear what the young man has to say. Go ahead, let's hear what all this fuss is about."

Bell's phone rang and vibrated. He looked at it and Fields.

"Go on and take your call, Bell. Seems like your deputy needs to talk to me alone anyway." Fields said with a smirk.

"I guess." Bell surrendered and then hissed at his deputy. "Tullos, you're out of place coming here. You need to get back on patrol."

"Stop your bickering about things." Field said as cherry cavendish smoke filled the room. He took another draw from the pipe and tapped his finger hard on his desk like a judge with his gavel. "You boys need to simmer down. This is the second time I've had to calm things between you. I don't want any more of this arguing. I've heard enough from both of you. Take your call Bell. Me and Tullos need to talk."

Sheriff Bell eyed both of them. He walked out of the office.

"Ran into Dalton like we talked about on the phone." Tullos said with gritted teeth.

"Stop right there. I don't want any names of your associates mentioned to me in person or where it can be documented. You got that?" Fields said as he glared at Tullos.

"Right Boss. I forgot. Won't happen again."

"We discussed everything earlier on the phone. There is nothing else to talk about. Josh Webb is not an issue. Despite his brother's actions, Josh is a smart man. He just needs to see the light. Did you know me and their father, Cyrus, worked the mines together? Damn hard work for anybody. Cyrus covered down for me many times, even saved my life once when part of a mine shaft collapsed. He pulled me out before the whole thing came down. I owe him for that."

"I understand, you have a connection." Tullos said.

"I need some time to think about things. Leave me."

Tullos nodded his head like a disciplined kid. He walked out of the resort to the parking lot. Bell was there waiting.

"Listen up, Deputy. Don't be going around me and talking to Mr. Fields about anything without my approval. You need to check yourself. We'll talk about the chain of command later. Understand?"

Tullos smirked and nodded his head. A smile appeared on his face. A grin that Bell did not like.

"Just trying to be helpful and keep things running around here. Sometimes things don't get taken care of like they should be. Plus, law and order has to be maintained." Tullos laughed.

Bell took a step toward Tullos, but stopped. This was not the place and time for this. Bell looked up and noticed Fields watching through his window. With a moment of silence, both officers calmed down. They stood and waited for the other to say something.

Tullos' cell phone vibrated and he silenced it. His eyes didn't leave Bell.

"Listen, whatever business you have with G.W. Fields needs to be conducted on your own time. Another thing, you need to respect the chain of command. Now, finish your patrol. Then go home and reset...think about things." Bell said and gripped his gun belt.

Tullos watched Bell head towards Etham. He looked at the resort and then the surrounding hills. Thoughts hit him.

Josh is a stubborn man, especially since his twin brother was shot. It will take a physical message to turn him around and back to the university. I need to make sure this is done right. Maybe Fields doesn't want him hurt too bad, but he does need to understand the severity of the issue. I've got some other business to take care of as usual.

Tullos grabbed his cell and texted the number that had texted earlier. Within seconds, he had a reply. A smile came on his face. Then, he made a call.

23

Billy Dalton watched the whole scene from his beloved Blazer parked a half block away, concealed by a rusty old sign and some overgrown shrubbery. His pal, Dave Clemmons, was watching from a bench on the other side of Fudd's. He had seen Josh Webb go into the restaurant and had given Billy the heads up, prompting him to send word to Tullos. Hopefully they'd get the go-ahead soon, because Fudd's parking lot wasn't well lit when the sun was setting and traffic was at a minimum.

Billy's phone rang as Josh Webb came out of Fudd's and turned the corner. Josh nearly trucked over Mrs. Boyd and Ms. Price, the old librarian hag, as Billy called her. He was laughing as he answered the phone.

"Hey Tullos, give the word, brother. We've got him right where we need him. And get this, he is literally talking to Mrs. Boyd right now. Looks like he's in a hurry though."

"Get it done, Billy. But, check it out, you've got to hold back a little. Like I said before, the Boss has a thing for this guy; just wants him to leave town. But give him a good one for me, I've hated him since high school!"

"You've got it, my man. I'll give him a little something permanent, just for you."

"Good deal. But remember, nothing too permanent."

Billy hung up the phone and immediately called Dave to give the go-ahead. Dave would get there first, but Billy hoped to make good on his promise to Tullos. Not really for his friend, but because he liked to hit people.

Mrs. Boyd was waving as Josh started to walk away; it was time to get moving. Dave began running towards the parking lot. Billy could see Dave was gaining ground quick. Josh wouldn't even make it to his truck.

Both women screamed out and Josh turned to see Mrs. Boyd leaning over to help Mrs. Price. She had been knocked over by one of those guys he had seen at the Boyd place. He was coming at Josh hard and fast. Though surprised, Josh quickly assessed the situation and knew that talking was not in the plan. This man was raring back to swing for the fences.

Josh stepped to the side and narrowly escaped a sudden knockout, but the man quickly recovered. With the element of surprise eliminated, it was now a fair fight. At least, Josh hoped so. He hadn't fought anyone since his freshman year at college. He didn't lose that fight, but he didn't necessarily win it either. It was obvious this man not only fought a lot, but he also enjoyed it.

Dave sent a couple lightning-fast jabs that connected, bringing home the message that if Josh didn't start retaliating then this would soon end unfavorably. Another long swing, this time Josh didn't dodge it all the way and took a stinging graze. Things whirled in his head, but he quickly got his bearing. While the man was catching his breath, Josh sent his own jab and followed it with a clumsy uppercut that connected enough to stun the crazy bastard, but probably damaged his hand more.

Holding his wrist, Josh looked over to see the two women being led around the corner of Fudd's. He didn't see the good Samaritan's face but was happy that someone else was there to help. He looked back at his very angry opponent. Before the man could attack again Josh took the low road and punted the man's groin area. The man folded forward and fell to the ground on his knees trying in vain to find his breath. Josh reached back for a long swing, looking to finish the ordeal. Instead, he took a 2x4 board across the back by someone behind him.

The cheap shot took out his breath causing him to fall forward adjacent to the first man. Rolling over he saw the second man, Billy Dalton, with his smirking yellow teeth and snake tattoos, was holding the board. Billy began taunting him, but it didn't register. Josh could only hear the panic in his lungs and he was desperate to remember how to function. Billy's words echoed, as if calling him from another dimension.

Josh looked past Billy and swore he could see a blurry figure watching nearby. Something was familiar about the man. He reached out to him, mouthing for him to help, but no sounds were coming out. A person can't talk without having air in his lungs.

Billy's voice became recognizable, "That's right, beg! Beg, you piece of trash!"

Those arrogant words gave Josh new strength. Air found its way back into his lungs and Josh could see Billy's friend beginning to stand. That wasn't good, he needed to make a last-ditch effort to neutralize the situation before it was too late. Josh looked past the two men to where the other man had been watching, but he was no longer there.

Billy turned to see what Josh was looking at and sneered, "There ain't no one going to help you, scumbag. You listen to me and you listen to me good. You're a lucky man today because I don't get to finish you here and now. If you don't leave this town and never come back, I'm going to get the thumbs up to bury you deep. You understand that, boy? And I want to bury you real deep!"

Josh nodded that he understood. He meant it, too. He intended to get the hell out of this messed-up town and never come back. Still gasping, he looked to the Dave who was slipping on brass knuckles. He wasn't planning on missing this time.

Damn.

"One more thing, dumbass. I'm gonna pay the Boyds a visit and remind them how things work around here. Probably gonna visit their whore daughter, too. Time to be done with those losers, anyway." Billy said.

"Leave them alone you son of a–" the brass knuckles cut him off mid-sentence as they collided with Josh's forehead and a flash of light was quickly replaced by darkness.

Billy grimaced at the blood stream flowing out of Josh's freshly gashed head. "Damn, Dave. We were supposed to go easy, brother. Got a little personal, didn't it?"

The men laughed and walked away; Dave with a limp and busted lip. Billy called Tullos and they both headed to Banetown.

24

Sluggishly, Josh awoke from an unconscious state and his eyes focused on flickering light. Numerous scented candles pushed back the darkness of the carpeted room and their lavender aroma irritated his bloodied nose. Off-balanced fan blades clicked in rhythm overhead. Each click pierced his ears and made his head ache even more than multiple lumps and bruises. He felt his forehead that hurt like hell. His body was limp and drained of energy. He could barely adjust himself on the couch he was on. As much as he wanted to look around and see where he was, his neck was not hearing it. Fear ran through his veins. This place, and everything in it, were totally unfamiliar. Vague memories of getting attacked fluttered through his throbbing mind.

The two deadbeats from the Boyd place. Those bastards are going to pay, if I make it through this alive.

Adrenaline shot through his body and he pulled his torso up. Pain radiated through every inch of his frame.

"Now, lay back down. You're beat up bad and need to rest." A familiar female voice said as they gently pressed him down.

A sense of comfort arose due to the voice and he did as he was told. Kristol looked down at him. He smiled and his vision blurred. Darkness closed in around him and once again faded into a void.

A couple hours passed and Josh came back to reality. Kristol was sitting in a recliner scribbling on a pad of paper. Light from a vintage tripod lamp in the corner sieved through her sandy brown hair. His eyes widened and he moved his arm.

"Good to see you alive and moving. I know you are wondering about being here. You're safe. Nobody will come up here and kill you or anything like that."

Despite only knowing her from a few encounters, he believed her. The stainless-steel revolver on the coffee table reinforced that.

"Now, don't you be thinking I'm going to shoot you with my .357 Magnum. I just shoot groundhogs and possums that get into my garden with that hand cannon." She giggled.

"I think I remember everything that happened until I was hit in the head. How did I get here? Where is here?"

She put her pad and pencil down. Silence overtook the room and she got up.

"That's a couple of questions for sure. Let me check your bandages first. Looks like more than a natural fist caused those wounds. His forehead and the back of his head pulsed with pain. He could feel his heartbeat as blood seeped from the lacerations into his eyes.

"You need stitches, and some fluids. You've bled a damn lot. I could sew you up, but I'm not an expert. You need a medical professional."

Josh's eyes widened and he felt his stomach twist. Words formed in his mouth but could not bring himself to say them. His manhood had been just overridden by good sense. Kristol applied a new bandage and walked to the shades. With care, she pried them apart and looked outside.

"Don't be feeling all ashamed about not winning that fight. It wasn't fair. It may be a good idea to keep you clear from the hospital and Etham. I've got a friend who is the head nurse over at Estill Hospital. She's a real lifesaver. Let me go call her."

Julie Bell and Kristol had crossed paths years earlier when Kristol had hit rock bottom and nearly overdosed on pain pills. The image of a nurse standing over her when she was revived was permanently etched in her mind. She owed Julie for saving her life and giving her the motivation to get off the drugs. Many wayward females had gone through the ER doors and were brought back to the land of the living, but sometimes there were casualties. Kristol had seen Julie in town visiting her husband and always made a point of waving to the angel that had saved her.

Mumbled words went in and out as Kristol paced back and forth in the kitchen with her cellphone. Josh made out a few words, but none of it made any sense to him. He felt the bandage on his forehead that was already saturated with blood. Sharp pain shot across his ribs and into his core every time he took a breath. Seeing Kristol in her tight jeans and even tighter black t-shirt, which both hugged every part of her, made him have temporary numbness in his mind and body.

"You're in luck. She is off work and willing to come over. She'll get you up and kicking soon."

"Appreciate that. This pain is hell. Never had brass knuckles used on me before."

"Got something to help. I know it's not a good thing to let you have any, but I think you're tough enough."

Kristol walked over to a well-stocked liquor cabinet in the corner and poured two tumblers of bourbon. She handed one to Josh and smiled.

"I figured you liked it straight and neat from the looks of you. Just take it easy on the stuff. It's Kentucky's finest bourbon and aged twelve years."

With one sip, Josh smiled. He took another and she took a large swig.

"Now, that's some smooth stuff. Probably the best I've ever had."

"I think so too. A friend gave it to me as a birthday gift." Kristol said with a smile.

"Great gift."

"Great friend." She laughed and poured herself another drink.

Her tattooed sleeve caught Josh's attention as it had every time when they had encountered each other. Again, his focus immediately went towards the hummingbird.

"Awesome tat work you have. Very detailed and colorful." He said and coughed.

"Well, thank you. I get some weird looks from the older locals, but most of the time I get compliments. You got any tats?"

"No. Thought about it a few times over the years. Just never pulled the trigger."

He took another sip and leaned his head back on the sofa arm. Rage ran through him. Thoughts about being beat up by those two degenerate pieces of white trash made him clench his fists and grit his teeth.

"Calm down. You're in no condition to be getting yourself worked up."

"I would've kicked their asses, if it had been a fair fight." He said and coughed deep.

"I know that for a fact; saw the whole thing myself. You're a damn wildcat, ain't ya?" Kristol growled playfully. "I saw them knock over them sweet old ladies and jump you. Those thugs are lowlife scumbags to me, just minions."

Her words piqued his interest, as well as his self-esteem. For a moment, no pain radiated through his body. Kristol's blue eyes enamored him and he focused on them. Her hair draped over her shoulders and petite neck, which ignited chills in his body. Then, a sharp pain brought him back to reality.

"Sounds like you know those guys."

"Everybody around here knows those two; Billy Dalton and Dave Clemmons. Two no-goods who think they are big time hustlers. Let me tell you, they are nothing."

"Why would they jump me like that or try to hurt Mrs. Boyd and Ms. Price? They told me to leave town. I guess they don't like me asking questions about my brother's murder."

With her tattoo-sleeved arm, Kristol threw back a shot of bourbon. She looked at him with an intense look.

"Well, I'm not from around here, but I've learned a lot since coming here seven years ago. Drugs and all the bad stuff that goes with it, rots people's brains. Them boys are so messed up on meth, pills, and who knows what else. They may have been high and seen you walking down the street. Then, decided on having some fun with you. Who knows why? With them, it all depends on the hour of the day."

Josh's mind drifted to that day at Randall Boyd's place and seeing the "snakes," as Mrs. Boyd called them for the first time. To Josh, they were definitely messed up and some real lowlifes. Kristol confirmed that.

"Where are you from and what brought you here? I did everything I could to get out of this place, so I can't imagine someone coming here on purpose." He said and rubbed his sore ribs.

"Well, those are awful personal questions. Would you like for me to ask you things like that?"

A lump formed in Josh's throat. Every pain from the beating he had endured hit him at once. Oxygen and energy were sucked from him. Maybe, he had been forward with asking too much.

"Listen, I was just poking at you to make you smile. I don't mind answering at all. For some reason, I trust you. You look so much like your brother. So, it seems like I know you."

Her words comforted him and made him think about what connection she had with Caleb. He decided not to push anything, due to his physical condition and his fascination with her.

"I was a college student pursuing a degree in environmental science. Came down here to do an internship. Loved the vast and beautiful nature of the area. Got my first tattoo. Fell in love with substances. Fell in love with a man that didn't really love me, so that didn't work out. Fell out of love with substances. Fell in love with a job. Now, here I am loving life and not falling for anything else. At least, not too quick or without careful deliberation."

"That's the best summation I've ever heard. If you don't mind me saying, you impress me."

"If you don't mind, I appreciate your kind words."

Both grinned at each other and laughed. Headlights accompanied the rumble of a car engine and spotlighted the small house as it pulled into the driveway. A few moments later there was a knock on the door.

"C'mon in. I appreciate you coming at short notice. He's not too good and needs more care than I can give. Don't feel safe taking him to the hospital; you know how things are around here."

"Yes, I do. All too well. Show me where he's at."

The conversation was muffled in Josh's ear, as if he were listening underwater. His mind drifted for a second, but awoke with noises getting louder and coming toward him.

"Julie…Julie Bell? I didn't expect to see you here. You're the nurse?"

"Josh, I would say it is good to see you again, but not under these circumstances. Kristol called me and told me you had been beat up pretty bad." Julie did a quick study of his face and forehead, "Yeah, she is right, they did a number on you. Anyway, I came to see what I can do to help. I am a nurse and can help you. Enough on me. Let's take care of you."

"Okay. I don't understand this place anymore. I come home to bury my brother and just want to bring the person who murdered him to justice. I see things I don't understand and then I get beat up for no reason. This is crazy. Everything is crazy."

Julie opened her medical bag and pulled out a syringe and vial. With precise and well-exercised motion, she filled the syringe.

"Please relax. I'm giving you something to calm you down."

"I don't need anything to calm me down. Those bastards jumped me and I gave them hell before they knocked me out. I'm sure of that." He said and drifted out.

Kristol paced back and forth. Her eyes could not be pulled from Josh. Concern was written on her face as well as knowing the nature of things in Etham.

"Is there anything I can do, Julie?"

"Why don't you go out on the porch and have a smoke? I'll work on him and then I'll need a smoke."

"Okay, he's all yours. Please take care of him. He's a good person. I feel it in my gut."

"Go on now. I know he is. Just like Caleb."

Kristol eyed her for a moment and walked out the front door. Julie looked at the wound on Josh's head. He came out of his haze.

"I did good, didn't I? Gave them hell, didn't I?"

"You sure did. Just relax and let me give you more to help with the pain."

Numbness hit his body as Julie pushed the second syringe plunger. Seconds slowed as he looked up at the fan circling and clicking. Josh drifted in and out. Thoughts about Caleb and Julie in the church played over and over as she weaved the suture into his skin and closed the lacerations. Despite the elixir pushed into his arm, uncomfortable pain radiated from each hole that the sutures went through and caused him to grit his teeth and squint his eyes.

"Try and hold still, I'm almost done. Just a few more left."

She smiled at her work as she cut the end of the thread. Her bright eyes caught Josh's attention. Sadness radiated from them.

"I'm all done. The stitches will dissolve in a couple of weeks. I've got a few days' worth of pain pills and antibiotics for you, but after that you'll have to use over the counter stuff. Just be sure to keep the wound clean. Most importantly, rest."

Josh smiled and nodded. His mind was induced to drift by the drugs, but he kept his eyes open and on Julie. Every move she made kept his attention.

"There's no denying Caleb and you are twins. You look just alike. Seeing you here makes me think about him. I wish I could have been there to help him. I miss him." Julie said.

Josh didn't know what to say. Questions formed, but he could not voice them due to his mind and pain killer. He stared at her.

"He was a good man." She fought the quivering of her lips and continued, "It breaks my heart that he's gone. He didn't deserve to die that way. This world is a wicked place. I just miss him so much."

A few tears ran down her face. She took a deep breath and attempted to pull herself together. Josh felt a surge of strength.

"Sounds like you knew Caleb well."

Julie straightened her back and wiped the final tears from her eyes. With precise movement, she put a bandage on Josh's stitches.

"You'll recover quickly. There's no internal bleeding or serious damage. You'll be sore for a bit, but you're tough. I'll leave the medicine with Kristol to administer to you. Don't be stubborn like your brother and take it. I'll check in on you soon. Yes, I knew Caleb. Everyone knew him. He was a pillar of Etham, a good man that loved everyone."

Julie walked out the front door just as quickly as she had come in. Once again, muffled words were all Josh could hear. Then, Kristol came in.

"You relax and take it easy. Julie says you'll be okay soon. She left me in charge to take care of you and make sure you take your meds. I'm going to make that happen just because I like you a little bit and need to keep an eye on you. Make sure you don't do anything stupid." She smiled.

"I need to get up and find out who killed Caleb. They are out there running free. Those two thugs that beat me up probably knows what happened."

"You don't need to be going anywhere. I'm going to make sure you do what Julie said and make sure you are recovered."

Josh looked up at her blue eyes and felt safe, comfortable. He had not felt that way in a long time.

"Just want to say you're a bit more handsome than your brother, Caleb." She said and rubbed ointment on his bare chest and face wounds.

That statement perplexed and excited Josh at the same time. It bounced around in his skull as his consciousness waned and sleep overtook him.

25

The newest home in the Green Valley Mobile Home Park was at least ten years old, but that didn't mean it was the nicest. There were some older ones dating to twenty-five years that were better kept up by original owners, who still took pride in what little they had. Everyone else was content to live in dented, unmatched vinyl, or rusted sided trailers. Trash lined the streets and carried over into most yards, which might have little to no grass.

About half had covered decks and most of those looked ready to fall in. Yard art was limited to a menagerie of gnomes, faded pink flamingos, and recycled toys. A few had small trampolines. Fewer still had barred windows and security cameras, some of which were decoys and others real, but which ones were only a guess. Those with less security resources had warning signs with pictures of handguns.

The Park, if such a place should be called that, was a long loop with a couple inside streets connecting to the main road. In between these streets, there was an old playground with rusted metal swings and monkey bars as old as the mobile home park itself. A cracked cement basketball court had opposing rusted goals. Neither had nets. No one was playing because most of the kids were in school and those that weren't were sleeping in.

Across from the park was one of the newer homes with two-tone green vinyl siding. A piece on the front right corner was swaying with the morning breeze. This unit had an old, uncovered deck with a couple plastic Adirondack chairs, a matching table, and a worn-out cushioned swing that screeched with different pitches depending on who was rocking in it. This morning it moaned a slow, melancholy rhythm, controlled by a single foot.

Elizabeth Dawn Boyd watched the motionless playground, trying to remember what it was like playing with her childhood friends. She sat on one foot while using the other to encourage the swing along. She wore kitty cat print pajama pants and an oversized gray sweatshirt with EHS imprinted in large red letters, which sometimes reminded her of her short time at Etham High School. Elizabeth held her cup of tea close to her chest with both hands. It began to cool, and the sweet jasmine aroma invited her to sip.

Only a few years had passed since she injured her back at cheerleading camp and was prescribed pain medicine. The doctors promised a full recovery, but the pain persisted long after her parent's insurance stopped paying for therapy and medication. Her friend Alicia had given her some pills to help alleviate the pain, and for a while it did. When those ran out, Alicia showed her how to earn enough money to buy more.

Alicia. Stupid bitch. I hate her.

Elizabeth's friend had gotten caught up in opioid addiction first and was also the first that Elizabeth had known to sell her body to pay for pills. She had introduced Elizabeth to the trade. For a while they both had fun, thinking it was a game they were playing with some of the younger, local guys they knew. It wasn't long, they realized they were sex slaves controlled by greasy, red-necked pimps.

Their current pimp was Dave Clemmons, a top-notch asshole with serious anger management issues. He wasn't allowed to hit them in the face, which was nice. But he thoroughly enjoyed slapping them in the back of the head and on the back. Elizabeth didn't know which was worse but leaned towards the back.

Two months ago, Dave had gotten drunk and in an uncontrollable rage beat Alicia to death for giggling with Elizabeth Dawn and another girl about her last customer's small physique. Dave overheard and thought she was making fun of him. He left her lying dead for nearly the whole weekend before disposing of her body to Lord knows where. Elizabeth was left to watch poor Alicia lie there dead, halfway on a deflated air mattress and halfway on the floor.

"You trashy whores will learn to keep your nasty mouths shut and have some respect." He had said after he took her life.

It wasn't an attempt to justify his actions, but rather a threat that the same fate might befall Elizabeth, if she got out of line. She remembered every detail.

She sipped from her jasmine scented cup again, enjoying the cool morning. She heard a truck coming up the road and figured the peaceful morning had been too good to be true. It was Dave. She could tell by the hum of the engine and the way the vehicle's all terrain tires grabbed the broken asphalt. She hadn't expected him so soon. He had just dropped her off last night after spending two days at one of the cabins with some rich pervert from West Virginia.

She wondered if Dave might at least give her a few cigarettes, along with the pills. Sometimes, if she did a really nice job and got a compliment, Dave would give her a few extras. An incentive to keep up the good work. The only real reward she needed was not to get slapped around, but a few cigarettes and pills would be nice.

Holding the cup in one hand, she wrapped some loose strands of her hair behind her ear that had escaped a messy bun. She hoped she didn't look lazy, even though it was her off day. Apparently, the people in charge preferred to let the cattle rest between customers. Somehow, Dave figured the ladies should still look the part no matter what day it was.

She wasn't going to get any cigarettes or pills today. She could tell that from the way he slammed to a stop and jumped out. No, it looked more like a getting-popped-behind-the-head day and the back too, judging by how he cleared the front steps in one leap. Elizabeth Dawn wasn't sure what she had done, but she was sure that she was fixing to get the Alicia treatment.

Before she could set her cup on the plastic table, Dave had crushed her nose with his fist. He began kicking her before she landed on the deck. She felt her arm crack after the second stomp and she braced for more. By some miracle, Elizabeth Dawn didn't know what happened, but he turned and walked away. She lay there playing a game of possum because she had no choice, but to stay alive. She wasn't dead and knew it. Being dead would be a dream come true.

She could hear his boots stomping back up and down the steps, a bit slower now. Had he calmed down? He jerked her up to a sitting position and yanked off her sweatshirt. She didn't feel it. Thank God for the effects of shock. Elizabeth Dawn wasn't sure what he was doing, but through hazy vision it seemed he was measuring her up. Then he spoke to her or maybe to himself.

"Damn, that's gotta hurt! The problem is you ain't bleeding from the mouth. That needs to be fixed."

Dave slapped her jaw and what shock was doing to hide the pain of the broken arm failed to do for her mouth. Elizabeth felt her throat tighten and her lungs begin to panic. Maybe, he was strangling her? Maybe, it would be over soon?

No, he's doing something else. I want to die.

Elizabeth Dawn fell forward and spat out the blood she was choking on and felt a fresh wave of air fill her lungs. She would just lay here for a while. Maybe, she could go back to sleep? Maybe, she would wake up and be back home again? Better yet, maybe she could go be with Alicia in a better place?

Dave jerked her back up by the hair and squeezed her face, turning right and then left. She hoped to God he found what he was looking for in her face. Perhaps he had, he stepped back and gazed at her, as if looking at a work of art. Elizabeth Dawn was fading.

"Say 'Cheese,' bitch."

Elizabeth Dawn passed out, oblivious of whether she would make it out of this alive or be laid to rest next to Alicia. Would anybody even care?

26

Over the next few days, Josh faded in and out of sleep with his only movements being sipping vegetable soup and water with his major one making the small distance to the bathroom with Kristol's help. The major one made him feel embarrassed every time. Few words with little content were spoken between them, due to his pain. An occasional smile and nod of the head were the usual methods. Sharp pain turned to soreness and Josh's mind became clearer with each passing day.

"I need to go to work at least one day this week. The resort can't run without me." Kristol said and took a drink of coffee.

"I bet. You seem to be someone that likes to make things happen. Manage things."

"You make me laugh. You think you can take care of yourself today and not get into trouble staying alone?"

Kristol handed him a cup of coffee and sat on the recliner to put on her boots. Josh watched her lace them up.

"You know better than to ask that. I'm feeling pretty good and I'll be out of your way before you know it." Josh paused, searching for the right words, "I want to say that I–"

"Don't be getting all mushy on me and tell me that you appreciate all that I've done. You don't owe me anything. I just wanted to keep an eye on you. You never know what kind of trouble you'll get into around here and some you can't get out of." Kristol said with a laugh.

Josh didn't know what to say at this point. Her words were not expected. She was a different person. Her raw honesty and sassy personality mixed with toughness complemented her beauty and slight softness. All together it made her adorable. It was a uniqueness that he liked and had never encountered before. Past love interests had parts of it, but never the whole package. That was one of the many reasons he had never settled down.

"Well, I'm off. Got a washed-out trail to fix and a tree fell on one of the cabins last night. I need to get the crew out to fix things. Plus, I have some administrative paperwork to do in my other job. The peak season at the resort is right around the corner. There's food in the fridge and cabinets. You need to make yourself something to eat. Keep your strength up." She nodded and put the revolver in her backpack.

A nod was all that Josh could muster. They stared at each other for a few seconds.

"A girl must be safe around this area. Just look at what happened to you. It could happen to anybody, even me."

"You're right. I'm convinced about that now. I need to ask you something."

"Go right ahead. I'm not one to hold back on anything."

"Caleb was a maintenance man at the resort. How well did you know him?"

Kristol turned toward him. Her eyes scanned Josh with detail and then her demeanor changed.

"Yes. He was a great maintenance man, the best I've ever seen. He worked hard and always made sure things were done right."

"I'm glad to hear it. He was a good man. Why would anyone want to murder him?" Josh said with a solemn face.

"I don't know. Caleb was a man of principle and faith. So, that tells me he was killed for a cause, out of passion, or even an accident. That's my opinion and you can take it for what it's worth." Kristol said, picking up her keys.

She smiled and walked out the front door. With pain, Josh leaned up, pushed open the shades, and watched her through the living room window. Once again, her untamed beauty and walk caught his attention. He shook his head and sipped the steaming coffee. His head felt better with each sip. Light from the windows lit up the place. More details caught his eye as he staggered around the house. Books overflowed from a large shelf in the corner with titles and subjects ranging from Hemingway to Renaissance Art. A lot of them made sense, but many topics and titles introduced speculation due to his limited knowledge of Kristol. Sketches were scattered on a desk next to the shelf. One was of a hummingbird, like the one on her arm and was finished. Another drawing was of him, half-finished on top. He picked it up and smiled. Details were brought to life with a variety of shading techniques contrasting with light. It looked like a black and white photo. Kristol was an artist and he liked that about her.

Not bad. Not bad at all. I'm going to have to ask her about her talent. Compliment her.

With the house filled with coffee aroma, he was pulled to the kitchen. As he sipped from the comfort of a rickety kitchen table chair, he looked out the back door. A well-kept freshly tilled garden prompted him to enjoy its view. Adjacent to the garden was a stone patio with a firepit in the middle. It beckoned him to go and enjoy a perfect place to enjoy more coffee. Pain filled his body as he made his way to the patio and he sat down in a cedar lawn chair. Sounds of the woods made him smile. Squirrels squawking and birds chirping made everything peaceful. The sun glowed down on him and put his mind at peace for a moment. Gunfire in the distance pulled him out of his meditation. Rapid shots and then spaced-out ones. It had been a long time since he had heard gunshots. They were common when he was growing up; someone trying out a new gun or sighting in their rifle for deer season. Now, the familiar sounds brought images of his brother dying in the hospital from gunshot wounds.

Why would anybody shoot Caleb? He was a preacher, maybe not a perfect man, but a man of the Bible no less. There's something wrong with this place, even the people. It's different now. That resort is giving something in the way of prosperity, but it is taking the soul of Etham. It took the life of my brother and it will take more.

Tears ran down his cheeks and he tried to fight each one. As much as he didn't agree with Caleb's actions and hypocrisy, he loved him and he himself had flaws. Everyone has flaws. Nobody was perfect in this world. All we can do is strive to be a better person every day. All of these thoughts culminated in his brain as he looked out into the woods. Movement caught his attention.

"What the hell was that?" He leaned up from the chair.

His heart pulsed fast as every detail of the wood line was scanned. A fox ran to the edge and stared at him. The elusive animal that Josh had only seen one other time, when he was a teenager walking through the woods with Caleb. He stayed quiet as they both studied each other.

"Don't worry my friend. I'm not going to hurt you. Let me look at you for a minute."

The male fox paced back and forth. Each time he stopped he looked at Josh and wagged his tail. With each movement, memories of his grandfather telling him the significance of seeing a fox, especially during the day, materialized in his mind.

Little man, I'll tell you a sign of signs. If a red fox comes to visit you that's a mighty special thing. It's a sign that people around you are deceiving you, fooling you into something that will be your downfall. But there is a twist to that. He's giving you the wisdom to make sense of it and come out on top. Heed the appearance of a fox in your path. Think deep about it and step lightly.

As fast as the fox had appeared, he was gone. Josh slouched in the chair and looked up at the blue sky. Energy welled within him. Caleb's death needed to be accounted for. Things had become mixed up when he got to Etham, but his mind was different now.

Need to get up. Nothing is going to make me leave Etham without finding out who killed my brother. Nobody is going to deceive me again. Knowledge is my strength and there are ways of getting it around here. I'm from here and know the ways. There's no downfall for me.

Josh pulled himself up from the chair and walked with increasing speed toward the back door. Energy and rancid body odor prompted him to take a shower. Hot water seemed foreign to him, but quickly became familiar. Feelings of being alive again pulsed within him. As the hours passed after the shower, he found solace in mixing a pot of chili that his mother would have been proud of. While the chili was simmering, he cleaned the whole house in gratitude to Kristol mending him up and what he thought might be a relationship of some sort. As the chili cooked, Josh sat back and sipped some bourbon from the liquor cabinet. The grind and halt of an automobile engine out front focused his attention.

"Mercy, something smells good in here! You must be feeling better." Kristol tossed a small backpack on the coffee table as she closed the front door.

Josh got up from the recliner and smiled. He took a few steps forward and handed her a glass of bourbon.

"Appreciate you having a drink ready for me. I sure need it. Things were really busy today."

"A small thing for helping me to get mended up."

"That's nothing. What's that smell? Chili?"

Josh walked to the kitchen. She dropped off her revolver next to her backpack and sat on the couch. With speed, her hiking boots were off and she came to the kitchen.

"I've not had homemade chili in years. Not something I normally eat, but I love it."

"Just sit right down and let me serve you. I owe you more but it will have to do for now."

"That would be fine with me. I've not had anybody cook for me in a long time."

Rays from the sun disappeared over the horizon as Josh spooned out the bowls of chili. He tried to think of words, but they eluded him. So, he decided to make actions the priority. Glasses were filled with bourbon. Words were finally found.

"Thought I would try and repay you for taking care of me. Like I said, this is not enough payment."

Kristol leaned back and downed her glass. She looked at Josh with her blue eyes.

"Like I said this morning, you don't owe me anything. I do like chili and I'm hungry."

They ate in a silence that seemed to complement the atmosphere and everything that had happened. They watched each other eat through the light of a flickering candle. Awkwardness filled the air. They both sensed it and didn't know how to handle it.

"I appreciate you mending me up and getting Nurse Bell up here to sew me up. You didn't have to do all that."

"I guess I needed to get you mended up and I like you a little bit. Not too much, but a little."

Josh smiled and sipped on his bourbon. He stirred his bowl of chili and looked back at Kristol. She took a drink too.

"Josh, I need to be honest with you."

"You can tell me anything. I'm here to listen." Josh said as he finished his glass.

"Your brother, Caleb, was a special man. He was a servant to the people around here."

Kristol poured both another drink. She walked over to her desk and took a small leather bag from one of the drawers.

"Let's smoke some good stuff and talk. I have some thoughts on things. Will that be okay with you?"

"Why not? It's been a while, but Lord knows I could use it."

Kristol rolled a large marijuana joint. She held it up to the light and made sure it was perfect. With precise motion, she took a lighter from her pocket and lit it. Two tokes made the end turn bright orange. The pungent earthy aroma penetrated Josh's nostrils and he breathed heavily to take it in.

"Here, have a drag."

"I don't know. It has been forever…way back in college."

"Relax, it will help your recovery." She teased him. "Don't be scared. I haven't steered you wrong yet, have I?"

Josh thought of the fox he saw earlier but reflected with clarity. A moment of resolution materialized.

What the hell?

He obliged himself with a deep toke, which prompted a deep cough and a laugh. The aroma quickly grew on him and its effects helped to numb his pain and sooth his mind.

Just what the doctor ordered.

"Kristol, I sure appreciate you taking care of me. Not many people would have done that."

"No big deal. Quit saying I owe you anything."

Josh touched Kristol's hand and looked into her eyes. She wanted to look back, but turned away.

"Listen, Josh. I'm not who you think I am. Things around this awful place have made me different and I'm ashamed. You just need to get out of here before things get worse than they already are."

"I'm not leaving. I need to find out who killed Caleb. That is what I'm here to do. You know that. Why would you want me to leave before I find out the truth?"

"I just…worry about you."

As he leaned over to kiss Kristol, she pulled back. Both of them felt something they had never felt before. The night of passion took them to a level that they had never been to before.

Candlelight flickered and produced dancing shadows on the walls. Kristol watched them and thought about what had just happened. Wind swayed the trees and cold air swept through the drafty house from hidden cracks. Her heart weighed heavy and images of the past reeled over and over again. Many memories mixed in a blur; as when she worked at the Honeycomb or was juiced-up on whatever drug she had hustled from customers or her usual connections. Hours passed and the flame ran out of wax. Darkness shrouded the bedroom.

27

Randall Boyd heard a growing and incessant horn blowing louder as it approached his house. The racket grew more deafening as he made his way out of his shop. Billy Dalton's Blazer turned onto his gravel drive in an almighty hurry and nearly flipped in the process. Randall finished wiping his hands on a towel as he stepped up on the front porch. Olivia stared at the fast-approaching vehicle. She heard Randall talking about who it was, but kept her eyes on the vehicle, not sure if it intended to stop or just crash into the house.

"Will these thugs ever leave us be?" Olivia asked and turned her head.

Randall searched for an answer, wishing they could find a way out, but they were prisoners. They would remain so as long as their daughter depended on it. If only they could find her and get away from the wretched town of Etham. He had a place in mind. An old Army buddy from the Gulf War had a few hundred acres in Montana and had made an open offer to sell him a section with an old cabin already in place. He was still young enough to make a fresh start and he figured Montana was as good a place as any. It was far enough away, but they couldn't make a move without Elizabeth Dawn.

He knew their daughter was somewhere around Etham. At least he thought he did. Otherwise, why would these clowns keep pressing them? He knew they could be stringing him along to keep using his place to warehouse their drugs for distribution. For all he knew, his daughter could be long gone by now. No, Randall refused to give that thought a place in his mind. He held onto the hope that Elizabeth Dawn was near, and he would wait as long as it took. Even, if it meant putting up with these idiots.

The Blazer skid to a stop inches from a cluster of pre-blossomed canna lilies and two men burst from its doors. Randall thought how nice it would be to simply shoot them both in the head. He wasn't a violent man. His last year in the Army was spent in Iraq. He had seen his share of the action, but he had never shot anyone, at least, none he knew about. He had fired a full magazine once in a botched roadside bomb attack. No dead enemy bodies were found in that incident and besides minor damage to a Humvee, no harm was done. He had always counted himself blessed to have avoided the most violent parts of the war compared to other Soldiers in his unit. He loved peace and when his enlistment contract was up, he came home. In this moment, he would shoot these two men in the face, if given half the chance. Then, he would enjoy a peaceful night of sleep and a cup of coffee in the morning.

"Randall, do you know what your dear wifey's been up to?" Dave was normally the quiet one. Whatever stirred him up had him in rare form. "Olivia, you stupid hag–"

"Enough, Dave. Let me do the talking," Billy reasserted his authority, "Give me that phone."

Randall cocked his head, wondering what the men were going crazy about. Billy took the cellphone from Dave's shaking hands with red knuckles. Randall's cheeks were flushed and his vision narrowed to a pinpoint. Their voices were muffled.

"Look at this, Randall. How do you like that? Tell us your thoughts."

Billy showed him a picture of Elizabeth Dawn, lying on a wooden deck with a twisted arm and bloodied face. She looked dead.

"My God, no!" Randall hunched over, sick from the picture. He wanted to throw up but couldn't. He couldn't breathe. Olivia's pale face was half-covered with prayer-like hands. She started for her husband, wanting to help him. She hadn't thought about the image he had seen, only that he must be having a heart attack.

"Not so fast, Olivia."

Billy grabbed her arm as she tried to pass him. Olivia slapped him and tried to work herself free.

"Hold up, old woman. Don't you want to see?" He shoved the phone into her face. Olivia growled.

"Get off me, you–"

She froze as still as the young lady in the picture and was unable to breathe through her pressed lips, but leaned in to confirm what she had seen. Was this real? Was this her little girl? The image nauseated her, but she couldn't turn away. Randall was no longer there, a broken forgotten presence. Olivia tried to wet her lips to talk. "Is she...is...?"

"Dead? Is that what you are asking?" Dave interjected himself again, as an artist excited about his work. "I don't really know, old hag. I just kind of left her there. She may still be there–she could be dead."

Olivia tightly pressed her hand over her mouth as if to hold in the last of her remaining air. She studied the picture of Elizabeth Dawn crumpled on a patio with a disfigured face and her arm bent in the wrong direction. She looked lifeless. Could this be real?

"My dear Liz, my poor baby." She said and cried.

Billy tossed the phone back to Dave. They both laughed.

"Listen to me, Olivia. You, too, Randall. This is your fault. We've told you time and time again to keep your mouths shut. Didn't we tell you? We know ya'll have been talking to Josh Webb and now he's been snooping around."

Randall had summoned the strength to go to Olivia. They held each other and cried, not hearing Billy's words. It didn't matter what he said, the picture said everything. Elizabeth Dawn was dead.

"No, Elizabeth Dawn isn't dead. You better hear this and you better both believe me when I tell you that if you ever cross us again, we'll not only kill her, but we'll kill one of you maybe both of you. Do you hear me?" Billy said with a fist in the air and a scowl on his face.

"What did you say? She's not dead?" Randall's words came out as if he had just been released from a chokehold and then prayerlike. Olivia wailed out as if the air had just found its way into her lungs, with uncontrolled sobs.

Dave found the pair to be hilarious and laughed his way back to their vehicle. Billy walked up to them and searched their eyes.

"You better take this seriously. We will kill your girl. There's no telling what else Dave will do. He's a crazy one, you know. Keep your mouths shut."

Billy and Dave got back into the Blazer and drove away leisurely, as if on a Sunday drive.

Randall and Olivia faced each other at their kitchen table while staring at the vinyl place mats and cloth napkins. They had cried, yelled at one another, cursed God, begged forgiveness, and cried again in cycles for hours. They were out of tears and sat unsure of what to do next. What could they do?

"Olivia, honey, I don't know what's next. I just don't know." Randall closed his eyes, shaking his head. "But I know one thing, we have to be ready. If we get the chance–if we can get Elizabeth Dawn–we've got to have bags packed and be ready to leave this place at a moment's notice. When we leave, we've got to leave here for good. Do you understand what I'm saying?"

"Yes, but," she wanted to cry, but was already feeling woozy from the events had caused.

"Yes, you're right. We've got to leave. There's no other choice." Olivia said.

Olivia grimaced and put her face down on the table, reaching out a hand to her husband. He held it softly, hoping in some way to offer comfort not just for her, but for them both. It wasn't much, but it was all they had.

"There's something else I need to say. I'm done waiting for a miracle. It's time to stand up to these guys. Maybe we'll get burned, but we've got to go down swinging. We're not doing Elizabeth Dawn any good. If we keep doing what we are doing, she'll continue to suffer. If we're going to die, let's die trying." Randall said with gritted teeth.

Olivia lifted her head and looked out the window. The yard used to be so pristine. They had built this home and always prided themselves in a manicured yard. The house was always perfect. The past few years had brought cancer upon it. It had deteriorated so fast she hadn't noticed. Cancer meant death for those who sat around and did nothing. That's what they had been doing. Sitting around and hoping for the best, but the best wasn't coming. It was time to do something.

Olivia turned to her husband, "Just tell me what to do."

28

Her favorite country song sounded from the radio and Susan Rawlins tapped her fingernails on the steering wheel. Muscles in her forearms ached from typing invoices and her jaws were sore from the smiling that she did all day at the Stepping Stone front desk. The aches, pains, and complaints were nothing compared to the physical beatings she endured back in the day when she performed the lower type of work at the resort. Thoughts of pulling herself out of that made her feel better as she went through the entrance of The Green Valley Mobile Home Park with its faded sign that had been there more years than anyone could remember.

"What the hell?" Susan yelled as she gripped the steering wheel and slammed the brakes.

A blurred flash of a thin-framed human stumbled in front of her jeep. The half-naked form collapsed onto the junked-up yard of a trailer lot. Susan got out and ran toward the crumpled body. Anxiety and fear welled within her as she recognized the girl. It was one of

Dave's girls, but she couldn't just leave her here. The girl's moaning pulled her closer.

"You okay, Elizabeth? What happened to you?"

"You...know."

"You need real medical care this time. Let me help you into my jeep."

"Leave me to die. I want this to end and end for good."

As much as Susan tried to pull Elizabeth up, only inches were accomplished. Susan sat down on the pavement and took a deep breath. With determination and a second wind, she pulled Elizabeth Dawn up and put her into the jeep. As she sped out of the park, she thought about the implications of being a Good Samaritan. Going back now was not even a choice. The girl needed help. Susan pushed the gas pedal harder as she took every curve faster than was safe.

"Snap out of it, Elizabeth. You've got to stay awake. Stay with me. We'll be at the hospital soon. Don't you die on me. You hear me!"

Slurred words came from Elizabeth. Her slumped body shook and then she was still. Her skin turned blue. Susan slapped her face hard and she started breathing again.

"I...can't keep..."

You can and you will. I'm going to take care of you."

The lighted hospital sign appeared. Susan pulled into the ER entrance and the doors slid open. She opened the jeep door and yelled for help.

"You can't park here." A young security guard yelled as he ran out.

"Listen. She's in bad shape. Get me help!."

"I can see that." The guard said as he looked at the crumpled body inside the cab. He ran inside.

Within seconds, medical personnel ran out and put Elizabeth on a gurney. They rolled her in. A face stuck out to Susan. It was someone she knew, but she couldn't remember who or where they had crossed paths. A female RN supervised Elizabeth Dawn being brought in and eyed Susan. The familiar RN walked up to Susan.

"She'll be okay. Nobody is going to hurt her here. I'll make sure of that."

Susan nodded as they hauled Elizabeth into the ER with the RN following behind. Things became blurred, but the need to be by the girl's side overcame her physical weakness. She followed.

"You sure she's going to be okay?"

"Yes, like I said. You need to go to the waiting room. I'll come and talk to you when we get her stabilized. You've got to trust me."

Susan looked at the RN that had too much mascara covering up tired eyes. Time stopped and Susan searched her memories to place the familiar nurse. In a spark, it dawned on her who the RN was, Julie Bell. The county sheriff's wife looked at her with an authoritarian look. A feeling of being a small part of a bigger thing came upon her. The same feeling of being a damned Good Samaritan consumed her again. Saying nothing was the best thing at the moment. Susan decided to settle on a medium. She would not run, but she would not say anything. As she sat and looked at the white walls of the waiting room and soundless TV that spewed repeated news footage, thoughts of what to do next flowed through her mind. Time stopped for Susan, but an hour had passed in reality. Julie came through the ER double doors.

"Elizabeth will be okay. No internal damage. Besides a broken arm, she has contusions on her back, lacerations, and bruised ribs. Nothing that won't heal in time with the right care. Rest and time to recover mentally and physically are what she requires. She needs to get off the hard stuff, if she wants to live past her young age. You know what I mean?"

"Can I go in and see her?"

"Yes, you can. I'm signing her release paperwork, despite needing to stay overnight for observation. Do you know what I'm telling you by doing that?"

With a nod, Susan walked into the ER room. An IV dripped and the heart monitor beeped slowly. Elizabeth Dawn looked at her with a look that was understood. After an LPN unhooked the IV and the rest of the monitoring devices, both looked at each other and searched for words that eluded them. Minutes passed with fear consuming both.

"You don't need to go back to the trailer park. He'll kill you for sure." Susan said as she sat on the edge of the bed.

"I know. Maybe it is just better that way. I can't do without the pills and I'm trapped in my hell. It's one that I created. I need some stuff right now."

"Don't be hard on yourself. You can overcome all this. You just need help. I was where you are now. You just need to get headstrong and pull out of it. I did."

Elizabeth Dawn looked down at her hands and clenched them together. Thoughts of what to do crossed her mind.

"You don't need any of my trouble. Just leave and I'll be okay." Elizabeth said.

Susan looked at her friend and then at the clock on the wall. Time was not on their side. Word always traveled fast in the county. Someone is always watching and talking.

Don't worry, I'll make sure she is okay." Julie said as she walked into the room with a plastic bag in her hands.

"What do you mean?" Elizabeth Dawn asked as she watched the RN walk closer.

"I've seen too many young girls like her come into this ER, beat up and worse. They just disappear altogether. You remember Alicia, don't you? What about Beverly? Who knows where they are?"

Susan and Elizabeth nodded their heads in confirmation. Silence consumed the room and the air became thick with the familiar smell of a hospital with its sanitized and stale aroma.

"Susan, you go home. You don't need to be seen with Elizabeth any more than you already have been. I've got a plan."

"I can't just leave her."

"You will and it's for your own good and Elizabeth's too. Now, get on home. Let me take care of this. You have helped Elizabeth Dawn this far. Let me do the rest. One more thing, if anybody asks, you don't know anything."

Susan hugged Elizabeth Dawn and kissed her on the cheek. Tears ran down both of their faces. Without looking back, Susan walked out of the ER.

"You need to get dressed quickly. I'm going to call a friend, who owes me a favor. She'll keep you hidden, until you heal up. Then, you're going to get out of Etham and out of the state." Julie said.

"Who's this friend? What about my parents? Do they know I'm here and alive?"

"We'll talk about that once we get you out of here. You know who my husband is, don't you?"

"Yes."

Their eyes locked on each other. Each one wanted to talk to the other about what each one knew, but time was short. Elizabeth Dawn struggled to her feet with extreme pain. With a burst of energy, she straightened herself and looked at Julie.

"There's a pair of jeans and t-shirt of mine in the bag. Put them on quickly. You stay right here. I'll come get you when it's time. Please trust me."

"I trust you." Elizabeth said with a look of a lost puppy.

Sheriff Bell walked into the ER with his walkie talkie turned up too loud and blaring with traffic. He turned it down and looked at one of the nurses on duty.

"Sir, can I help you?"

"You can. Do you not know who I am?"

She looked at the man's badge and name tag in front of her. The name Bell jogged her memory. She scanned the authorized personnel list on the clipboard in front of her. Being new to the hospital and the local area didn't help the situation.

"I'll tell you what your list is going to tell you. I'm Sheriff Bell and I'm authorized. My wife works here."

The nurse stared up at Bell. He eyed her back. His anger was not with the young nurse straight out of school, but with the whole situation of hearing that another prostitute had been admitted to the ER for physical injuries.

"Nurse Bell. Yes. I'll go get her. Just wait right here."

Within a minute, Julie appeared. She held a patient case log in front of her as she looked at it with reading glasses.

"Honey. Good to see you. Thought we were having dinner later this evening at Fudd's, when I get off. Something wrong? You never come here, unless something bad happens."

"Got a call about an incident at the trailer park and that a subject was brought here as a result. Has anybody been brought in?"

Julie looked at her husband and then at her watch. Both stared at each other.

"The shift change brief is soon. I can't miss that if you want to have dinner with me. Yes, we had an unidentified woman come in that was beat up really bad. We patched her up and wanted to keep her overnight for observation. She was at herself mentally and able to check herself out. I insisted that she stay, but as you know with those types, she didn't want to hear that. She walked right out the door as fast as she came in. Who knows where she'll end up, just like all the others that come through those doors."

"What was her name? Maybe, she's wanted in some other active case. Like you said, just like all the others."

Julie went over to the desk and looked through the unending paperwork in a file. She fingered through them with deliberation, as a ruse. Bell paced and looked at his cellphone. His actions concerned Julie. Their relationship was on the rocks and with all his crazy behavior she did not trust him anymore. Divorce was on the horizon and both of them knew it.

"Here we go. Elizabeth D. Boyd. Is she on your case list?"

"Maybe, I've heard the name. I'll run it through the system and see what comes up. I can't make our dinner date tonight. There was some trouble at one of the resort cabins. Deputy Tullos is still too green with a hot temper that needs to be controlled. Not something he can handle by himself. I'll make dinner up to you, I promise. Hope you understand?"

"I do. We can do it tomorrow night?"

Bell walked out of the ER without responding. Coldness enveloped the room. Julie felt it and she knew what to do. As she typed in the first few letters into her cell phone contact list, the name she was looking for came up. She hit the call button.

"I need your help. I don't know who else to turn to. I have one of the Banetown girls at the ER. Beat up pretty bad. Need somewhere she can heal up and need someone to get her out of town. Do you understand? I'm sorry to call you, but you're the only one that can help. I fixed up Josh, so now I need the favor back."

Kristol thought about the girl and the situation. A dilemma was thrust upon her that she didn't want to be a part of, but Julie had saved her and patched up Josh. Anxiety pulsed through her body. A choice had to be made.

"I got you. You know that. You helped me, so I owe you. I heard about what happened through the rumor mill. I'll take care of Elizabeth Dawn Boyd. She needs to be taken care of. Can you bring her to my house later tonight, around nine?"

"Yes. I can do that. Just keep all this on the downlow. Thank you, Kristol."

The cell phone went silent. Julie felt good for once in a long time and a tear ran down her cheek. She walked back to the ER room.

"You are okay for now. Later tonight, I'm going to take you to a safe place to heal. Then, you can start a new life somewhere away from here."

"I can't begin to thank you."

"Just sleep and I'll come get you soon."

29

A mound of freshly dug earth was piled over Caleb's grave. Josh sat on the grass facing it with his legs folded, leaning back on his hands. He'd hoped visiting his brother might provide some kind of direction for what to do. He needed answers and wanted to see justice for his brother, but more was going on in Etham than he initially thought. Drugs were rightly assumed, the abuse of opioids had long infected the Kentucky Appalachian Mountains, but there were more things now. Josh figured prostitution was somewhat normal just about anywhere, but a full-blown human trafficking ring in Etham. That was altogether unexpected. He thought he would help point a finger at a guilty drug addict that had gotten carried away while robbing his brother. He could do something like that. Bringing down a trafficking ring was a completely different story. He was already in over his head and knew he was a target. Perhaps it was best to cut his losses, while he still could and leave.

One thing that nagged at him was why Billy Dalton and that greasy haired friend of his, Dave Clemmons, didn't kill him when they had the chance. Josh was convinced they would have liked to and would have gotten away with it. Had someone held them back? Why? It could be that whoever is in charge doesn't want to call attention to their operation. Maybe, they figured a little encouragement would be enough to get him out of town? They were right. Caleb was dead and there wasn't any reason for him to get himself killed. Justice, as sweet as it would be, would not bring Caleb back.

Of course, there was another factor for staying. Somewhere out there was a young woman being held against her will and forced to have sex with strange men to make someone else rich. It's one thing to know that happens. It happens every day. The only difference is that now he knows the victim. At least, he knows her parents.

Josh wondered how often he had passed someone in the streets who was caught in some kind of trafficking. How often had he not been aware that such an evil was in his presence. Sure, he had heard about it happening somewhere else. It was clear now that it could happen anywhere, even in a small town like Etham, Kentucky. Josh was certain it didn't matter what anybody did; what could he do? The most likely outcome of him snooping around is that he would be murdered and be discreetly disposed of. At least Caleb was found and someone had called the EMTs, but he might not be so lucky.

Standing up to stretch and pace around, Josh put his hands in his jacket pocket and felt a small, glossy card. He pulled it out and saw the face of a young lady with long, brown hair brushed and pulled around her right shoulder. It was one of those wallet-sized school pictures, probably a senior photo. He had forgotten that Mrs. Boyd had given it to him, just before he was attacked.

He had seen the girl before, but where? Maybe, she merely resembled one of the hundreds of young students that walked the university halls. But the face seemed so fresh. Then it hit him–at the cabin. Yes, he had seen her at that cabin where Caleb had been shot. She was the girl that Billy Dalton had dropped off! No wonder they had paid him a visit. He had come across her by chance that very day.

He studied the girl's face. She was a lot younger in the picture, but it had only been a couple years. In the photo she looked hopeful, graduation being the only obstacle holding her back from a very promising future. What had the young girl in the photo been planning for after high school: college, a career, marriage, and children?

Elizabeth Dawn Boyd, now three years out of high school. A sex slave, chained in broad daylight by drug addiction and fear. God help her. I can imagine Caleb trying to help her. I need to help her, too.

Josh squeezed the picture hard in his hand and raised his fist up in the air. Clenching his teeth with pressed lips, he wondered how he could even think of abandoning this poor girl? He was powerless and couldn't turn to the law for help.

Sheriff Bell is turning a blind eye to everything for some reason. Is he involved?

He realized it didn't matter. It had already been reported and the bastard hadn't done anything about it. Going to him would be a waste of time. If Bell was involved, then going to him would certainly be a bad choice. Maybe he was wrong about the sheriff, but it was too risky. Involved or not, the man was not trustworthy.

The best thing to do was to get out of Etham and report it to the FBI or some other agency. There were law enforcement departments that specialized in this kind of thing. He would seek them out and make a report. Yes, that was the rational thing to do.

Josh opened his fist and looked at the now-crumpled photo of Elizabeth Dawn Boyd. Going to the FBI was certainly sensible, but what about her? Those thugs had certainly given him a message and it was loud and clear. Randall and Olivia Boyd had likely received one, as well. Worse still, how bad of a message had Elizabeth Dawn received?

"Hi there, handsome."

Kristol's soft voice awakened him from his thoughts. She walked slowly, with three fingers of each hand tucked into her jeans pockets. Josh held his head up toward the sky, closed his eyes, and slowly released a sigh. He opened his eyes to watch her approach. Her normal tough exterior was replaced with relaxed shoulders and softened eyes. A new tenderness radiated from her. Had something changed within her? Whatever it was, coupled with the range of emotions digging at his soul, made it difficult for him to not burst out in tears.

Does she feel the pain, too? Maybe, she feels my pain.

"I came home to bury my brother. And I came to try and figure out why he had done certain things–to try and come to peace with it. To come to peace with Caleb."

Josh looked across the countless grave markers, searching for something more to say. A soft breeze reminded him of the wind chimes on the homestead porch and of his brother's Bible in his back pocket. He took it out and glanced at the passage that had started him on this journey.

"This was Caleb's pocket Bible. He was clutching it hard after he was shot. He gave it to me right before he died. I brought it out here to leave with him. I figure it ain't doing me any good."

"Maybe, he wanted you to have it for a reason."

"Yeah, to get me on the trail of the people who killed him. All it's done is get me into something deep. Deeper than perhaps he even knew."

"Maybe it was for more than that. You should keep it, at least to remember him by. He wanted you to have it. In my opinion, you need to keep it."

Josh considered her words. Maybe she was right? Maybe, it was more than putting him on this wild goose chase? Maybe, he needed to come to terms with the words it contained about life rather than whatever subliminal message his brother's blood meant on its pages? Besides, it would only get destroyed by the weather out here.

"Kristol, there is a lot happening here. It's more than what happened with Caleb, more than drugs. Girls are being forced into prostitution, maybe even more. I thought I could help, but I can't. I think I even made it worse for some folks. I'm going to leave Etham and never come back."

"Never come back? But…I thought–"

Josh hadn't considered how Kristol would feel about him leaving. She had been there for him when he needed help. They had grown close, fast. Maybe, too fast. That had accounted for her unguarded support towards him when she had helped him. Her normal strong mask was beginning to deteriorate.

"Kristol, I'm sorry. I didn't mean it like that. It's just the only way I know to help these people stay safe. The solution is to get away from here and report it to the federal agencies. Why don't come with me?"

Kristol eased a bit, considering the situation. She loved the mountains and she enjoyed working for the resort. It was the perfect place for her. She felt strongly for Josh, but there were other even stronger ties and considerations. Yes, it had happened fast, but it had happened. He made her feel…secure. She didn't feel the need to be so guarded around him. This was something that she had never felt before. Would he really want her to go with him? On the other hand, would she really want that?

"I've heard that there are a few girls being pimped around the county, even suspected it was going on in the cabins. I didn't know it was so big. I figured it was a couple wayward women that had gotten themselves into it by their own choice."

Josh reached out to hold Kristol's hand. He didn't want to leave her; he just couldn't stay here. It was too dangerous for him and probably dangerous for her now. But he knew this place was a paradise for her. It was as important for her finding these old mountains as it was for him to leave them. For Josh, everything else was paradise. He began to tell her how he felt, but her phone rang, making them both jump.

Kristol looked down at it to see who it was. "It's Julie Bell."

"You should answer it."

Josh didn't quite trust Julie, due to her fling with his brother and that she was Bell's wife. But she did patch him up and hadn't told anyone about him being at Kristol's place. At least, no one had shown up to provide further encouragement for him to leave. He also knew there was a rift between her and the sheriff, which made a lot of sense. Maybe, the deal with her and Caleb was a result of her husband's abuse. It didn't matter, he'd keep a close watch on her.

Kristol answered the phone, "Julie, what's up?"

"I need your help. I don't know who else to turn to."

Kristol looked at Josh who had gone back to flipping through his brother's Bible. He listened as the conversation continued.

"Sure thing, Sweetie. What's up?"

Julie summarized the events of the evening and how Elizabeth Dawn was in her care. Kristol knew the girl couldn't be released on her own and that certain people would be looking for her. She also couldn't stay at the hospital. Kristol turned to Josh who was studying her face.

"Judging from your reactions, something crazy is going on." Josh said as he moved and touched her hand.

Kristol let him squeeze it. She looked at him with an open-hearted look.

"It's one of the girls you talked about. She's at the ER, and Julie wants to hide her out until she can recover. She'll be at risk if she stays there. I've met this one before, her name is Elizabeth Dawn."

"Elizabeth Dawn Boyd?"

"Yes, do you know her?"

Josh started to pace back and forth. His eyes focused on Caleb's grave and then back to Kristol. He handed the creased photo to her. Every detail was studied.

"Where did you get this? You do know her. How?"

"She's the daughter of Randall and Olivia Boyd." Josh said.

"I know of them. He's an artist and does stained glass. She's a nice woman from what I know of her. They live off the main highway to Hazard."

Josh gently held Kristol's hand again. She handed the picture back.

I know you're going to help her, no matter what anybody tells you. Let me help. It is what I need to do. This whole thing can be fixed once and for all with the right solution." Josh said.

Kristol looked at him in silence, watching new life flood into his eyes. He had been broken and ready to give up. But defeat had been quickly dissipated by hope. He was back in the fight.

She smiled, "Okay, let's do it. You agree?"

"Yes. Let's make it happen, but I need to know who killed my brother."

"Okay. Maybe, that will come to light in the end, but knowing how Etham is you may never know. It might be better that you don't know."

30

Clouds blocked the full moon on the way to Kristol's house. Julie knew the road, having made the trip there recently to patch up Josh, as well as other times working as a mobile nurse years earlier. With all that, it still looked unfamiliar at night. Tall, silhouetted trees seemed to reach down, grab the road, and pull everything upward. The glare from the headlights reflected off the highway and blinded Julie as she slowed her car. Finally, the road sign came into view, Slate Lick Road. One last turn made her feel better; the stretch before she got to her destination. Elizabeth Dawn was sleeping in the passenger seat. Her breathing sounded weak. Julie rounded a sharp curve and looked over at her passenger. Questions about how old she was and how she had gotten mixed up with the bad elements crossed Julie's mind. She knew the answers, but still contemplated the questions anyway.

Then, images and fear of her husband filled her mind. Deep down, she was convinced he knew what was going on and maybe he was involved. She had always known and felt something, but it had never really registered. None of that is why she fell in love with Caleb. The passionate affair had brought a brief happiness to her sad life. True, it never should have happened, but it did. She had been blinded by years of mental abuse. She couldn't overcome the feeling of being a disappointment of not mattering to the one person who should have loved her unconditionally. Bell was different when they first got married. He treated her as if she were the queen of the world. He was good to others, too, and was proud to enforce the law. She was excited to see him elected as Sheriff, a crowning moment in his career which he had started as a deputy. Something happened along the way. He became distant. Maybe she was to blame for some of it, but not for the abuse she received. Caleb should not have happened, but he did. And though the affair was short, she loved him. Tears of sadness and love for Caleb ran down her face. She shook her head and focused back on the road.

As she pulled up to Kristol's house, the porch light came on. That made Julie feel better about what she was doing.

"We're here. C'mon, let's get out. You can walk with some help from me, but you've got to try and do it on your own. The owner of this place will respect you more. I promise you."

"I don't know if I can. My legs are numb and my back is on fire with pain."

"I know, but you can do it. Hold my hand."

Both walked up the stone path that led to the house. Kristol stood on the porch with her revolver in hand and scanned the driveway to the house.

"Get on in the house. It's not safe to be out in the open."

Julie and Elizabeth Dawn quickened their steps and Kristol herded them into the house. Quickly, she turned off the porch light and made sure all the shades were pulled down. With the lights dimmed, she dialed her cellphone.

"Come on in. They are safe. Use the back door."

Kristol hung up. She assisted Julie in laying Elizabeth Dawn on the couch and covered her up with an old Army wool blanket.

"I want to thank you for taking me in. I know you understand the danger of just talking to me. I know who you are. You work at the resort, maintenance supervisor or some boss like that. I appreciate you."

"Yes, something like that. Now, don't you worry yourself. You just go right on to sleep. Everything is going to be alright." Kristol said as she rubbed Elizabeth Dawn's forehead. Quickly, her eyes closed.

Kristol motioned Julie to the kitchen. The back door opened. Julie's eyes widened.

"Nobody followed them." Josh said as he laid his father's old 30-30 rifle on the kitchen table.

"Josh. What are you doing here? Thought it was just going to be Kristol. Figured you would be up and around; headed the hell out of Etham." Julie said as she was further amazed at how much he and Caleb looked alike. Memories of Caleb flooded her mind again.

It's my choice. I want to help all the girls that are caught up in this. I want to find out who murdered Caleb. Deep down, I know he wanted to stop all this. I'm going to finish his work."

Julie began to cry as she thought about Caleb. Inside her heart, she knew why Caleb had been killed. She looked into the living room at Elizabeth Dawn sleeping.

"We'll keep her here until she has healed up some. Then, we'll get her up to Cincinnati. I've got family and friends there. Maybe her parents can go with her. Their days are numbered, too." Kristol said as she poured glasses of bourbon.

"I appreciate that. Here's a bag of bandages. Don't give her any type of medication. She's coming off some bad stuff. Withdrawal will be rough for her."

"I know what she will be going through. In a week or so, she will be okay." Kristol said and handed Julie a glass.

"No. I don't need a drink. Just need to head home. Things will not look right to the sheriff if I'm not home soon. I don't want to draw any attention this way."

Kristol and Josh looked at each other. Julie's use of sheriff, instead of husband, struck a chord with them both.

All got up from the kitchen table and walked towards the front door. Julie looked down at Elizabeth Dawn and wished never to see her again.

"You know if things get bad your way, you can come here. You're always welcome." Kristol said.

"I know. I'll be fine." Julie said and then turned toward Josh.

"You know that your brother would be proud of what you're doing. I loved him. He was a good man and didn't deserve to die the way he did."

Josh took a few steps forward and looked at Julie. He could feel Caleb's Bible in his back jeans pocket. It seemed to heat up with each passing second. Something in him seemed to take over his words.

"Caleb loved you. I know that. The connection and love were there. Yes, I saw the looks that you and him exchanged the last time I attended church years ago. You both deserved the love that you both felt."

Julie stepped back. Knowledge of her affair with Caleb was sacred and unknown. She wanted to explain, but her words got stuck in her throat.

"Me and him being twins makes me see and know things beyond most people's understanding. Believe me, it is okay. I've accepted the relationship you both had. We just need to make everything right with his death and everything else around here. Don't you agree?"

"I agree. I'm sorry, but I loved your brother with all my heart. The affair was wrong."

"I understand and I know Caleb understood that, too. But the past can't change, and neither can those connections. Whatever he felt, I'm sure he'd want you to make things right with your husband. If that is even possible, but it's not wrong to remember Caleb with affection and love. I loved him, too–beyond words–as my brother."

Kristol took in what she was hearing. Not many people knew about Julie' affair, though she had known. She had her ways of knowing the going-ons in Etham, but she was good at holding secrets close. Besides, it wasn't her business. She had enough relational drama of her own and she had no right to make any judgments on anyone else. She decided to not bring up her knowing about the relationship.

"Well, I better go. If you need any medical supplies or if she gets worse, call me anytime of the day or night."

Kristol and Josh nodded their heads. They waved as Julie got into her vehicle. The clouds had moved out and the moon cast an ambience over the terrain. They watched Julie's tail lights disappear down the road and went inside.

Sitting back down at the kitchen table, Kristol felt Josh's stare. She could tell what he was thinking. Had she known about his brother and Julie?

"Nobody in town knows that she and your brother were seeing each other. I didn't even know that." Kristol lied, but felt it was better for him to believe that no one knew. "Trust me, I hear and know everything that's going on in Etham. I would have heard something."

"It's a twin thing. Seen it years ago and it caused conflict between us. It doesn't matter now."

"I learn something new every day."

"Let's talk about the plan." Josh said as he checked the loaded rifle and took a drink of bourbon, he had just poured for both of them.

"I agree. What do you have in mind?"

Both eyed each other. Kristol looked at the glass of bourbon and reflected on everything she knew, didn't know, and everything that had happened. Ideas burst into her brain. Details of each one raced into plans.

"We're going to stay right here. That scum out there will not come here." Kristol said.

"Why do you say that? They're bad to the core and fought me right in town. Why would they not come up here, which is isolated and miles from anything and anyone?"

"Thought you knew everything going on around here. Guess you would say I am close to Mr. Fields. He will be able to figure all this out and help. He has helped me so much and is like a father to me. Took me in when nobody would and let me work at the resort. I manage multiple things for him. He pretty much lets me have the run of the place. If they do come, I will put lead into them." Kristol smiled and gripped her pistol.

Josh looked at her in disbelief. Fields was a family friend through his father, but Josh had never trusted Fields when he had seen him picking up his father to go to work at the coal mine. That one day when Fields had made fun of Josh and Caleb for wearing matching plaid shirts. Josh could hear the words in his head.

You both look like clowns with those striped shirts. Going to school looking like that will get you some beatings for sure.

Josh and Caleb had picked out the shirts and their father had bought them when the money was tight. The brothers were happy to have new shirts without rips and stains. They didn't say anything because their father was getting a ride to a job from their supervisor that was twenty miles away, due to their car not running. Both Josh and Caleb knew why their father bit his tongue. His memories joined with reality. He decided not to say anything about his feelings just like he had put this memory out of his mind when he had recently seen Fields. Yes, Fields had helped their father with the job and when he got sick, but Josh kept that memory and distrust in his head.

Kristol looked at Josh and she hesitated for a moment, which made him feel uncomfortable. Then, she smiled with her bright teeth showing.

"I agree with you. Staying here until Elizabeth Dawn is healed enough to travel is the best thing. We can defend this place. We have enough food, water, and ammo."

"I'm glad you agree with me. I would hate to do all this alone." Josh smiled back.

"The time for action will come. Let's get some sleep. We will need all our energy when it is time. Time to react to whatever comes out of this." Kristol said and checked the rounds in her revolver.

"The couch is taken, so you need a place to sleep." Kristol said and swallowed another shot of bourbon.

"I can bed down on the living room floor. I'll be good there." Josh said with a subdued smile.

"No sense in that. Come sleep with me. There's enough room, plus you like me some, don't you? If you don't, you better tell me now."

Josh looked at her and she smiled. He nodded his head.

"I like you some."

Passion, lust, and whatever you could call it embraced them in Kristol's bedroom. Sleep eluded them for most of the night, but they were happier, nonetheless.

31

Sheriff Bell had just returned to his office from the day's patrol. His last check was the long-abandoned coal mine up on Jack's Creek. Many decades had passed since any coal had been loaded on the rusted carts at that old place. Another reminder of days gone by. Fears of ghosts and routine patrols by the Sheriff and his deputies deterred anybody trespassing. With the day winding down, he leaned back in his desk chair and put his black leather boots up on his desk. A long draw from a cigarette eased the tension but didn't erase bad memories. A sharp knock at the door pulled him to his feet and prompted him to look at his watch.

1800 hours. Too late in the day for most folks and Tullos never knocks.

"C'mon in."

"Hey, my friend. I let myself in. The front door was open. How are you?"

Bell flashed a smile and walked up to the tall man with a military haircut in a gray heavily starched uniform. His badge shined as much as Bell's. Authority was written on his face and projected from his stature.

"Alexander, what brings you down here from Frankfort? Don't you have a comfortable chair to be sitting in up there?"

"Good to see you, too, and your sorry excuse of humor. You've not changed a bit since our academy days.

They shook hands hard and looked at each other knowing that this was not a reunion visit. Uncomfortable silence lingered for a couple seconds too long. Each one sized up the other, but both understood the pecking order of law enforcement jurisdiction and authority.

"Have a seat my friend." Bell said with a smile.

"Don't mind if I do. The two and a half hour drive up here tires a person out."

Bell walked over to an old wood cabinet in the corner and pulled out a bottle of well-aged bourbon and two glass tumblers.

Let me pour you a drink and we can toast our reunion visit. Let you relax after the long drive."

Colonel Alexander P. Hall, Kentucky State Police Post 17 Commissioner, leaned back in the chair. He looked around the office and smiled.

"That would be fine, since I'm off duty and visiting an old friend."

Those words made Bell cringe, but he hid his reaction. Both had endured the academy together and he knew that Alexander was never off duty. That's why he had become commissioner with a spotless record.

"It's good to have a drink with an old friend." Bell said as he handed the glass to Alexander.

Bourbon aroma filled the office air, twinged with a bit of uneasiness. Each took a sip, savoring the warmth of the drink while hoping the visit would remain warm as well.

"Bell, you know I'm not down here this evening to sit around and drink your expensive booze."

"No, Alexander, I reckon not. The long ride, coupled with whatever reason you are here warrants my gratitude. I figured a drink couldn't hurt. What's on your mind?"

They both had another drink after they downed the first one. Bell took a seat behind his desk.

"I guess we need to get down to the core of it." Alexander said as he leaned up from the chair.

"I agree. You're right. I didn't figure you drove so far while off-duty to hang out with me in Etham."

Both finished off their tumblers. They eyed each other just as they had during hand-to-hand combative training at the academy.

"We received an anonymous call a few days back. A female caller stated that she feared for her life and wanted to come forward. She went on and said that a number of young women were caught up in some bad stuff in Etham. Stuff like drugs, prostitution, and theft. Even said a couple of them were killed a while back and dumped somewhere. Another was beat up really bad in the last few days. She went on and said that Preacher Caleb Webb's death was connected to all of it. That's some real bad stuff and can't be ignored."

Alexander looked at Bell. Each one stared at the other and Bell reviewed what he had heard with speculation and apprehension.

"Your boys were up here when we airlifted Caleb Webb out of here. A full investigation was carried out. The case is still open with no leads. I've run the traps around the area. Nobody is talking. As far as the women, I've not had any reports of anyone missing, not like what you are saying. Sounds like a lot of unsubstantiated rumors to me. Yes, we have drugheads get up and go to other towns and don't tell anybody, so that may account for what you heard. I'll keep my ears open for anything that sounds suspicious. Did the person on the phone give names of the women? That would help me a lot."

Alexander eyed Bell and put his empty glass on the desk. He got up and walked to the window.

"No names. I'm sure you are handling everything down here. Things seem to be booming around here, a big change from the last time I was here. A few years back this place was on the road to being a ghost town. What's your opinion on the change of Etham?"

"I would tend to agree. Things seem to have a way of working out. Don't you think so? The resort has brought an economic boom."

"They do. I have seen that a lot in my career. I've heard about the resort and it has people talking at the Capitol."

Alexander walked towards the door. He looked around the office and then back at Bell.

"You've got it pretty good here. I came down as a friend and I'm leaving as a professional law enforcement official just as I hope you are. We both went to the academy, and we took our oaths required by our positions. We both uphold the law no matter what."

"Yes, we do. I'm the same as you and you can't deny it. You have a boss and I have a boss. In the end, the people are our true bosses. We are the same." Bell smiled.

"You are wrong on one thing. I will have peace when all this is done. Maybe you will and maybe you will not. You must ask yourself that. I just came here to see a good friend." He looked at the empty glass, "and shared a good drink."

Heartbeats of both men seemed to beat together for an instant. The bond that they had before that brought them to this juncture was realized and now had ended.

"Peace is a matter of perspective. Your definition of peace is maybe not my definition. So, here we are." Bell said and put his hands on his gun belt strapped around his waist.

"I understand you and your position. I'll leave you with this. People above me are interested and things don't seem right in Etham. You take that how you want. I come as a friend now, but next time it may be different. Only you can decide."

"Okay. I take it how you gave it. Hope you have a safe trip back to Frankfort."

Both projected disturbed and concerned looks at each other. They nodded.

"I'm headed back to post. Good to see you, my friend."

"Thanks, Alexander. I've got things covered down this way. If I need your help, I'll hit you up.

Alexander walked out of the office, leaving Bell to grit his teeth. Blood began to boil as Bell paced the hardwood floor; the creaking boards sounded like a nagging noisy fan with each step. He drew his tumbler back to throw it but poured another drink instead. He watched his old friend get into the car outside the window. Alexander was right, he wasn't the same law man he started out as. He used to be as clean as anyone, the real deal. But his career spiraled out of control the past few years after that damn Mr. Fields found out about his cheating wife and used it to control him. He should have told him to go to hell, but he was in an election year and he was afraid of being exposed. Things had escalated quickly and he was now just a lap dog for the man that he despised the most. He shook his head and took another drink from the tumbler.

What a damn mess. I need to make this right.

He picked up his cellphone and hit the call button. After a few rings, it went to voicemail. He dialed again.

32

Five days had passed since Dave beat up Elizabeth Dawn and left her crumpled up like a wad of paper on her porch deck. He left, not knowing whether she was dead or alive. That was a mistake he'd likely not hear the end of any time soon. When he and Billy returned the next morning, she was nowhere to be found.

The girls normally understood to stay within the boundaries of their assigned trailers. If they got out of line, then Dave would be obliged to smack them around a little until they got the point. It worked for the most part, but Dave and sometimes Billy felt the need to impose their power just for good measure every once and a while. Dave was usually good about not damaging the goods, but every once in a while, he'd go too far and cause one of the girls to miss a few days of work. This was usually overlooked by the Boss, who figured it was a small price to pay for a man of his skills and the effect on the girls to keep them in line. The Boss wasn't happy at all this time, and that was made clear from phone calls and promises of repercussions.

Somebody must have helped Elizabeth Dawn because she wouldn't have been able to get far otherwise. Dave and Billy asked around the trailer park with their usual firmness, but they got the same answers that the police always got when they asked questions. No one saw anything. Billy was frustrated with all of this.

Stupid trailer trash idiots. They don't know who they're messing with.

By the time they checked the hospital it was too late. Elizabeth Dawn had managed to get there, get patched up, and leave. The mystery was to where? The obvious first choice was out at Boyd place. Dave and Billy went out there and had come up with a way to search the property without tipping off the girl's parents. From all appearances, the Boyds had no idea their daughter was unaccounted for. If they were, it was likely they would be gone, as well.

After that search, Billy was keeping tabs on the Boyds if anything had changed. Deputy Tullos was patrolling around, searching for any signs that turned up. Dave was stuck watching downtown Etham. He had spent the last three days moving between Fudd's restaurant, the courthouse, and his current position, the alley off from the town square. If he saw anything it would be at the crossroads of town, though it was a long shot.

What the hell do they think I'm going to see here? They're just mad at me for screwing up. Just keeping me out of the way. They will regret messing with me.

Dave thought about just driving off and leaving everything behind. He couldn't explain it, but he had a gut feeling that this operation was on borrowed time. Maybe, he was too. It would probably be best to get out of Dodge while the getting was good. The question was where he would go. He had a little money saved up, but it wasn't exactly enough to make a brand-new start far enough away from here. He needed more, so he always stayed and here he was.

A few more months and I'll leave these clowns for good. They think they're so smart, we'll see about that.

Dave was about to crank up his rusted-out Chevy Nova and move positions when Julie Bell pulled up in front of the corner market. She was pretty and easy to look at for a woman in her forties, so he figured he'd hang out for a few more minutes and indulge himself. Thoughts of her being the sheriff's wife and a bit older didn't bother him. He figured she needed some attention, since Bell didn't give her any. In his opinion, she was not too far out of his league; maybe she'd like to hook up.

Julie came back out with multiple bags hanging from each hand. Tossing the groceries into her SUV, she sped around to the far side of the square and pulled into the library. After five minutes, she came out empty handed and left with the same urgency.

Then it hit him. She was the one that helped Olivia Boyd and that lady from the library, after he had knocked them over. That was the day they beat up the preacher's brother in Fudd's parking lot. Dave fired up his Nova and shot out after Julie. He noticed the librarian slipping out the back door going toward her car as he passed. He couldn't follow them both, so he slowed and grabbed his phone.

"Billy, check it out. I just saw Sheriff Bell's wife slip in and out of the library real sneaky like. She's the one that helped old lady Boyd and the librarian when we beat up Josh Webb. She's acting weird and speeding out of town. After she left, I started following."

"Why? Do you think she is connected? How? She's Sheriff Bell's wife for god's sake!"

"Listen, I'm not sure, but that day we roughed up Josh Webb. I turned back to see her helping Olivia and that librarian. She had a look on her face that was really crazy. Now, I see her slipping in like that, and then, after she leaves, the librarian makes a beeline out the back door. Doesn't that sound suspicious to you?"

Dave heard Billy's breath as he considered what the man had said. He had met Mrs. Bell at the emergency room once when he had broken his leg when he fell off his porch drunk a few years back. She seemed to be the do-good type to him.

"Yeah, it does, kind of. Okay, keep following her. She may have seen Elizabeth Dawn at the hospital and helped her. Who knows, best case scenario it's nothing. If not, you get back to town, pronto. I'm headed over to Boyds to see what they're up to. They're really sneaky."

"Too easy, Billy. I think I may be onto something, though."

"Yeah, maybe so. Don't do anything stupid. Sure don't need the Sheriff on us. You know how he is. Call me, if you see something."

33

Billy slid his phone into his jeans and pulled into the Boyd's driveway. Things were quiet as he walked out back to Randall's shop. Too quiet.

"Hey, old man! Where are you at? What are you up to?"

No one replied. As Billy opened the shop door, he looked at Randall and studied him to determine what the man knew. He is either a good actor or didn't know anything about what was going on in and around Etham. Most folks didn't, at least, they don't know who's doing what or how they were doing it. Billy wasn't sure whether Randall knew much about anything at all. He had been going through the motions, meandering back and forth around the homestead like an ancient spirit, who had missed his ride to the hereafter.

Whether Randall Boyd knew anything about Elizabeth Dawn's profession or if he even knew she was missing was a mystery. Something had changed in the man over the past week. The picture of his daughter had crushed him. He'd never seen a man implode like this. He'd thought the man was going to die when he saw the picture of his daughter. In a way, he did.

Billy had seen men die. Hell, he had killed a few himself; at least two in Iraq and another here in Woodridge County. That man had walked in on his wife paying Billy for the opioids the man and wife were to enjoy later. The woman's husband had taken issue with her explicit method of payment and gave Billy a quick ultimatum: kill or be killed.

He had disposed of the body in an old mine shaft that was home to some other unfortunate souls. He had left the man's wife on her couch, well preserved, and staring at her ceiling fan with mournful woes. No one else would ever know. Not Dave, not Tullos; no one except the man's wife who was threatened and ensured an endless supply of pills.

It is true that you can watch a man's life fade away through his eyes. He had seen it as a kid when his father passed away from the Black Lung. His eyes had fogged over and the slow pace of his chest coasted to a stop like a car running out of gas. He'd also seen it with his Army infantry brother, Kevin Jenkins, when he bled out after getting hit in an ambush in Iraq. It was much quicker with Jenkins, but the same result.

Billy had seen that life fade out of Randall Boyd's eyes. Instead of blood, he was depleted of life through tears and sorrow. He had dried up inside and then flat-lined, a dead man left walking in a world created for the living. For several years, Billy felt contempt for the man and pushed it towards him like adding sticks to a small fire not because he needed it, but because he enjoyed the flames. Now it was different.

He thought about a time when he and some friends were shooting a stray dog with their BB guns. One of the older kids pulled out a .22 and shot the dog in the back side. Not enough to kill it, but enough for it to wish it was dead. Billy remembered its wailing howls echoing through the woods. That had haunted his dreams then and sent chills down his back now.

Damned old dog and damn Randall Boyd!

"How are you doing, old man? What's on your mind, today?"

Randall didn't even acknowledge him. It was eerie, as if he were watching a ghost replaying its former life or perhaps it was the other way around. Perhaps he was the ghost watching Randall live out his days. Whatever the case, it was agonizing to watch. Perhaps the old man needed to be put out of his misery for good. It seemed like a good idea at the time and he felt the pistol grip tucked in his pants, but just as he committed himself to the idea a car pulled up the driveway. Billy walked out from the shop to see the librarian step onto the Boyd's porch. He was sure she could see him, but she ignored him, the same as everyone else around here. He started towards the house then turned back to Randall.

"You stay out of trouble and don't you move. Hear?"

He walked away, figuring the real trouble was inside with that librarian and Mrs. Boyd. When he opened the door the two ladies went on talking in hushed voices. He could hear what they were saying, but acted like he couldn't. Not that it mattered, they were talking about stupid books. Billy shook his head and helped himself to a soda from the refrigerator.

"Just go on and help yourself, Billy. Might as well eat all of our food, too. I'm heading to town with Beatrice. There's a sale at the Corner Market."

Corner Market? Books? Yeah, right you stupid old hags. Whatever you say.

Billy watched the ladies walk out to Beatrice's car. He looked out the back window at Randall, who was milling towards the yard. That man was clearly no threat. Billy downed the rest of his soda and missed the trash can as he rushed out to his Blazer. The answer to Elizabeth Dawn's location was with the women and Billy had a gut feeling they were going to see her now.

Randall saw the message as soon as he stepped into the living room. There was nothing new in there. No notes lying about explaining where his wife went off to, but something was off. It was his first stained glass work that he had been proud enough to display, a project that he had started several times and discarded because it hadn't been right. Finally, he managed to finish it. This one was pretty good for a beginner. It was a mural of the sun dawning over the horizon with an inscription of the Psalm, "Weeping may endure for the night, but joy cometh in the morning."

It was a reminder to him that dawn brings with it joy, and with that hope. The verse meant so much that he had named his daughter after the sentiment. As the girl grew, so had his joy and hope. Nothing went on their walls that wasn't meant to inspire happy memories. After many years it had been absorbed into the total decor, only noticed at times of cleaning or occasional reminiscence. There hadn't been much cleaning or nostalgia the past couple of years.

The mural was off balance. One of the hanging hooks must have slipped off the nail. The small brad nail was still solid in the wall, which meant that someone must have bumped against it. That was unlikely because it was hung over a side table.

Randall studied the mural, wondering where the joy went. Hope was a lie, something people boasted about in good times and conjured up when things were bad. He had held tightly to it–until the picture of his precious girl, curled up, beaten…dead. If he had any tears left, they would fall. A hollow groan escaped from somewhere in him as he reached to straighten the mural. He felt something on the back, a note.

Randall,

Elizabeth Dawn is alive and staying with that woman from the Resort, Kristol Engel. She lives at Frank Burton's old place. Hopefully, Billy followed us.

-Bea

A fresh spring of tears sprang from some previously unknown source and with it, a resurrection of hope. Randall started towards the door and stopped. Going back to his bedroom, he reached into a hidden compartment in the nightstand by his bed. It contained a fully loaded Model 1911 .45 pistol.

Randall Boyd was alive again. In the past, he had failed to protect his daughter and failed to rescue her. He had thought if he did what the thugs said then she might be safe, at least from death. He had been wrong. Now, it was time to bring her home.

34

Billy started to doubt his decision to follow the women. They had indeed gone straight to town and into the Corner Market. He sat in his Blazer contemplating on whether to hang around and see what happens or to hightail it back to Randall's place. Perhaps the two old hags were really that excited over some stupid sale at the grocery. Did they really have no clue as to what was going on? Could Olivia Boyd be so petty as to get worked up over a sale just days after seeing pictures of her half dead daughter? That seemed odd. Still, he fired up the Blazer to head back out to the Boyd place. He figured he'd first swing into the gas station around the corner to pick up some smokes, since he was in town. When he turned the corner, he saw a truck take off from the back alley of the market. It was Olivia and Beatrice.

You sneaky old biddies!

Olivia had arranged to borrow a truck from a friend that worked at the market, saying she needed it to haul some compost for her garden. It was a pretty good plan and had accounted for Billy's impatience. They knew he would follow.

The cigarettes would have to wait. Billy gave the women a little space and then followed. He thought they had seen him, but they made no show of it if they did. They headed north out of town and after about half an hour rolled into Wolfe County.

Alright, ladies, where are we going? Take me to the girl, so I can end this babysitting routine.

The sun was getting to the horizon with each passing minute. Why would they head to Wolfe County this late in the day? It perplexed Billy. The women pulled into a small garden center outside of Zachariah, a small town that made Etham look like a metropolis. Olivia pulled the truck up to a gate and a few minutes later a front-end loader was dumping compost into the bed of the truck. Billy watched as he seethed.

Really? What the hell? Who has been played a fool here? They are getting a load of crap.

The women pulled out heading back to Etham. Billy watched as they passed. Beatrice laughed as she waved, then blew him a kiss. Olivia gave him the finger.

The realization that he'd been brought on a wild goose chase had settled on him as the women passed. Billy slapped the wheel and then hammered it twice to drive home the point. He sat for a while, hoping his rage would calm. Going ballistic on two old women wouldn't set well, even in the corrupt mountains of Kentucky.

Billy figured if the women were decoys, then that meant Randall Boyd was playing him, too. True, it could be that none of them knew anything, but the look Olivia gave him as she held up her finger stated the obvious. They had led him away, so that Randall could make a move. Billy didn't know what that might be, but his gut was screaming Elizabeth Dawn. He fired up the Blazer and pushed south towards Etham.

About four miles into Woolridge County, he began seeing the compost filled pickup truck doing its best to make good time. Billy reckoned running the women off the road would easily look like an accident, especially with the way they were driving. If he planned it right, they wouldn't live to give their account, because Rock Lick Gorge was coming up and it was at least a hundred feet drop from the road to the creek below. Billy pressed the pedal to the floor.

Beatrice saw the Blazer gaining in the rear-view mirror. "You best hold tight, Olivia. That crazy idiot is behind us and has lost his mind."

Olivia leaned over to see Billy coming in fast in the side mirror. Then, she saw blue lights about a quarter of a mile behind him.

"Billy ain't the only one coming in fast. I see the lights?" Beatrice said as she pushed the gas pedal harder.

"Yeah, but does that mean anything around here anymore? I swear the law dogs are just as bad as Billy and his kind."

"Maybe so, but Billy is slowing down. Thank God for small miracles."

"Praise God! It ain't no small miracle."

———————

Deputy Tullos pulled up beside Billy and pushed the switch that rolled his passenger window down. Billy's arm was resting on his open window as he hammered the door with his finger. He waited for some attitude-laden comment from Tullos, who had a history of getting in his way, more out of fun than for purposes of the law and business.

Tullos wasn't laughing. "Why the hell aren't you answering your phone?

"Stupid thing went dead; what's going on?" Billy said with a snaggle-toothed smile.

"You need to get off this wild goose chase. I figured you were getting ready to do something stupid like running them off the road. We don't need that attention right now."

"Me. I would never do anything like that." Billy chackled.

"Shut up and listen. Get back to town and wait for me to call. Something is brewing. I don't know what, but something."

Tullos rolled up his window and squealed his tires towards Etham. Billy slammed his hand on the steering wheel.

"One of these days. You don't know who you're messing with." Billy said out loud and gritted his teeth.

He watched the sun go down over the ridgeline in front of him. An orange and purple glow radiated upward. At that moment, even Billy appreciated the beauty of the Appalachian hills.

35

Plastic grocery bags rubbed together as Julie rounded the curves and turned onto the bumpy gravel road up to Kristol's place. Whether or not Elizabeth Dawn was physically able to leave town with her parents raced through her mind. Only examining her personally would make her feel better. As she pulled up, she noticed how dark the place looked and the sun lowering over the hills behind the house added to it. A single lamp was on in the shade-drawn picture window. A smothering feeling came over her as she grabbed the bags and walked up to the house. The door opened and Kristol walked out with her revolver.

"Sorry, I have a gun in my hand. It's just that you don't know who to trust these days. Hell, you don't even need to trust me." Kristol laughed. "I guess I better trust you, since you brought some groceries. You didn't need to be doing all that. I can go get groceries. I ain't got nothing to worry about or anybody watching me."

Julie looked at her for a moment. She thought about all the corruption in Etham and the Resort. Then, her mind shifted to the task at hand.

"I figured you all needed some supplies and I was in town anyway. No use for you to be moving around town with the circumstances."

Kristol put her revolver in the small of her back which held it in place by her jeans. She walked down the porch steps.

"I appreciate it. Let me help carry some of those bags in. Can't let you do all the work."

Kristol walked down the porch steps and grabbed most of the bags. She looked towards the road at the end of her driveway.

"Let's go inside. You have a patient to look at." Kristol said and gripped the bags.

They both walked in. Kristol closed the door, while she scanned the front yard and driveway again, as if she was expecting someone to roll up.

Elizabeth Dawn pulled herself up from the couch with some groans and Josh straightened himself up from the recliner with a smile on his face. Julie sat the bags on the floor and walked over to Elizabeth Dawn with a detailed eye.

"How are you feeling?" Julie said and examined each wound and bruise.

"I'm sore as hell, but I'll survive."

"I know you will." Julie grinned as she replaced the bandage on her ribs.

Elizabeth Dawn winced as she leaned back on the couch but returned a smile as a small compensation for the nurse's work. It made Julie feel good about her calling and it motivated her to help her patient no matter the cost.

"In my opinion, she doesn't need to move for a week or so." Kristol yelled out from the kitchen as she was putting away the groceries.

"Josh, good to see you. Looks like Kristol has gotten you fully recovered. I can see it by the smile on your face." Julie said with a grin.

"Like I said when you brought Elizabeth Dawn here, you mended me up. I owe you for that. Kristol has followed your instructions and more." Josh said and smiled back.

Julie walked into the kitchen and started taking items out of the bags. She looked at Kristol.

"I think she needs to get out of here as soon as possible, no matter her medical condition. The people searching for her are dangerous. We need to get her out of Etham." Julie said.

Kristol looked at Elizabeth Dawn and then shook her head as she glanced back at Julie. "They're not coming up here. She's safe, I assure you. All those people will not come up here and bother me or anybody I have here."

Julie looked at Kristol with a mixture of assurance and fear. She could not explain it in her head, but understood. She nodded her head.

"I trust you. I'll check on her in a few days and then we can get her and her parents out here for good. They deserve a new beginning. Don't you think?"

Kristol looked at Julie and smiled. She reached over and put her hand on Julie's.

"Thank you. I'll keep her safe, until you come to take her to her parents in a few days. Deal? Don't worry. I got this."

Julie smiled and walked to the living room. Kristol watched her closely as she moved across the kitchen.

"Elizabeth Dawn, you are healing great and you should be ready to travel soon. Your parents will be waiting for you at the end of all this."

"Really, they will hate me for what I've done. I'm dirty and I turned on them when they were trying to help me. I don't know if I can see them, or…even talk to them."

"They love you. They told me so and can't wait to see you. Heal up and you will see them soon. Okay?'

"Okay."

Julie kissed Elizabeth on the forehead and touched her cheek. They both nodded. Julie walked to the door and looked at Kristol.

"Take care of her, like I know you will."

"I will, you can trust me. I've got this situation under control." Kristol pulled her revolver from the small of her back and smiled. She looked at Julie.

"I see that she is in good hands. I would not want to meet you as an enemy with that gun in your hands. I'm sure everyone else around here knows how tough you are."

"I'm quite sure everyone around here knows me and how I am. Due to that, she is safe."

Julie nodded her head and looked at Josh. They looked at each other with concerned eyes.

"Keep your wounds clean, Josh?"

"I'm keeping them clean and they are about healed. I owe you." He nodded his head and touched his rifle standing next to the recliner.

"You don't owe me anything, except making sure Elizabeth Dawn gets out of here to her parents."

"I promise that. Don't you worry. I'll make sure of it no matter what happens."

Julie nodded her head at Josh and Kristol. She walked out of the house without looking back. She felt in her head and soul that something permeated from them. It was something that she couldn't put her finger on and not enough to ask them about. She was assured that Elizabeth Dawn would be safe and get to a far-off place. Something told her to trust Kristol because she was a woman and by the eyes darting back and forth that she was in love with Josh. Jealousy filled her heart as she thought about how much she loved Caleb, Josh's twin brother. After thinking about everything that had happened, Kristol was like all the others in Etham. She could not be fully trusted. Julie felt that deep in her soul but had to risk it.

Julie got into her car and backed out of the driveway. So much was rolling through her mind that she didn't notice the old Nova parked on the side of the road watching her leave. She turned onto Route 15 and headed home.

36

Julie felt in her heart that something was wrong with everything in Etham. She had seen and heard things. Working at the hospital had given her a front row seat. Things had to change and it might as well start with ensuring Elizabeth Dawn got a new start and maybe herself too. With a turn of the steering wheel, she headed toward Etham.

Harris and I need to work things out. It's been going sour for way too long. Plus, he needs to help me get Elizabeth Dawn and the Boyds out of here. I know there is still goodness in his heart. It was there when I fell in love with him years ago. Caleb had that goodness too and I fell in love with it. If Harris had not grown distant and cold, maybe I would not have given myself to Caleb. He's gone now. Maybe, me and Harris have a chance. I know he has a reason to be mad at me, but he messed around too. I just don't have evidence, just rumors I hear around town. Maybe he was never dirty and if he was now he has changed.

Sadness and excitement ran through her veins as she pulled into the sheriff's department parking lot. Harris pulled up next to her and got out.

"What brings you by? I'll be home late tonight. Things are crazy around here. There's some activity down at the trailer park that is getting out-of-hand." Harris said and looked at his watch.

Damn, it's 6:46. She's probably mad because I'm not home for dinner, before she goes in for the night shift at the hospital.

Julie went up and hugged her husband. Surprise took over. He didn't know whether to pull away or hug back. A memory of the last time they had hugged was elusive.

"I just wanted to come by, give you a hug, and talk. Can you spare a few minutes from the Etham crime wave?

Harris nodded and smiled. They walked to his office. Nobody was at the department and quietness added to Harris' bewilderment at his wife's sudden demeanor change.

"Honey, I need to tell you some things and I need your help." Julie said with tight lips.

Uneasiness took over Harris' body as he tried to figure out what "some things" and "help" meant. Could it be worse than finding out about Caleb? A sudden wave of anger shot through his mind, but he decided to listen to her. Only because of her sudden enthusiasm.

"Go ahead, let me hear it." Harris crossed his arms and eyed her.

"I know things are not exactly perfect with us due to me and Caleb. We fell in love for a reason years ago and I don't regret that at all. Things need to come back together and we need to make amends. We have both done things we are not proud of. Yes, I know things about you and other women, but I have forgiven them. We can get past everything. What do you say?"

Harris stared at her and walked around the office. Her words had hit deep in his heart. He thought about her affair with Caleb. Then, he thought about all the times he had looked the other way when a drug deal happened at Green Valley Trailer Park or being asked not to investigate a Honeycomb dancer being beat up because she held out some trick money from her lowlife pimp. Even worse in his mind, when he took the physical benefits of his position when an attractive female had crossed the line and he had to put her back in place. All of it swirled in his head and he felt his blood begin to boil. He closed his eyes and turned away, partly away from her, and partly because he realized that much of his anger was with himself. She was right, things were as much his fault as they were hers. He turned and looked at Julie.

"You didn't need to be hooking up with that backsliding preacher man. I may have my bad traits and done things that weren't right, but I didn't preach to people about the good book and tell them how to live when he was deceiving them. Bet his flock would have taken a different view of him, if they knew he was in the pews with you after church." Harris seethed and glared at Julie.

Julie looked at him and squinted her eyes. She put her hands on her sides. Her look penetrated his soul and he could feel it.

"I have said I am sorry hundreds of times. I bare my heart to you and asked for forgiveness because I actually love your sorry ass. Just think about all the things you have done to me and the people of Etham. You should be more ashamed of yourself than me about my misgivings. Either you want to be with me or not. This is your choice right here and right now, because I'm tired of all this. This is the only time I'm going to do this and give us a chance. If you are not invested in us, then I'm going to walk away."

Harris took a seat and gripped the leather padded arms of his chair. They eyed each other for several minutes. Harris thought about mean things to say, like maybe she had fallen for Josh because he was Caleb's twin brother or that maybe she would be better suited for working at the Honeycomb than at the hospital. He held back, again noting that he was just as guilty as her. He remembered why he had fallen in love with her years ago: her beauty, both inside and out. She genuinely cared for people and loved helping them. She was good at it. To be honest, she really hadn't changed that much, though she was more callous and protective of herself now. That made him smile because she used to believe everyone was good. She still wanted to, but she was more realistic now. He realized she had stayed with him, even after all the crazy stuff he had done. Her comment about him doing bad things to the people of Etham pierced him deeply, but she was right. He stood up.

"Okay."

Julie's stiff gaze softened, and she leaned her head to one side. "Okay?"

"You're right. We have both done wrong with me being the worst. It's time to get things back on track with us and me. I took an oath for our marriage and for the badge. All, I have failed. I'm ready to make things better." Harris said.

He didn't believe the words he had just uttered. Once again, memories of all the bad things he had done played across his mind like strips of film rolling through an old movie projector. Reel after reel crossed his memory exposing to him his own faults.

Julie ran over and hugged him. Both of them felt right and the bond was reestablished between them instantly.

"You said something about help. What do you need help with?"

A look appeared on Julie's face that Harris didn't like seeing. Something big was getting ready to come out of her mouth.

"You remember Elizabeth Dawn Boyd, the one that you were looking for at the hospital?"

Harris didn't expect to hear that name. Why would she bring her up?

"Yes. I need to talk to her about some things that happened at the trailer park. Nobody knows where she is. Probably better that way. I've heard that some bad people are looking for her. What about her?"

"You're right about it being about that. Some bad people don't need to know where she is. I know where she is."

Harris was shocked by what he had just heard. He sat in his chair again and poured himself a drink.

"You want a drink, honey?"

"No. Don't you want to know how I know?"

"I figure you're going to tell me and you did say you needed help." He gulped down the bourbon.

Julie took a breath and sat in a chair facing Harris' desk. All of sudden she felt like Harris was the judge and she was confessing. That made her feel nauseous again when she was talking about her affair with Caleb.

"She's at Kristol Engel's place."

Harris stood up and went around to Julie. His eyes locked on hers.

"Why? How do you know that? When did you know that?"

Fear ran through Julie as she slowly stood up. She put her hands around his waist and looked up at him.

"Remember the oaths you talked about. I took one as a nurse." She said as she thought about the last line she had memorized years earlier.

May my life be devoted to service and to the high ideals of the nursing profession.

Harris stared at her for a moment and then smiled. He put his arms around her.

"Yes, you did and you are an awesome nurse. I can imagine you wanted to help her and make sure she heals."

"You do know me. I took her to Kristol's because I helped her out once and figured she could hide Elizabeth Dawn."

"Kristol Engel?"

"Yes, why? Is that bad?"

"Well, I'm not sure."

What Sheriff Bell did know was that Kristol Engel was connected to G.W. Fields. She was like a daughter to him and he had set her up pretty good at the resort. He also knew that Fields was bad to the core. The man had been a thorn in his side and was the reason he had taken a turn to corruption, but that didn't mean Kristol was dirty or that Fields was even involved with the dealings at the Honeycomb. It was obvious, though, that despite any protections Fields might provide, Elizabeth Dawn would be found and then there would be trouble for everyone involved, Kristol Engel included.

"Honey, I want to help her and the Boyds leave town to start a new life, to go somewhere and start fresh. Please help me get them out of there. It's the right thing to do. Please, Harris. They need our help. We can drive them to an airport, buy them tickets, and give them a new start."

Field's face crossed his mind. The logistics of the plan would be easy but keeping it quiet was a whole different story. Pondering the idea and execution consumed him as he looked at Julie.

"Okay, I'll help. You go home and look up some tickets to wherever. I'll go up and check on Elizabeth Dawn to see if she is okay. Talk to Kristol. Make some things happen."

"She's okay. I was just up there."

Julie decided not to tell Harris about Josh being at Kristol's house. Right now, was not a good time. She hoped Josh was not there.

"I'll feel better about all this if I see her in person. I need to talk to Elizabeth Dawn Boyd."

37

Kristol put the rest of the groceries away as Josh looked out the front door. The orange sky had already turned to a dark purple and shadows danced with the wind singing along the tree line.

"Hope she was not followed. No matter what, I will protect you and Elizabeth Dawn from anybody that comes up that driveway." Josh said as he walked to the kitchen window and looked out back.

"My knight in shining armor." Kristol teased with a smile and wink, "But I'm a strong damsel and not in distress, I will be fine and Elizabeth Dawn will be, too. Who knows, maybe, it might be me saving your skin at the end of all this."

"Maybe, I wouldn't be mad about it."

They both laughed. Elizabeth Dawn was asleep on the couch.

"I can at least help put the stuff away, and maybe get started on supper." Josh poked through the bags looking for some items to slap together. Hamburger meat for burgers and potatoes to cut up for French fries; eat your heart out, Fudd's!"

"You're a better chef than me. I'm sure of that. As you can see from the time you have been here, I don't cook much. Being a single woman doesn't add incentive to cook for myself."

Josh began washing the potatoes and heating a skillet. He laughed.

"When do you think Elizabeth Dawn will be ready to travel? You think Julie will come through with helping her. It's a big risk for her."

"Not sure, it depends on her wanting to heal up. The mind has a lot to do with it. As far as Julie, that could go either way. At the end of the day, she is still married to Sheriff Bell. I don't care much for him. Many in Etham, the good and bad, don't like him. He will have a tough time in the next election. Then again, Julie may surprise us all and be a woman of her word."

Kristol picked her phone up and texted. A beep followed.

"I have to trust my gut and maybe everything will work out. Julie said she'd get the word to Olivia and Randall. I'm sure they will be ready to leave and excited to have their daughter back. Now, back to this business about you cooking for me and making a good woman out of me."

Kristol's giddiness was contagious causing a smile to beam across his face. Josh lassoed a quick fist pump from Kristol and followed with a light drum roll on the countertop. Both erupted in giggles.

"What are you two going on about, in here?" Elizabeth Dawn had gotten up and caught the sense of excitement, but not quite sure of the occasion. An aching smile reminded her of the damage to her face. She held herself back, but just enough to not hurt so much.

"Julie said she will get word to Beatrice, at the library. She's agreed to talk to your parents. She will tell them to be packed and ready to go when you're healed up." Kristol said.

Elizabeth Dawn hugged her arms close to herself and then held her mouth with warm hands. Soft laughter soon turned to tearful joy. Kristol looked at her with stoic eyes thinking about Elizabeth Dawn leaving. She looked over at Josh. He was looking out the living room window again.

"You two get down in the basement."

"Babe, what's wrong?" Kristol asked.

"Just do it, now! Take the rifle with you."

Kristol didn't argue and fled with Elizabeth Dawn down to the basement. She trusted Josh, but thought he was in over his head with whoever was driving up the driveway. Hiding in the basement was the best course of action for Elizabeth Dawn and she wouldn't hesitate to use the rifle, if needed. Julie had been followed, and now things were going to get messy.

Josh grabbed Kristol's .357 that was resting on the countertop and looked through the window. He thought he had seen movement and again wondered if it was possible that someone had followed Julie. There were a lot of eyes in town, and he figured most were somehow connected. He hoped he was wrong, but at this point, who knew? Josh went to the back door and checked out the most vulnerable entrance.

Josh barely heard the well-oiled hinges of the unlocked front door slowly open and turned to see Dave Clemmon's incomplete set of teeth. He was holding an antique .44 six-shot revolver. It was pointed straight at him and he had clicked back the hammer for good effect as Josh stared at him.

"Well, looky here. Isn't this a nice surprise? You go ahead and put that pistol down in there. Walk this way, nice and easy."

Damn, I must have left the front door unlocked after Julie left. Distracted by cooking for Kristol.

———

Randall Boyd slowed to a stop about 200 feet past the turn into Kristol's place. He hadn't pulled in due to a familiar car that was parked just up the gravel driveway. It belonged to Dave Clemmons. He turned off his headlights and backed up. He parked his truck to block Dave from being able to leave. He wasn't sure what Dave's presence meant, but Beatrice had been too close of a friend to lead him into a trap. Besides, wasn't he already trapped? Something didn't make sense about it, but whatever was going on he felt he was close to seeing his daughter. He decided to approach from the concealment of a small, wooded knoll at the side of the house.

All was quiet on the property, which meant everyone was inside the house. Despite the sun almost being gone, Randall observed the place from the wood line about twenty-five feet from the side of the house. He couldn't see through the lighted windows because of the curtains but was sure they could see him if he approached from the wrong angle and every side of the yard was wide open.

If he remembered right from when old man Burton lived there, he was adjacent to the side that had a bedroom. If he could make it to the side of the house without being seen, he could sneak around the back and try to get a feel for where everyone was at. It would be a sprint.

Here we go.

Randall charged at his target with gritted teeth and to his surprise there was no response. Stooping to be out of view of the bedroom window, he tried to quiet the pounding of his heart and slow his breathing. The charge was a small victory and he wasn't sure if that was a good thing or bad.

———————

Dave's voice carried through the house and into the basement. Elizabeth Dawn watched as Kristol held the first part of an unrecognizable sentence in and then changed it to a hushed, "Be quiet...get behind those boxes." Once the younger woman was in place, Kristol eased off the lights. The only light came from underneath the door at the top of the stairs.

"Whatever happens, you've got to stay down here. Understand?"

Kristol's voice was barely audible as she moved up the stairs, but the message was loud and clear. Nausea rushed through Elizabeth Dawn, as she trembled in the dark. She had been so close to freedom, but now Dave had found her.

She wondered what he would do to her. He had slapped her around several times and nearly killed her last time. And what about these people? They had tried to get her away and now they would probably be killed. He was here, after all and probably holding a gun on Josh. There was no chance he would change his mind. There was no backing out. Either Josh would find a way to get the upper hand or he would die and so would Kristol. So would she, not that she cared anymore. Elizabeth Dawn knew that death would be better than going back with Dave. She hoped he would kill her if she was destined to go with him.

Suddenly, a thump came from the small basement window close to the ceiling. A shadow outlined the front it and stooped down to peek in. Elizabeth Dawn didn't move and stared at the window. The dark figure stopped and then continued around the house.

"Dad?" Elizabeth Dawn covered her mouth, trying not to give anything away. She thought about pushing past Kristol, who was still at the top of the stairs, but stopped. Bursting upstairs would only make things worse. She was scared for her father, if that was him.

Her body convulsed, unable to cope with the roller coaster of emotions; twists and turns from hope to loss of hope and now, hope again. Kristol looked down at Elizabeth Dawn and put her finger to her lips by the light of a small flashlight. Elizabeth Dawn willed herself to hold it together, unsure of how much more she could take.

Dave walked around the house while he kept his gun on Josh. He picked up Kristol's .357 from the kitchen floor and put it between his belt and jeans. He only looked away from Josh long enough to take quick glimpses through all the rooms.

"No one else is here." Josh said and watched every move Dave made.

"Shut your stupid trap!" Dave took another turn around the room and poked Josh in the head with his gun. Then, he laughed as he walked back towards the front door. "Why don't you stop lying to me and tell me where the girl is? I will go one step farther. Where is Kristol? I need to talk to her about some things, too, important things."

"What girl? This is my friend Kristol's house and she's not here. She went down to Etham."

"Kristol is here, moron! Her truck is out front and I know Elizabeth Dawn is here, too. You want to know how I know? Because you're a lying sack of shit. I know that they are both here."

A soft squeaking floorboard alerted the men to another presence and the men eased their looks from one another and turned to see Randall Boyd. He had eased in unannounced, listening to the interrogation with a gun pointed at Dave.

"If you move one inch I'll blow you to hell. If you doubt me, go on try me." Randall said.

Dave didn't believe him, but he wasn't as stupid as he let on. He kept his gun on Josh as his mind raced to determine how to get back the upper hand. He knew he would. Randall Boyd was no killer; he was a pushover. Dave figured he would kill Josh and then he would do bad things to the girl in front of Randall. And then he would kill them. Kristol would have to sit by and watch. Heck, he might just go ahead and shoot her too because she deserved it. He'd even track down the old Boyd hag, Olivia, and the librarian, Beatrice, and kill them both. He was sick of the whole game. He would kill all these people and leave this god-forsaken place for good just to get it over and done with. He needed to move on.

Dave cackled back to Josh. "Now, why in the world would Randall Boyd be here? And pointing a gun at me to boot?"

"I don't know, but if I were him," Josh looked at Randall and back to Dave, "I'd just shoot you right now. Then, put another bullet in your head for good measure."

"There doesn't have to be any shooting," Randall offered. "Dave, you put the gun on the table and leave. Don't you ever mess with my family again. That is a warning."

Dave grinned and gave Josh a wink and looked back around. "Sure thing, Randall." Dave threw his gun on the floor away from himself and Josh. "You've got me. I'm just going to leave."

"Careful, Randall, he's got another gun." Josh pushed the coffee table into Dave, but he was ready and stepped away, minimizing the force of the table. Dave lifted Kristol's .357 from his belt for a point-blank shot at Randall's head and two shots echoed throughout the house.

The shots were followed by silence. Kristol crept up from the basement with the rifle in her hands. The scene took her breath away.

"Is Dave dead?" Kristol asked the question but knew the answer from the way he was lying on the floor in an increasing pool of blood.

She eyed both Josh and Randall with a semi-automatic pistol in his hand. Initially, she thought that he didn't have it in him, but apparently the old man had grit after all. She didn't know what to say with Dave dead in her living room.

"So, what do we do now?" Kristol said and leaned down to look at the bullet holes in Dave's trunk.

Elizabeth Dawn ran upstairs and was stunned to see Dave dead on the floor, but more so by her father being at the door with a gun in his hand. Her bad dream had ended. It was dead on the floor and bleeding out. Relief filled her body as she ran and hugged her father.

"It's over Elizabeth Dawn. He won't hurt you anymore. Nobody will ever hurt you again." Randall said hugging her as tight as he could.

Tears ran down his daughter's cheeks. This was the end to her hell, and she rejoiced. Knowing her father had ended it was bittersweet.

"Randall, I know this is a great time for you both," Josh broke in, "but you and Elizabeth Dawn need to find Olivia and get as far away as possible. Julie Bell is going to help. Just get out of here and don't come back. Me and Kristol will clean this up."

Kristol looked at Josh. Her eyes scanned the room and looked at the reunited family. She thought about her Mom and Dad. Then, about the good times that they had until they had been taken from her. As she looked at Elizabeth Dawn, she thought about herself. Something clicked within her, something deep.

"Yes, both of you get out here as fast as you can. Like Josh said, we'll clean this up."

Josh nodded his head. He pushed Randall and Elizabeth Dawn out to the porch. Kristol didn't follow. She kneeled and looked at Dave's body and thought about what to do next.

"Get Olivia and get as far away from Etham as possible. Like I said, we'll take care of Dave, so don't worry. Your family has suffered enough. Don't ever come back to Etham, at least until all this is worked out."

"I'm happy that you are back with your family." Kristol said as she stepped out onto the porch.

"Thank you both." Elizabeth Dawn said and tearfully hugged Kristol and Josh.

"You are both good souls for helping my daughter. I know I pulled the trigger to end this, but you both made this miracle happen. I can't begin to show my thanks. If you ever need anything, I'm your man." Randall said and then escorted his daughter down the moonlit driveway towards his truck.

The Boyds left Josh and Kristol to somehow work through the mess on the living room floor. Dave had underestimated Randall's resolve and it cost him everything.

38

Four bells chimed from the wall clock as they stared red-eyed at Dave Clemmons' lifeless body in silence. The incessant ticking kept pace with the thumping in their chests. They wanted to talk more about what had happened but were too exhausted from the trauma of the night's events. The shooting connected them even more now, but each one looked at the situation differently.

"I can't believe Dave's dead in my living room. This didn't need to go down like this. Dave should have stopped and Randall should have thought about not pulling the trigger." Kristol said with second thoughts about everything.

"Yes. It is very real. In my opinion, he deserved the bullets. Randall was in the right." Josh said as he hunched over to study the body again.

Dave was stiff and his blood had thickened on the carpet over the hours that had passed. A stench had begun to fill the room and became stronger with the passing of time. The smell was unforgettable and settled over everything, even Josh and Kristol.

"We are going to have to do something. Can't stay up here forever with Dave rotting on the floor." Kristol said and pulled an unopened cigarette pack from the end table drawer.

"A smoke would be nice right now." Josh said.

"I could use more than a cigarette, to be honest. But this will take off the edge. Take one."

Kristol handed him the pack and he fished one out. With a light and draw, he sucked the nicotine in. For some reason he thought of the time he and Caleb had snatched a pack from their aunt's carton when they were in the eighth grade. She had never noticed. Josh chuckled at the memory, then felt bad about laughing.

"We need to call the law, but I don't think it should be Sheriff Bell. We need to call the State Police." Josh said and took a hard draw from his cigarette.

"I don't think we need to call any law. They're not worth a damn, not a single one of them."

Josh didn't like that idea, but he couldn't disagree with that statement with what he had seen. He got up and paced. After circling the body a few times, he went to the living room window and fidgeted the curtains back to look outside.

"Why do you say that? We need to call the law. That's the right thing to do. How else would we handle this?" Josh said.

"We just need to be calm. There are ways to take care of issues like this. It just takes some thinking and knowing the right people."

"Really? Maybe we should find a plastic tarp and a couple shovels, huh?" Josh hoped she was joking, but part of him was feeling her out. Would she really want to do that? There was enough unbothered land to do it if they wanted to, but he couldn't imagine himself burying the body.

Kristol shook her head with a smirk. She got up from the couch and looked at the body on the floor.

"I am going to the bathroom. Please, calm down. We need to keep our heads straight and come up with a solution. Is it okay if I go to the bathroom? If you want to join me, you can. Just turn your head when I'm doing my business. Deal?"

Josh could not help but smile, even with everything that had happened tonight. The smell increased and disrupted their conversation.

"I'll be back in a jiffy." Kristol said and walked to the bathroom.

After the door was shut and locked, she texted.

Need some help. Something crazy has happened.

Minutes passed and no return text. Kristol became frustrated and looked into the mirror. Her reflection caught her off guard. Each face contour pulled her deeper into contemplation. She had not noticed her face for what must have been five years. It was unrecognizable to her now. It amazed and distressed her. How did this happen? She washed her face and hands.

"You okay in there? Do I need to come watch you?" Josh laughed.

"Yes, I'm fine. Just finishing up. Don't need an audience. Give me a sec."

Kristol looked down at her phone and no reply. Sadness and anger ran through her. It was something she had never been able to deal with before. She looked in the mirror one more time and opened the bathroom door. She lit another cigarette and slouched on the couch.

"What do you think we should do, Josh?"

That was a question that he did not expect. He immediately started to formulate a course of action based on many different emotions that he could not control. He knew that silence was not the right answer.

"We need to call the police. We didn't shoot Dave, but we need to protect Randall Boyd. He came here to save his daughter and it came down to Dave's choice. Above all, we need to protect Randall in my opinion."

Kristol looked at Josh. Her heart pulsed for him and she thought about all the implications of all the possible choices. She didn't want to share all of them with him. Back and forth, thoughts moved in her head. Finally, she came to a way forward.

"Josh, I need to talk to Mr. Fields. He will take care of all this. He has taken care of everything for me before."

The reference to Mr. Fields made Josh think. Seems like he had been brought up a lot in many conversations.

"Why him? What can he do?"

"He has taken care of me and has been like a father to me. Things like this are just problems to him and he is good at coming up with the right things to do. Trust me."

Josh looked at her and studied her eyes. Her demeanor had changed, something he had not seen before. It was as if a totally different person was in front of him. In a second, she projected a different look.

"Alright, we'll call the law. Is that really what you want to do?" Kristol said.

"I think that's the only choice we have."

"Who do you want me to call, Bell and Tullos?" Kristol said and readied her cellphone as Josh thought about that question.

Then, his thoughts turned to how the whole scene looked. Things didn't look right for a self-defense case, if it came to that. Josh grabbed Dave's .44 caliber revolver from the floor and exchanged it with the .357 Magnum pistol in Dave's hand. He took the pistol outside and fired two shots into the air.

39

An eerie quietness blanketed Green Valley Park and gave Deputy Tullos the creeps. The absence of the normal lower-class activities made things appear peaceful and uneasy at the same time. Most of the time there was music blaring, yelling, and county dispatch receiving calls about alleged domestic violence or some crazed addict harassing fellow residents more than usual. That was normal for any night, especially a late Saturday night. Something was not right and his radio being quiet confirmed it. He had never seen or felt this before, even to the point of wondering if everyone was watching him and staying on the downlow for some reason. He scanned the area with focus on the lit areas and then decided to drive down to the circle, which was the center of the trailer park. The same quietness there heightened his anxiety and convinced him that something was going on.

His phone burst to life from the dark silence and startled him as if a ghost had suddenly popped into view. He recognized the number and knew it wouldn't be good, especially at this hour. He answered and listened to the frantic voice at the other end of the line.

"Hello."

The voice on the other end was fast but concise. His eyes widened as he listened.

"You have to be kidding me. That doesn't make any sense. Okay, don't do anything stupid. I'm on my way." Tullos put his cruiser into gear and hit the gas pedal.

Kristol Engel. What the hell?

Wild thoughts ran through Tullos' mind. How would it be handled? Kristol was Mr. Field's protege at the resort. The man adored and protected her as if she was his own daughter. Tullos had only met her formally in Fields' office a few years back. She was a loner, and he didn't mess with her. Nowadays, she managed a lot of stuff at the resort and stayed quiet. But Tullos knew she was a lot more to Fields than a resort manager, significantly more.

Nothing was stirring or moving about as he rounded the curve up to Kristol's house. Kristol's truck was out front, along with Josh Webb's vehicle. Dave's car was parked up from the driveway and somewhat hidden.

This is messed up from all that I'm seeing so far.

Tullos pulled up closer to the house and got out. He gripped his pistol that was still holstered and a flashlight in the other. The hairs on his arms stood straight as he walked up to the lit porch. Nothing seemed right and he resisted the urge to call for backup. Once again, quietness draped everything. He knocked on the door, but no one answered. Movement inside caught his attention, which prompted another round of knocks, this time with more authority. Finally, the door opened.

"Deputy, I'm so relieved you came as fast as you could. Everything is a mess. I figured the law can make sense of all this and straighten things out." Kristol said with fake eyes.

Tullos was stunned to see Kristol at the door acting the way she was. She looked at him with wide eyes and nodded her head.

"Did you, now? Well, what's going on? I saw Dave's vehicle down the way. Is he about? And what about Josh Webb? I see his car here, too." Tullos said pointing his flashlight beam at it. He gripped his pistol handle hard.

"I guess you will find out, when you figure things out, Tullos." Kristol said.

"Slow down. First, let's get all the facts. I see a few vehicles in the driveway. Who is all here? I need to figure out what is going on?"

"I'm here." Josh came to the door.

"Josh Webb, why are you up here?"

He eyed Tullos and both felt the friction. They let it go for the moment.

"Kristol invited me up for dinner. She claimed she owed me for helping her when her truck broke down in town."

"That's very interesting." Tullos said as he looked at Kristol.

"No use in hiding anything. C'mon in, Deputy. Get on in here and take a look at Dave Clemmons on the floor dead in my living room. We need to take care of this." Kristol said, stepping aside to let the deputy in.

Tullos could not process Dave being dead on the floor. His eyes widened and his stomach tightened. Words eluded him.

"Dave came up here and started threatening me and Josh. Accusing me of hiding some girl. Somebody named Elizabeth Dawn. I don't know the girl personally. I've heard her name around and that's it. She doesn't have a good reputation." Kristol said and looked at Tullos with intense eyes.

"Yep. We had this piece of trash come in and try to kill us." Josh affirmed.

An uncomfortable moment of silence ensued. The three exchanged looks as if in a poker game. Kristol and Josh decided to stay silent for a moment out of fear and not wanting to incriminate themselves. Kristol eyed Tullos and he looked at her. Mr. Fields popped in his head.

Tullos walked further into the house with his eyes focused on a stiff body in the living room. His attention was heightened. Despite the victim's face turned to the side with a pool of blood seeping from the body onto the carpet, he knew it was Dave Clemmons. The red hair, black t-shirt, and cheap leather boots gave it away. Thoughts of how to handle this situation rushed into his mind. He looked at Kristol as he ran courses of action through his mind.

"Let me look the crime scene over. Both of you just stay where you are at."

"There's no crime scene here." Josh said.

"Need to make sure this is all legal." Kristol chimed in.

"I'll be the judge of that." Tullos said as he walked around the body.

Dave had been shot two times in his front torso by a high caliber firearm. A .44 caliber revolver was still in his hand, and it had not been discharged. Seems like he was caught by surprise and gunned down going toward the front door.

"So, who shot Dave? A lot of things don't look right here. What do you both have to say about all this?"

"I did it. He threatened to shoot both of us. He was trespassing and threatening us. I told him to leave three times. He would not stop harassing us and started towards Kristol to hurt her." Josh said as he handed the .357 Magnum pistol over to Tullos.

"Interesting. You must have got the jump on Dave from the front door judging from the wounds." The deputy inspected the pistol and confirmed that two rounds had been shot.

"I was in the corner next to the window. That piece of trash came at Kristol accusing of hiding a girl and threatened to shoot her. He walked forward to shoot Kristol and I fired."

Kristol sat down on the couch and lit a cigarette. She took a long draw and breathed out smoke through her nose. The wavering tails rose to the ceiling.

"This is crazy, Deputy Tullos." She took another drag from her smoke and continued. "This scumbag came up in my home with a gun threatening us and now he's dead in my living room. Why are we getting accused of anything?"

Tullos eyed both as he continued to examine the body. He felt in charge, even though he wasn't qualified due to his lack of training and experience in things like this. The fact that Dave was on his back and looked as if he had been going toward the front door along with the possible caliber inaccuracies of the wounds caught his attention more as he reviewed his knowledge of bullet wounds from the academy. He stood up from his crouching position and stretched his back.

"I'm not accusing either of you of anything. The truth is, I believe what you're saying, but the problem is that your story doesn't add up. Kristol, you must have been at the front door for him to come at you like Josh said. Plus, the wounds don't really correspond to the caliber of weapon that Josh says he shot him with. As such, you both could do a lot of hard time for this."

Kristol thought of every reason not to have Tullos up at her house and tell him to go to hell. She regretted calling him. Things had to be kept in order at this point and she knew it. Josh thought about explaining what really had happened. Hard to explain a dead man in a puddle of blood on the floor in any case and keep Randall's name out of it. Kristol looked at Josh. Then, Josh looked at Tullos.

"I'm going to ask something that you both need to come clean with." Tullos said with a smirk on his face.

"Go right ahead. I guess we don't have anything to lose now, according to you, deputy dog." Kristol said.

Tullos looked at her with a mean look. He knew he needed to keep his cool in this situation.

"Was this girl Dave talked about ever here?" Tullos said and thought about how hard they had been looking for her.

Josh and Kristol studied the deputy and considered what to say. Kristol went first.

"Like I said, I have heard of her. That is all I know about her. She has never been here. What's the big deal about this girl? Did she kill someone or talk too much?" Kristol put out her cigarette in an ashtray on the coffee table.

"Things are messed up around here. She's part of another investigation I'm involved in. That's all I can say right now," Deputy Tullos said.

"What do you mean? Another investigation? How are things messed up? Is Caleb's murder somehow part of the messed-up things?" Josh said.

"It all depends on how things pan out. I'm going outside. You both need to come with me."

Tullos walked out of the house and up to Dave's vehicle with his flashlight. Both windows were open with trash scattered all around inside. A small notepad was in the passenger seat. He opened it. It had dates and times of multiple transactions that Tullos was familiar with due to his police work and included dates of when he dropped certain named females off at cabins in the resort. As he watched Kristol and Josh, he carefully slipped the notepad into his pants pocket. He knew this was insurance for any situation.

"Deputy, I need to call someone. Do you mind?" Kristol said with her hands on her hips.

"Who would you be calling right now?" Tullos said and then it dawned on him as he said it.

"Go right ahead and make your call."

"Thank you, Deputy Tullos."

Tullos thought about the consequences of not letting her call, but his decision to go ahead and let her make it made him feel a lot better. At the moment, he was confused about everything. Then, thoughts of normal legal procedure came to mind. A struggle erupted within him but was overpowered by self-preservation and the natural order of things as he knew them in Etham. He thought about and weighed out what was happening with his well-being and him being sheriff one of these days in his mind.

Josh watched Kristol walk away from them. Her being allowed to make a phone call during all this shocked him, but his attention was brought back to the reality of Dave being dead and Tullos questioning them.

"I'm just going to examine the body once more. Josh, follow me up to the house. I need to ask you some more questions when I'm done."

Josh looked at Tullos and held his tongue as they both walked back to the house. Kristol pulled her phone from her back jeans pocket and dialed Mr. Fields. Within two rings, he answered.

"Are you okay?"

"It's bad here. Need some help cleaning this up. It's real messy." Kristol said with a big breath.

"Tell me. No matter how bad it is."

"Okay. Dave Clemmons came up here looking for the prostitute he beat up. That's some bad business in my opinion. A business that is bad for everybody. He was up here to find the girl and kill anybody that got in the way. I don't know how Randall Boyd found out about his daughter and Dave being up here. Randall came in and shot Dave. He's dead with his blood covering my living room. I figured someone needed to shoot him but didn't think it would be Randall. Tullos is up here acting all big. I called him. Josh Webb is here and taking responsibility with self-defense of me and him. I need help."

"Don't say anything, just listen. Stay with the story of Dave coming up there threatening and getting crazy. I'm very surprised Josh Webb is there, but we can talk about that later. Listen to Deputy Tullos for now. He'll lead you in the right direction. This all needs to be settled discreetly and quickly. Etham is getting enough unwanted attention as it is with Caleb Webb being killed. Get Josh to play his part. Do you understand what I'm telling you?"

"Yes, I do. I appreciate you."

"I'll help you. I know how this will play out. Listen to me, my Hummingbird. Things will be fixed. Just trust me."

"Okay, I trust you. Goodbye."

Kristol walked back into the house to the living room and Josh stepped up to her. Tullos was leaning down examining the pistol in Dave's hand and his wounds. With precision, he used his cellphone to take pictures and then looked up at Kristol as she walked over.

"What did Mr. Fields have to say about this?" Tullos said and continued taking pictures with his cellphone.

"What makes you think it was Mr. Fields?" Kristol said and eyed him.

"It is my job to know everything that's going on around here. Don't lie to me about it not being Mr. Fields, because I know better. I know what is going on in Etham."

"I guess I will tell you since you are so sure of yourself. He told me that you are the law and do exactly what you say."

Tullos stood up and looked around. His face glowed.

"It's good that you talked to Mr. Fields. Everything here seems to point to Dave coming onto your property with a gun and threatening you. Then, he was shot by Josh in self-defense of you and him, but I have my doubts about that."

Josh's heart skipped a beat. Kristol stared at Tullos as he continued talking.

"From my preliminary observations, he was shot in the front torso by a different caliber weapon than the firearm that you say you shot him with. Ballistics would have to confirm or deny that. Different calibers is a problem for any investigating officer and jury. I'll throw out that I know Dave carried a .44 revolver, just pointing that out as a fact that can be confirmed. If he was on this property threatening you in your face, how did he get shot going towards the front door? I do understand that Josh says he was in the corner and shot him as he was moving toward you, Kristol. Seems to me there's more to the story than you both have told me, but it does not really matter to me. Probably should matter to you both. One thing is certain, something is not right here and in my opinion, both of you are going to do some time for this unless you both start talking to me."

"What the hell are you talking about?" Josh yelled.

"Keep that volume down. Understand who you're talking to and what's going on here. You talk when I say you can talk." Tullos said.

Josh decided to listen to the nonsense. He looked over at Kristol, who had zoned out. Silence was the best course of action to take at this point.

"Just for your consideration, the dead man on the floor, who was supposedly shot by you, was being investigated for the death of your brother, Caleb. Strong evidence points to him and I'm convinced of it and the rest of the world will agree. I'm not sure how you view things, but it does seem that justice has already been served for your brother. You or somebody, shot the man that killed your brother. Don't you agree?"

Tullos smiled. His grin and wide eyes made Josh feel crazy. In an instant, he was torn between being happy and scared due to facing charges for a killing that he didn't commit, but now wished he had. Knowing that the man that had killed his brother was dead in front of him made everything right. He wished he had pulled the trigger.

Josh looked at Kristol who had a troubled look on her face. Her thoughts and the words Tullos were saying didn't sync. Josh and her eyes connected and each sensed similar feelings. All of it meshed between them. They needed to let this play out, until there was an opportunity. Josh and Kristol nodded their heads. They didn't take their eyes off Tullos as he walked towards them.

"We just need to clean all this up. Josh, I need to tell you something." Tullos said.

"Go ahead."

"As I just told you, I've been investigating your brother's murder aggressively since it happened. A few leads came my way and I followed up on them. From the evidence I've discovered, Dave is the man that shot Caleb up at the resort cabin, there may be another person involved. I can't be sure."

Josh wavered and kept himself standing. All eyes connected. Kristol looked at Tullos with mixed feelings. She could not believe what Tullos was saying.

"Another person? Are you sure of that? I want the truth. Don't lie to me." Josh said.

"It is true. I pieced it together with evidence last night. So, Dave has paid for his crime in my opinion like I said earlier. Don't you think so?"

Josh paced back and forth. Things swirled in his mind. All of it pieced together with what Tullos had revealed.

"That dirt bag." Josh said as he kicked the body.

"Now, now. Don't let your anger take over. Justice has been served and he's dead as a doornail." Tullos said.

"You got any idea who the other person might be?" Josh said.

Deputy Tullos put his hands on his gun belt. As he scanned the room, he looked for anything out of the ordinary."

"Nope. Nothing definite. Be happy you have the trigger man."

Josh nodded his head. Thoughts engulfed Kristol. Too many things that she had heard and seen did not make sense to her. Now, a dead body was in her living room.

"So, what do we need to do now, Deputy? We need to make sure that everything is taken care of correctly. Don't you think, Deputy?" Kristol asked.

"Things need to be cleaned up. No use in making this a big thing. Etham doesn't need the publicity and you both don't need the charges. Dave was a drain on society and a murderer. He killed Caleb and tried to kill you both. We just need to do away with him without any other trouble." Tullos said with arrogance.

"I agree. I can't believe the man that killed my brother is dead in front of me."

Tullos walked up to Josh and patted his shoulder. Pain pulsed within Josh. Revenge and fulfillment mixed with sadness of another human being killed ran through his veins.

"Don't we need to call the coroner and make this all legal like?" Josh said with wide eyes.

"No need to do all that. Who would claim his body and attend a funeral? He's a drug-head pimp with no family. Plus, if I call this one in, there will be a lot of paperwork for nothing. Let's just take the body to a place I know. He doesn't deserve a proper burial, anyway. He's a murderer, isn't he Josh?"

"Hell, yes. He killed my brother. I'm not doing hard time for that scumbag. He deserves what he got." Josh said and grabbed a cigarette from Kristol's pack. He lit it and put the lighter in his pocket. It felt good to inhale the nicotine. In that moment, relaxation and contentment overcame him.

Kristol looked at both and then thought about Mr. Fields telling her to do what the deputy said. A suspecting look appeared on her face.

I don't trust Deputy Tullos. Never have and never will. He may know some stuff, but he doesn't know everything and the way things should be.

"Okay. Where do we need to go? What do we need to do?" Kristol said.

"Load up the body and we'll all go there. It's not too far away. You're both in on this, right?"

Kristol and Josh nodded their heads. They looked at each other and then back at Tullos.

"Help me load up Dave into the back of Kristol's truck. We need to get this all done before daybreak. Don't need people around here seeing blood leaking out of the truck bed, now do we?" Tullos said as he lit a cigarette.

"My truck? Why my vehicle?" Kristol asked with a look that Tullos didn't like.

Smoke traced his forehead as he smiled. He knew that he had at least one of them hook, line, and sinker.

"Because it's easier to load the body into the back of your truck and easier to spray out the blood with a garden hose. My cruiser is not a suitable choice for that. Plus, nobody would ever stop you or think you were doing anything crazy. Josh and his truck would draw more attention. Don't you agree?"

Kristol nodded her head and turned on a spotlight she had installed on the porch to light up her driveway. She lifted Dave's legs as Josh and Deputy Tullos lifted the upper torso. Josh took deep breaths with a smile in between. Blood made a trail to the vehicle. They loaded up the body and covered it with a tarp that Kristol kept in the back of her truck. They wrapped the body up to contain some of the blood.

"Now what, Deputy?" Kristol said as she put her hands on her hips and breathed heavily.

"First of all, don't think about bringing the guns in the house. You won't need them and I will feel a lot better. Both of you jump in your truck and follow me. That is all you need to know for now. Didn't Mr. Fields tell you to do what I said?"

"Yes, he did up to a point."

Josh looked at Kristol. They didn't say anything to each other. They got into Kristol's truck and turned on the headlights.

"Let's just see where he takes us. There's more to all this. Caleb was killed and I want to find out why and by whom. I don't really think it was the low life in the back of your truck bed and who is this other person he mentioned? Don't you agree?" Josh said.

"I'm sure glad you think like me. I sure don't feel good about leaving the guns at the house." Kristol said as she put her truck in gear.

Tullos made sure to keep their headlights in view. He reached down and picked up his cellphone. A groggy voice answered.

"Damn, you know what time it is?"

"Shut up and listen, Billy. Get your ass up and get over to the mine ASAP. We've got some work to do."

"The mine. Are you kidding me? Who is it?"

"I'm not kidding and you'll find out when you get there. Now, get to moving."

40

Things were quiet as Sheriff Bell pulled up to Kristol Engel's house. The porch spotlight was on. He scanned every detail of the place as he got out. Josh Webb's vehicle was in the driveway. Down the road, Dave Clemmons' car was parked. That was not something he was expecting. The place and feelings he had prompted him to pull out his 9mm as he walked up the stone path to the porch. He noticed a trail of what looked to be blood from the house to the driveway. The front door was cracked open. Bell gripped his pistol tight as he pushed the door open and eased into the house. With precision, he shined his flashlight around and walked in with attention to anything that moved. Slowly, he flipped the light switch. Immediately, he noticed the dark stain on the carpet.

What the hell has happened here? That's a lot of what looks like blood here and outside.

With caution and gun pointed, he went from room to room with no one to be found. He made sure to look behind each door, in every closet, and under the beds. A final look was done in the basement. The backdoor was locked from the inside.

I figured Kristol would be living better, since she was Field's chosen one. Something crazy has happened here.

His focus adjusted back to the blood-stained carpet in the living room. Things started to become clear in his mind. He made one more check of the house to make himself feel better. Nobody was there. With a quick look at the couch next to the front door, he noticed the two pistols and rifle, which he had missed as he came in. Odd for them to be left and gathered up together. Next, the blood pulled him closer. As he looked at it and thought about all the possibilities based on what he saw and what he knew, he deduced what had happened and where he needed to go next. Bell took some pics of the scene with his cellphone camera.

These may come in handy later.

Bell gathered up the guns and took one final look at the living room. Something about the whole scene made his gut churn; whatever happened here wasn't over yet. He got into his SUV and headed down Route 15. The destination pulled him as he pushed the gas pedal harder.

41

Gravel peppered the truck fenders and echoed inside the cab. Along with the rumbling engine, everything else was canceled out. Kristol and Josh looked at each other every mile or so with the dashboard gauges lighting up their faces. Thoughts plagued their minds of where they were being led through the darkness and if they could trust Deputy Tullos in the cruiser in front of them. Josh didn't have to think too hard on that, but he had no choice at the moment. They had turned onto Shank Bottom Road and each mile pulled them farther into the hollow.

"I know where we're going." Josh said as he put his arm out the window and let the cool breeze hit his arm and convinced him that everything was real.

"I've not been up this way before. Where is that bastard taking us?"

Josh looked out the open window and could make out the stream below by the reflection of the moon through the dark trees. He and Caleb had spent many hours fishing in it and trapping crawdads. Their Dad had brought them here when they were very young. He'd let them play in the creek and tell them about the old days when this hollow produced top-grade coal. A scent of pine trickled into his nostrils, and he closed his eyes. Years of memories passed in seconds.

"We're headed to the old McCreary Mine. Dad used to work it back when coal was booming. It all dried up and this one was the first that went out of operation. It's been abandoned since I was a kid. Perfect place to hide a body."

Kristol bit her lip as she watched the deputy's tail lights. She knew there were rumors of people disappearing around the county and never seen again. That's the kind of thing you expect in a movie, or maybe in some faraway place. But here in Etham? Tullos' brake lights lit up and he turned the cruiser onto a side road and stopped at a gate. It automatically opened.

"Damn, he must have a remote opener with unlimited access. Something must be important down there." Kristol said as she followed Tullos.

Josh nodded his head and looked through the back window. Under the light of the moon, Dave's body moved under the tarp as they hit a couple of ruts. Had he really killed Caleb? At this point, the shooting of Caleb all pointed toward him. The fact that Dave showed up at Kristol's house ready to shoot everyone down was pretty good evidence, too. But Tullos had mentioned someone else possibly being involved. Who would that be? Billy Dalton, perhaps, or someone else? Whoever it was would be a crucial piece of the puzzle and he felt the deputy was purposely holding back on the name. Why?

Deputy Tullos pulled up to the entrance of the mine next to a weathered coal tipple and kept his headlights on. Josh thought back to the days when he'd watch the coal drop from the tipple into the railroad cars, followed by a dark cloud of dust. The tipple seemed like an iron dinosaur, ferocious, and at the same time mesmerizing. It was no more than a fossil now, frozen in time. Tullos got out and motioned Kristol to pull her truck up next to a rusted old rail cart.

"I guess this is the place." Kristol said as she walked toward the end of the truck bed with a flashlight.

"Yeah, this is definitely the place." Josh said as he walked in the same direction as her.

Both looked at each other through the flashlight glow, when they got to the end of the truck bed. Then, they stood still.

"This place will work nicely for old Dave. He doesn't deserve a proper burial. What do you think, Josh? He shot your brother down in cold blood." Tullos said, fighting back a smile as he walked up.

"I know you said that and say the investigation points toward that, but what evidence do you have? That piece of dirt doesn't deserve anything in my book, but I want to know for sure he shot my brother down. Who is the other person you mentioned?"

Tullos put his hands on his gun belt and then took out a cigarette. He lit it with an old flip-top lighter. Smoke spewed out of his nostrils. The end of the cigarette glowed in the darkness.

"Dave was the trigger man for sure. We have people that say he was up that way doing no good and got too involved, like he did at Kristol's place. He always had an out-of-control temper. I've arrested him a few times and always on some hot-headed crap that normal people don't do."

"From what I have seen, I agree. What about the other person?" Josh said and his teeth glowed from the glare of the flashlight.

"Like I said. I don't have anything on him."

"Him? So, you know the other person is a male?"

Tullos stopped and the two men locked eyes waiting for the other to make the next move.

"I didn't say that. I said I thought there was another person possibly involved. I don't have any more to provide than that. That information comes from an unreliable informant. There's not enough to go on."

Josh looked at the deputy and opened the truck bed. Blood ran out onto the ground. Kristol thought about the words Tullos had said about loading and washing out the truck bed.

"I guess he's the guy that killed my brother and he needs to go away. Just like he wanted Elizabeth Dawn to go away when he was looking for her at Kristol's place. I do have a question for you, Deputy." Josh said.

"Okay, sure. What do you want to know?"

"It's the same question I asked before. What's the evidence you have on Dave for killing my brother; other than being a crazy hot-headed psychopath? I just need to know to make my mind right on all this."

Tullos walked back and forth. His mind drifted towards past days he didn't want to remember. He looked towards the mouth of the mine and then back towards them.

"Okay, listen. We've been investigating a prostitution ring going on in Etham."

"Yeah, I know about that, but what does that have to do with...."

"Your brother had been snooping around. We believe he was trying to help some of the girls. We also know old Dave here was involved in it. Rumor is he was one of the strong arms. I think he caught your brother trying to help one of the girls escape and shot him. And something else I realized tonight back at Kristol's adds something new. We got the forensic report back last week that described the slugs that were in your brother. Want to guess what caliber?"

Josh chewed on the deputy's words and remembered the gun Dave had been waving around. Things connected in his head.

".44 caliber?"

"Bingo. So, we may not have everything we need, but I'd say we have a preponderance of evidence. Don't you think so?"

He made sense, but Josh's gut was telling him there was more. He began to ask again about who the other involved person might be. If the Tullos knew about the trafficking and about Caleb's part, then he must have an idea of who else was involved. But headlights flashed the three and the roar of an engine grew louder as it pulled through the gate. They all turned to see who it was. The engine stopped as the door opened. Tullos shined the flashlight and Billy Dalton stepped out.

"Tullos, why the hell is he here? He's probably as deep into everything as Dave was. Maybe he is the other person involved in Caleb's murder?" Josh said as he postured his body.

"Easy, Josh. Billy's here to help get rid of Dave. He's my informant and not the other person involved."

Billy bit a piece of his fingernail and spit it out as he walked forward. Tullos kept the flashlight on him and continued, "Now, we are all in this together. We are all going to clean this up and be done with it. Everyone understand?" Deputy Tullos looked at them all, one by one looking for buy in, but the fluttering wings in his gut was all Josh could stand.

"No, I'm out. We've got to report this and do things right. Especially with that ass around," Josh pointed at Billy, who sneered back with a slight bobble of his head.

"You're nothing but a dead man, Webb," Dalton snorted.

"Shut up, both of you. Now, we are going down into that mine shaft and disposing of Dave's carcass. We've crossed the legal lines and there's no turning back. If either of you cause any more trouble you'll be joining Dave. Yes, you too Billy. Capiche?" Tullos said.

Josh muttered the f-word through his clenched teeth as he stepped away. He looked at Kristol and rubbed his head, hoping to find some kind of support in bailing out of this situation. He was disappointed.

"Josh, I know this is jacked up, but we've got to follow this through. I don't want to go to jail, not for something I didn't do. Not for that piece of trash." Kristol cupped Josh's face in her hands. "You don't need to go to jail for it either. Look, we can't change what's been done. We'll have to live with all this either way, no use in doing that in prison."

She was right, the only way to get through this was to get it done and the sooner the better. The problem was, he figured, they weren't planning on him getting through it anyway. He was going to have to play along with it and hope for the best. He turned back to Tullos.

"Okay, let's just do it and get it done, but Kristol stays out here. If I don't come out of that mine with you and Dalton, then she can get the hell out here." Josh said.

Kristol started to interject, but Josh held up his hand. She knew he wouldn't let her go in the mine, but she felt she needed to protest.

"That's fine with me. You ain't got any reason to think anything bad is going to happen inside the mine. Right, Billy?" Tullos said.

"Yeah, whatever. Let's just do it and be done."

Billy's voice was a growl, and his look wasn't convincing to Josh. The men reached into the truck bed and began to assist Dave on his final journey.

42

Kristol stood under the tipple as the three men pushed the rail cart with its deathly cargo into the mine. She was torn. The events of the last few weeks and hours replayed in her mind. The murder of the preacher and then the arrival of Josh made her uneasy. She wanted to laugh as she remembered almost passing out the first time she saw him. He looked just like Caleb and she thought she was seeing a ghost–perhaps coming back to haunt her. It now seemed funny, but she couldn't laugh because Josh was going down into that mine and wasn't coming back.

She had never meant to fall in love with him. In truth, she had sworn off relationships. Men had always let her down. She learned at a young age that men only wanted one thing and they would do everything in their power to get it. When they got it, they were done with you. It was like when her high school boyfriend finally sweet talked her into sleeping with him. She had been terrified and didn't really enjoy it, but he had been gentle and slow. The next day his attitude towards her had changed, as she would find out to be normal. It had been a switch for them both. For him, he got what he wanted and turned his sights on someone new. For her, it was regret, but the switch awakened something inside her that she couldn't turn off.

College had been a vicious cycle of the same letdowns. No one wanted a real relationship, only a good time. She grew to accept it and eventually to embrace it. But that changed, too, the first time a man slapped her. She had been certain he was Mr. Right and for a while, he lived up to it. In the end, he couldn't handle her doing things on her own or telling him, "No." It had been a painful lesson; the better a man seemed to be the worse he turned out to be. She also learned that justice wasn't much of a thing for young women, especially when it came to boys with rich parents.

When Kristol went to work in Etham, she swore men off for good. She fell in love with the mountains and hoped to land a full-time position at the end of her internship. She would give her heart and soul to her career and nature. One could spend their whole life studying the intricacies of the Appalachian ecosystem. The small bit she'd already learned had given her great joy. That was it, then; she would be married to her passion.

Of course, that didn't last. One of her fellow interns talked her into getting her first tattoo at one of the local parlors. The artist was a smooth talker and it didn't take long to get her hooked, both on tattoos and his bed. Then, drugs came into the picture. The next thing she knew he was selling her under the guise of making money to buy her drugs. He was pocketing most of it. When she brought it up, he smacked her around.

She left him at the same time her internship ran out. She didn't want to go home and besides, she really loved the mountains. She got a job at the Honeycomb as a bartender hoping that a permanent job would open at the resort trail system. She had told the Honeycomb management she was done selling her body, but she'd be happy to flirt and pour drinks. That was it, nothing more. They agreed due to her beauty. That is how she met the one man who would get her out of her mess. G.W. Fields had come in on business and at the time she didn't really care what kind of business a man like him might have in such a place. He walked directly to the back office, taking no time to look at the girls. When he came out, he stopped in front of the bar and looked her over. Not in lust, but in a sad way, as if he recognized her. She asked if he would like a drink and he just nodded as if his words were lost. She'd learn later how rare that would be. Words were always in good supply with him.

He wanted water, that was it. They chatted for about an hour as she had time between a few customers. No one gave him the usual hard time about not buying any alcohol and no one got on to her about spending too much time talking to a non-payer. He told her he saw his daughter when he looked at her. Samantha died fifteen years earlier in a car wreck on her way home from college. It devastated him and his wife, Becky. She eventually left him and moved away to God knows where. Kristol was the spitting image of Samantha; even laughed in the same way he said.

She already knew that Mr. Fields ran the new resort and was responsible for the trail system. When she said that she had been a university intern there, he got excited. He wondered what she was doing in a shithole like the Honeycomb and she replied she was still trying to figure that out herself. They both laughed, not because it was funny, but because they didn't know how else to react. Kristol began working full time on the trail crew the next day and never looked back.

Since that time, he had looked after her. He even helped get her off the opioids, which wasn't too difficult. Most addicts required medical treatment to get off the drug, but Kristol was one of the luckier ones. She preferred a good drink and an occasional joint. She cleaned up easily enough once she got away from Banetown and the Honeycomb. After a year, she got promoted to a trail supervisor position and then to manager of the Outdoor Recreation Department.

As good as Mr. Fields had been to her, he could never erase the bad taste men had left in her. He was a father figure, so that was different. But as much as she cared about the man, she knew he was involved in some shady dealings. She learned in time that she was no angel herself. It's a tough life and a girl had to do what a girl had to do, especially in a world run by power-hungry men.

As such, she did what was needed and only that. True, some had suffered, but she couldn't be blamed for that. People had a responsibility to look after themselves if they couldn't then that was on them. She had risen from a bad situation and felt others could do the same. Kristol thought about Elizabeth Dawn. The girl had gotten herself into a bad situation and had no one to blame but herself. Now, she was fighting to make things right, and whatever the cost might be to Kristol and the business, she could certainly respect the girl. She wished her the best going forward and that was the truth.

As for relationships, she had renewed her commitment to swear off men. Besides, the single life suited her. She could come and go as she pleased, and that made her feel secure and happy. She could run the business without answering to a man.

When she first saw Josh that day when her truck broke down, she thought she had seen a ghost, Caleb's ghost. In her mind, he'd be in his right to come and haunt her. Caleb had reached out to her for help and she had betrayed him. Not that she meant to, but rather she had to. Seeing Josh had frightened her, at first. Maybe that is why she let down her guard. Maybe, that is why she couldn't help herself? She only wished now that she had never gotten involved; that she had never fallen in love with him. Then it would be easy to just walk away, but it was too late now.

A car pulled softly through the gate that had opened automatically nearly an hour before. She hadn't realized before, but the first light of day had come, and she could see who was coming. She crossed her arms into a self-hug and smiled as she walked to the car. Mr. Fields got out frantically, but calmed himself when he saw she was alright.

"Thank God, Kristol, I was worried sick. How did you get wrapped up into all this?"

"It's been wild, but thanks for coming. I thought I was going to have to wait out here by myself."

The old man's shoulders softened and he let out a slow breath. His face relaxed.

"Well, I wouldn't make my little Hummingbird do such a thing, could I? How long have they been in the mine? Did Josh go in there alive, too?"

"Yes, he did. It's been about twenty minutes. G.W., I'm so sick about all of this. I don't want Josh to die."

The old man looked at her with a bit of amusement. "You really like him, huh?"

Kristol blushed and felt silly for being embarrassed, but he knew about her resolve to stay away from relationships. She also felt ashamed for feeling silly. Josh was in that mine with no possible likelihood of coming out.

"It's unfortunate, it really is. I was hoping Josh might come around, perhaps understand what we are doing. We've already done so much for Etham."

Kristol nodded, trying her best to hide her doubt. "Yes, but it's at a heavy price."

"What's bothering you, Kristol? Yes, there's been a price, but there always is with progress."

Kristol sat against the side of the car, fidgeting with a piece of grass in her hands. A small sliver of the sun peeked over the ridge warming her neck, teasing her with the hope of a new day. She certainly understood that progress came at a price, but it was much higher than she cared for. If not for the grace of the man standing in front of her, she'd be part of the payment. She had accepted that and even learned to sleep at night. The alcohol helped. Something new had factored into the equation and that was the man down in that mind shaft and the love she had for him.

"G.W., I want Josh to come out of there and if he does, I'm going to leave Etham."

"Kristol, my sweet Hummingbird, surely you know you can't do that. Right? We've come a long way and you have played a vital role in it. You've got to see it through."

"No, I've made up my mind. Josh has given me back my perspective of right and wrong. I'm getting out.

"I can't let you do that, Kristol. What would Josh do if he found out, if he comes out of that mine?"

A pistol blast echoed out from the mine shaft, interrupting the conversation and was quickly followed by a second. The two squatted down and fixed themselves on the opening, pondering whether to dive for more cover or head down to investigate. They opted to watch cautiously from the other side of the car.

43

Metal wheels ground and squeaked as Tullos, Billy, and Josh pushed the rusted steel mine cart along the tracks. Musty air greeted them as they progressed through the mine. All of them dug their heels into the ground and pushed forward with deep grunts, while Tullos held a flashlight in one hand. Josh thought that the heavy iron cart was from the 1920s and was just the right size to haul a body.

I'd bet that a lot of bodies had been hauled in it. Damn, it's heavy and hard to push.

With each step, Josh's heart thumped faster. He war-gamed his next move to save his life and Kristol's. Uneasiness about the two behind him plotting his death pulsed in his mind. They moved deeper into the mineshaft with flashlight beams bouncing here and there.

"Bet you don't know a damn thing about what is really going on around here?" Tullos yelled out as he half pushed the cart.

"He thinks he knows everything. Uppity college professor and all, thinks he knows everything." Billy added to the barrage of insults between deep breaths.

"I don't know a damn thing like you say. Why don't you educate me or maybe you don't know anything your damn selves?"

Billy gritted his teeth and pushed harder. Tullos just laughed.

"You better know who you're talking to, boy. If you don't, you'll be dead quicker than you will be at the end of this trip." Billy yelled.

"Now, now, Billy. Don't be lying to Josh. Mr. Fields wants all of us to come out of this shaft. He has a plan."

Josh gripped the cart hard and dug his fingers into the rusted metal. He pushed his heels into the gravel.

Did he hear what he heard?

Each step fueled his anger more. Sweat poured down his forehead. He could not hold back.

"Fields? How does he call the shots for you, lowlife scum?"

"I told you to shut that mouth of yours." Billy said.

They pushed forward inch-by-inch. Their chore became easier when the tunnel sloped down. After another twenty-five feet, a vertical shaft appeared with the help of a flashlight beam.

"We're here. Get on to dumping Dave into his final resting place." Tullos said and lit a lantern that was hanging from a shaft beam. The cavern lit up and shadows danced on the rock walls.

"Before we get to dumping, tell me more about what I don't know starting with Mr. Fields and who shot my brother. Why not since you are going to kill me anyway?"

"Josh, you're a fool. All your education and you being gone for years has made you real stupid." Tullos said as he lit a cigarette and turned the lantern towards Josh and Billy.

"I'm stupid in many ways, but smart in others. Tell me who killed my brother. I am smart enough to know you're going to put a bullet in my head soon, so let me die knowing the truth. How about it?"

Grins appeared on both Tullos' and Billy's face. They looked at each other and nodded their heads.

"So, the professor wants to know the truth. I guess we can give him that before he meets his maker. What do you say, Billy?"

"I'd say let him have it with no holding back. Then again, he don't deserve to know anything, just like his serpent-tongued brother."

Josh's heart pounded hard. He wanted this to end. Still, he wanted to beat the hell out of both of them. Send them to whatever hell they deserve, but he knew that wasn't likely.

"Your brother got to inquiring about the business, maybe by accident or wanting to be a hero. Regardless, he didn't need to be poking around. He paid for it fair and square." Tullos said.

"I need more than that and what about the business. What business?"

"Well, let's get everything out in the open. Caleb tried to be a hero and save messed-up prostitutes that do what they do for whatever reason, drugs or they know nothing else. You know, born into it. They are meant for the business." Tullos said and laughed.

"A sex trafficking gimmick, is that it? That business is the low of the low. Is Fields involved? Caleb would have been against the business, and I know he was trying to combat it in his way."

Tullos and Billy laughed. Their eyes lit up as lantern light reflected off them. Their teeth glowed and the hue of their skin gave them an even more sinister look.

"I don't believe that this dead piece of work in the cart shot Caleb. He didn't have the grit to do something like that. So, who had the balls to do it, Mr. Fields or you Tullos? I'm sure Billy doesn't have the grit to pull any trigger." Josh yelled and tightened his fingers against the cold metal.

Anger radiated from the men's faces. Billy gripped his fists as Tullos put his hand on his pistol and toked his cigarette hard.

"Let's kill this bastard right now." Billy said and took a step toward Josh.

"Not yet. You need his help to throw Dave in the shaft. Get moving. I'll cover you both, so nobody gets any ideas on doing something stupid." Tullos smiled with the cigarette in his lips. Each toke made it glow brighter at the end.

Josh's thoughts and eyes moved around the area trying to figure out his next move. His eyes centered on an old mining pick a few feet from the cart. An idea burst in his mind.

"C'mon Billy. You heard the bossman. Let's get this done, so he can put a bullet in me just like he did Caleb." Josh said and gritted his teeth. His heart beat hard and veins in his forehead raised.

"See Billy. Josh is an educated man. Figures things out real quick like."

Josh looked at Tullos and contemplated how to kill him with his bare hands. Patience and calculation kept his temper in check. Billy laughed and reached down into the cart to get hold of his former partner in crime. Josh leaned down and grabbed Dave's legs. With grunts, they lifted the body out of the cart.

"Boys, don't drop ole Dave. You might hurt him." Tullos said and laughed.

"So, it was you that killed my brother." Josh said and glared at Tullos.

"Does it really matter who killed him?

The idea of Tullos killing Caleb confused him. Yes, he was a henchman, but there was something that didn't seem right with it. Rage raced through him as he thought about all the different people that could have shot his brother.

"Let's get going. We need to get this done." Tullos said and puffed on his cigarette.

Both men laughed. Josh saw his chance to come out of the mine alive. He pushed Dave's body into Billy, which made him fall down. With speed, Josh grabbed the mining pick he had seen earlier close to his foot and slung it towards the lantern. It went out upon impact. Total darkness engulfed the room. Gunshots flashed. Groans followed. Josh ran toward the flashes of the pistol. With all the force he could muster, Josh slammed into Tullos. The gun fell to the ground. Each man struggled for life and was fueled with adrenaline. They rolled on the ground with punches thrown here and there in the darkness. Tullos reached around to find his pistol, due to him beginning to lose energy and momentum. Luck did not shine on him at the moment. Both men got to their feet and tried to figure out where the other was.

Caleb, give me strength and vision right now. I need it. Show me the light. Let me bring justice to all that have wronged you. Revenge is wrong, but it seems right now.

Hard breathing gave Tullos away. Josh ran towards the giveaway sign. He had some bearing on where he was facing and hoped he had made the right decision. With a leap of faith, he slammed into his opponent and Tullos yelled as he fell down the shaft. His yell became fainter with each second until a crashing thud which was followed by silence. Josh breathed heavily and crawled in the opposite direction. With each inch, he felt for the Tullos' flashlight or lantern which he hoped still worked. Finally, his hands found the lantern.

I guess I'm damn glad I had that cigarette at Kristol's.

With a flick of the lighter that he had in his pocket, light radiated from the lantern. Dave was cold as he was when he was wheeled into the shaft. Billy lay in a pool of blood with most of his head plastered against the tunnel wall. Another bullet had ripped through the man's chest. The dark shaft beckoned Josh. He inched to the edge of the shaft and looked down.

"I'm glad you're at the bottom of a hell that you created. You're in the same hell you created on earth, darkness. By the way, my gut tells me Mr. Fields pulled the trigger on Caleb. He's going to pay just like you did."

Josh leaned down and pushed Billy and Dave into the shaft. Their weight was deceiving. He sat down and breathed hard.

"They helped create this hell, so they should enjoy it themselves. To hell with them, too."

Josh took a deep breath and stood up with the lantern in hand. He took quickened steps towards the mine shaft entrance. Thoughts of Kristol pushed him harder. He had to get to her. She was unprotected and amongst evil at the surface.

Light from the end of the shaft made him run faster towards it. Every muscle in his body hurt, but the thought of Kristol made him push without thought to physical pain. Each step made him breathe with more intensity. Light welcomed him and he embraced it. Caleb seemed to guide him to the light as he pushed forward closer to Kristol.

44

A sharp pain pulsed violently on his right side as Josh made his way to the opening of the shaft. It occurred that a rib or two may have been broken in the fight with Tullos, but he hoped they were only bruised. He slipped the deputy's pistol into the back of his pants and stepped out of the shaft. He stopped to catch his breath and let his eyes adjust to the sunlight. The cool fresh air was a welcome feeling and brought a promise of relief. It was short lived. He scanned up the gravel path to the parking lot to find Kristol. She was not alone. A familiar figure stood at her side, dressed in a business suit, a matching fedora, and smoking a pipe. Mr. Fields stood with Kristol and told her everything was going to be alright. The words of Deputy Tullos from inside the mine played again in his mind.

"Don't be lying to Josh. Mr. Fields wants all of us to come out of this."

It had been said with deceit and malice. Josh had thought that Tullos and Billy might let him live, but he knew better now. They had meant to kill him all along, but they had failed. Enough had been revealed to know that this man who had been a close family friend was a fraud. Why? Mr. Fields had built something great. Why would he need to get involved in sex trafficking? None of it made sense to Josh, but that seemed to be the reality of the situation. Now, Kristol was here with him. Josh felt bad for her. She had trusted the old man like a father. He wasn't sure how to break this to her. She had been scarred by her past and Fields' betrayal would add to that now. His blood began to boil and his jaws clenched as a new wave of energy surged. Kristol saw him first, limping up the rocky path to where she and Mr. Fields were waiting.

"Josh? I can't believe it, you are alive! I thought for sure—" She fell into his arms and held him, not wanting to finish her thoughts.

"Kristol, we have to get out of here." Josh spoke softly to her, almost in a whisper and turned to lead her towards her truck. She stopped and turned back to Mr. Fields.

"What about Mr. Fields? He's been waiting with me and keeping me safe."

"She's right, Josh," the old man took a draw on his pipe, "We've been waiting for you and the others. I was expecting to see Deputy Tullos and Billy Dalton come out of that mine shaft with you. What happened in there? We heard gunshots."

Kristol stepped back towards Mr. Fields, hoping to break whatever tension Josh was feeling. Josh looked at both of them.

"Kristol, step away from Fields. He's not what you think." Josh tried to coax Kristol from the old man, as if he were a dangerous ledge and she might fall off at any moment.

Fields stepped forward, "Josh, I don't know what's gotten into you, are you okay? Obviously, something happened down there and you've been–"

"Stop it, old man! I know about what you've been doing. Maybe, I don't know everything right now, but I know enough." Josh motioned for Kristol to follow, but she stayed centered between the two men, as one standing before two diverging roads and not knowing which one to take.

"Kristol, please. Let's go." Josh yelled.

Kristol's face relaxed and she looked down at the ground, as if the discovery of which path had been settled. "I can't Josh. I want to, but I just can't." She stepped towards Mr. Fields, "I can't keep having men tell me what to do. I am making this choice. Please, let's just talk this out, please. I think that would be best, don't you?"

"Kristol, look, I know Mr. Fields has been good to you and you trust him, but–"

Fields began to clap, slowly at first and then faster. He sneered, "Okay, smart guy, you've got me. Obviously those two morons at the bottom of that shaft down there told you something. So, what is it that you think you know? If that's the case, explain why I've let you even make it this far? If I'm such a bad guy, surely, I would've shot you down already."

"Probably because you like to keep your hands clean or maybe you're just a coward. I know about the sex trafficking and murders. But why? You've got the resort, isn't it enough?"

"Really, Josh. Do you think a broke old coal miner has the kind of money to do what I've been doing? You're just as stupid as your old man was."

"You son of a–" Josh said and started to reach to the small of his back to pull the gun but checked himself. He was already in enough trouble in his mind, it would be better to get the man talking, at least Kristol would know enough to come with him.

"No, you're the son of a bitch, Josh. Look around. Our way of life–our prosperity–has been crapped on by our own country. They've taken away the mines and left us destitute. We've had nothing but poverty and drugs for over thirty years, for goodness sakes. Someone had to take it back and Josh, that is what I've been doing!"

"At what cost?" Josh waved his arm across the horizon as if presenting a case before a jury. "Your resort is nice enough, but when I drive through Etham, I still see the same old poverty and drugs. The only one I see being helped is you!"

Josh saw Kristol step back in his peripheral vision and was glad she was getting to a safe space. He couldn't stand the thought of her going through with this and surely hoped they could get out of this alive.

"You are wrong, Josh. Yes, I've made a lot of money, so sue me. So have others. True, a lot of people are still suffering, but the truth of the matter is that they will always suffer. They bring it on themselves. Okay, so I'm using them. I'm selling them like slaves. It's ugly, but you know what they say about making omelets…..got to break some eggs."

Josh thought about gripping the pistol again and another haul down the mine shaft wouldn't be too difficult. Fields had played his cards. It was best that he and Kristol get out while they could. He decided not to go for the pistol and reached for Kristol's hand.

"Don't you want to know who shot your brother?" The old man said and watched Josh stop in his place as he lit his pipe.

"What the hell did you just say?"

"Well, since they spilled the beans down there in that mine, I thought maybe they told you everything. Obviously, they didn't," he blew the smoke as he placed a lighter into his jackets inside pocket and returned with a .9mm pistol. The old man laughed, "Well, first of all, it wasn't Dave."

Kristol stepped further away from Fields with a growing awareness that everything was going to hell. She looked at Josh with concerned eyes.

"Well then, who? If it was you then why don't you just say it. Don't look like you have anything to lose now."

"You're right, Josh. First, I'll start by saying it wasn't me," the old man sneered, "If that makes you feel any better. To be honest, I was disappointed when I found out about your brother's affair with the sheriff's wife. I couldn't believe it, but I figured since he was into that kind of thing, I'd get him on the team. But Caleb figured differently and tried helping some of the girls, maybe even help some escape. The problem was that they didn't want to escape, just like I've been saying. Pigs love to wallow in their own mud, you see? Your brother persisted, until one day my little Hummingbird came across him trying to get one of the girls out from one of the cabins. You know where, up on the trail."

A wave of nausea rushed through Josh's gut, and he turned to Kristol. She stood with trembling hands, slowly shaking her head. With a muted voice, she whispered, "Josh, I'm so sorry."

Fields snorted, "Yeah, she shot him down. I couldn't believe it myself." The old man rambled on saying who knows what. The words faded into silence and Josh could only hear the thump of his heart. It wasn't possible. Kristol had taken care of him and nursed him back to health when he'd been jumped. A special bond had been built; they had made love. She had even helped save Elizabeth Dawn. None of this made sense, but the look on her face gave way to the truth. Kristol had killed Caleb.

Josh clenched his fists and turned to attack Fields but stopped at the site of the man's gun. He reached back for his own weapon, but Fields got off a quick shot before he could pull his gun from his back. The hot bullet ripped through his left shoulder and sent him hard to the ground. The old man stood laughing over Josh and taking in the victory.

"You know, I really did like your father. I can't figure out how he got it so wrong with you two boys." Fields looked over at

Kristol who had buried her face in her hands. "Sweet Hummingbird, don't be upset. I have to finish this now, are you with me?"

Josh lay on the ground gasping for air and looked over to Kristol. She looked back down at him, not needing words. Her silence spoke for her, *"Yes, finish him."*

Fields took another moment for self-appreciation and then lifted his pistol to complete the job. He looked back at Kristol for one more look of approval. Josh pulled his gun up first and sent a bullet crashing into the old man's chest, sending him to the ground with his smug face turning from doubt to shock. He tried lifting himself up and Josh pulled the trigger again, but the chamber was empty. Fields laughed again, but the movement brought on a wave of coughing causing blood to shoot from his mouth. After a short struggle, the old man's body fell limp.

Kristol ran to help Mr. Fields, crying for him to stay with her. She held his lifeless body while Josh worked to stop his own bleeding. It wasn't easy, but he managed and stood up. His mind shifted to what to do about Kristol and heard the gun cocking in her hand as he faced her.

"Are you going to shoot me?" Josh said.

"I don't want to. None of this played out like I thought it would." Kristol's hands trembled as she spoke. Josh figured she might shoot him accidentally, even if not on purpose.

"Kristol, why don't you put the gun down and let's talk for a minute. Tell me what happened. You killed Caleb? I don't understand." Josh's words faded into thought and he gripped the pistol. He waited for Kristol to talk, but she couldn't find the words. Finally, she began to explain everything about how she had come to Etham, about the internship, the drugs, and how Mr. Fields had taken her in. And how he had given her back her dreams and how she had sworn an oath to herself that she would do anything in her power to see him be happy.

Kristol looked back at her old father figure. She thought she'd never get out of that damn deep hole she had been in, but he had gotten her out. Yes, she owed him everything. She turned back to Josh, but relaxed her gun hand as she spoke.

"Things weren't going so well with the resort. The idea was good, but the money just wasn't there. The grants hadn't been enough to get things going. One day, I overheard him talking to one of his Cincinnati associates on the phone. They would front him with some money, but he'd have to let them run their prostitution ring through the cabins. He said he'd think it over and threw the phone when they disconnected. What struck me was that he wasn't mad about the trafficking, but rather because they would be making all the money. So, I went to him and suggested he start his own prostitution ring."

Josh eased his pistol grip and his eyes widened. "You...approached him? Kristol, what did you do?"

She was half covering Josh with the pistol and half brushing Mr. Fields gray hair, hoping somehow that petting him would help her old friend rest.

"I told him we could do better without help from any outsiders. We came up with a plan to lure in troubled girls, get them hooked on the pills, and then turn them to prostitution. Much like what happened to me. Only difference is we targeted kids with bad histories and addictive personalities. The ones that nobody really cared about."

"What about Elizabeth Dawn? She wasn't from a troubled family, how did she get involved?"

"That was one of the odd cases and should have never happened. In the end, she only caused more trouble than she was worth. I should have had Dave get rid of her a long time ago."

Josh resisted the urge to gag. "Do you even hear yourself? How can you talk like this?"

"I guess it all got out of hand. When you came along, I–" Kristol's voice trailed away to another place where her words might have made sense. "I thought I could get out of it. Maybe cut ties. Thought maybe you would want to help us out."

"Help you out? With what, pimping out the girls? What made you think that?"

"It doesn't matter now. Josh, I don't know what I was thinking. I certainly wasn't planning on falling in love with you!" Tears welled up, and the veins protruded from her temples gave witness to her pain. Josh could tell she really had feelings for him. Her tears slid down her cheek as she covered her mouth and lowered the gun.

Neither of them heard the rustling of footsteps headed toward them. Sheriff Bell had been awaiting with backup behind a knoll of trees but decided to approach after hearing the gunfire.

"Put down the guns, this is the Woolridge County Sheriff. Put them down right now and get on the ground!" He had his pistol on both of them.

Josh dropped his pistol and held both hands up. He stared at Kristol, hoping to ease the situation.

"Kristol, it's over. Please just put the gun down and we'll figure all this out." Josh said with a tear.

She lowered the gun further as the sheriff approached. With slow movement, she relaxed.

"All the way down, Kristol. Nice and easy. Once we're all clear, I'm gonna need somebody to start explaining stuff fast."

Sheriff Bell slowed his approach hoping to not make the situation any worse. He looked over at Josh, distracted by the bloodied mess that was the man's shoulder. He looked back at Kristol just in time to watch her pull her trigger. He wasn't sure if it was the hot lead ripping through his chest that hurt more or the thud of his head hitting the graveled lot. It didn't matter, he was fading fast. Only his instinct caused him to roll over and watch the person that shot him approach through the onset of blurred vision.

Kristol aimed at the Sheriff Bell again. "People need to stop telling me what to do."

Josh lunged his body into hers and they both struggled with the gun. His weakened state made it an even match. He felt his strength fading at an alarming rate and had to do something quick. He smashed his head into Kristol's nose, hoping to just stun her and she fell back grabbing at whatever to keep from falling. She caught Josh's arm with one hand causing him to come down with her and squeezed the trigger of the pistol with her other. Josh jumped at the blast of the pistol.

The two lay still with warm blood flowing between them. "I'm sorry, Josh." Kristol whispered hoarsely. "I'm sorry about this and about Caleb. Please…forgive me."

Josh rolled away from her and lay on the ground watching the lightened sky trying to make sense of it all. Kristol had killed his brother and now she lay dead beside him. He was sad for her and himself.

It wasn't long before Sheriff Bell's back up arrived on the scene and Josh could hear the ambulance sirens. It was over, at least the killing was. Now, it would take time to see where things went from here. Back to the university or to jail? He just kept watching the sky, feeling a soft breeze sweep across his face. The State Police were coming through the gate, spreading out to clear the area and tend to the bodies scattered about the parking lot. Josh concerned himself with another man, not in uniform, but Sunday church attire. The man smiled and waved at him as leaves swirled about and carried him away in the early mountain breeze and early morning dawn.

Josh returned the smile with a raspy whisper, "Thank you, brother." He faded into unconscious dreams.

Epilogue

A small assembly of students, supporters, and faculty members applauded as town officials joined the dean of the new Etham Community College in cutting the ribbon that would officially open its doors. Josh Webb pumped the giant scissors in celebration as he smiled at the cheering group and handed it off as he descended the platform. As quick as it had started, the small mass of supporters lingered in small talk and then slipped away one by one. One couple stopped for a moment and waved at Josh. Retired Sheriff Harris Bell and Julie Bell waved and Josh smiled. A slap on the shoulders turned him to find the mayor reaching for his hand.

"Well done, Josh, you did it. It's hard to believe this all happened in a little over a year."

Josh turned to wave at the Bells, but they were gone. He focused his attention back on the mayor. "No, sir; we did it. There's no way I could have done this on my own. If not for the town selling the old strip mall lot for pennies on the dollar, we would have had to wait for at least another year.

"Thanks again." The mayor said and walked towards his car.

"It's an investment, not just with the town, but for all of us." Josh turned to the familiar voice approaching. Rita Long, who had previously been Mr. Fields' executive assistant, had assumed control of the Stepping Stone Resort and Trailhead Center. The enterprise had suffered a major public relations blow from the trafficking scandal and the newly established board felt her as chairman would be the best thing moving forward. They had figured correctly, and Rita had worked her fingers to the bone to get the business back in favor with the public eye. In addition, one of her focus areas had now come to fruition, leading the community to build the new private not-for-profit college. She had donated funding and established scholarships to be granted. Her donor base harvested from rich resort patrons ensured young people of the area would be able to attend for free.

"We're not just changing our image as a community, but our trajectory, as well. We need educated citizens in order for this region to prosper." She said and looked at Josh with a smile.

The couple eased into less serious talk. It was a perfect day for the event, albeit on the hot side. They discussed how it would be nice when the weather cooled. Hunting season was coming quickly; so was football. The conversation went on for several minutes, until Rita looked over Josh's shoulder and smiled in recognition of a familiar face.

"Well, if it isn't our first enrollee of many."

Josh turned to see a bright faced young woman approaching with parents in tow. She had been awarded the first enrollment, along with a hefty scholarship from the resort.

"Elizabeth Dawn Boyd! How are you doing, young lady? And how are Mr. and Mrs. Boyd?" Josh said with a big smile.

"Doing great since you brought our girl home." Olivia smiled and hugged Josh.

"Yes, we can't thank you enough for bringing her home and taking care of other things." Randall said. Both shook hands and nodded at each other.

Rita shook all their hands. Then, Elizabeth Dawn hugged Josh hard.

"I just wanted to say thanks again for everything. Mr. Webb, if it weren't for you...." Elizabeth Dawn tried to hold her tears back, "I wouldn't be here at all, much less starting college."

Josh smiled, "We've all made mistakes, some worse than others. None of us are where we are today without the help of those before us. It is up to us now–those who have survived chaos–to pledge ourselves to help those who come after us. It's how we pay it forward, a sacred oath. I know you will live up to that and much more."

Classes would start the following Monday and students would begin the cat and mouse game of being taught and completing assignments. It would be normal, as a small town should be. Josh smiled again as Elizabeth Dawn walked away with her parents. He was happy with normal.

Made in the USA
Las Vegas, NV
04 November 2024